Fire Dancer

Book 2
Spellbound in Sedona

Anna Lowe

Copyright © 2024-11-30 Anna Lowe

All rights reserved.

Editing by Lisa Hollett

Cover design by Kim Killion

Contents

Contents   i

Other books in this series   iii

Free Books   v

Chapter One   1

Chapter Two   11

Chapter Three   19

Chapter Four   31

Chapter Five   41

Chapter Six   51

Chapter Seven   59

Chapter Eight   69

Chapter Nine   77

Chapter Ten   85

Chapter Eleven   93

Chapter Twelve   103

Chapter Thirteen   113

Chapter Fourteen   123

Chapter Fifteen   129

Chapter Sixteen   137

Chapter Seventeen   147

Chapter Eighteen   157

Chapter Nineteen   161

Chapter Twenty   165

Chapter Twenty-One   173

Chapter Twenty-Two   183

Chapter Twenty-Three   191

Chapter Twenty-Four   199

Chapter Twenty-Five   207

Chapter Twenty-Six   217

Chapter Twenty-Seven   231

Chapter Twenty-Eight   241

Sneak Peek: Dream Weaver   253

Books by Anna Lowe   255

About the Author   265

Other books in this series

Spellbound in Sedona

Wind Whisperer (Book 1)

Fire Dancer (Book 2)

Dream Weaver (Book 3)

www.annalowebooks.com

Free Books

Get your free e-books now!

Sign up for my newsletter at *annalowebooks.com* to get three free books!

- *Desert Wolf*: Friend or Foe (Book 1.1 in the Twin Moon Ranch series)

- *Off the Charts* (the prequel to the Serendipity Adventure series)

- *Perfection* (the prequel to the Blue Moon Saloon series)

Chapter One

PIPPA

My back ached as I bent over the workbench, rolling my latest creation back and forth. It was shaping up to be a real beauty — a pitcher of clear glass splashed with sunrise colors. There was ruby red, blood orange, and sunflower yellow. Blue like the dazzlingly clear sky in Sedona, and vibrant green like fresh shoots of juniper.

I had my hair done back in a braid, but a few long blond strands had worked their way loose. I puffed upward, getting them out of my eyes. A bead of sweat dripped from my forehead, sizzling faintly as it hit glass heated to the temperature of planet Mercury or thereabouts. Unlike a painter, I didn't sign my artwork, but a little bit of me marked every one of my creations.

The bell over the hot shop door chimed, and I called out without looking up. "Welcome to Sedona Glass. I'll be right with you."

In addition to the new arrival, there was already a family browsing through the shop, but I couldn't put down my project at this crucial stage. Luckily, folks were rarely in a rush in Sedona, and most enjoyed watching the creation process the same way they enjoyed taking in the spectacular scenery — slowly and with a hint of awe.

"Hi, Pippa. No rush," a familiar voice replied.

I glanced up and smiled at one of our best customers, a friendly redhead.

"Thanks, Stacy. I just need a minute," I said, focused on the finishing touches.

With a pair of pincers, I widened the mouth of the pitcher, then stopped spinning it long enough to notch a spout into the lip.

"Wow. Look at that," the mother whispered to her daughter.

"Amazing," the girl breathed. "Like magic."

I grinned. No magic on this particular piece. The vase I'd made earlier, on the other hand. . .

Reaching out, I dipped my pinchers into a vat of molten glass, then hooked a thick vein onto the side of the pitcher to make a handle. I tapped the joints a few times, then rolled out the imperfections with a steel cylinder. Finally, I heated the base with a blowtorch and tapped it on my workbench to make it even. Then, voilà! Into the annealer it went to cool down.

I brushed off my hands, pleased with my work. Art wouldn't save the messy world we lived in, but it sure could make life cheerier.

Wiping my brow, I finally turned to my customers. The original trio seemed happy browsing, so I brought out the box containing Stacy's latest order.

"Here you go. Another fifty." I counted the pinkie-sized vials nestled in recyclable packaging. "Two, four, six, eight. . ."

Stacy raised one to the light, checking it briefly. "Perfect, as always."

That caught the interest of the first customers, a mother with two teenaged kids. The twelve-ish daughter looked fascinated; the slightly older son, bored.

"What are those for?" the girl asked, intrigued.

"They're love vials, like this." Stacy tapped the vial hanging on her own necklace, making the small pegasus pendant beside it jingle.

The girl leaned closer. "What's in there?"

"Blood. Just a tiny bit," Stacy hastened to add. "Couples exchange them as a symbol of their love and connection."

"Cool," the girl breathed.

"Gross," her brother muttered.

I was firmly in the boy's camp when it came to those vials. But they were surprisingly popular, and, well...when money talked, I listened.

Stacy shut the box and pointed to a foot-tall glass pegasus in a tactful change of subject. "Now, isn't that a beauty? Pippa made that."

The mom looked relieved, the daughter impressed. "That's amazing. It's so lifelike..."

"Except pegasuses aren't real," the killjoy brother added.

"Pegasi," Stacy murmured as she signed the invoice. Like most of our regular customers, her company handled the billing separately. She started scooping the box into her arms, then stopped and pulled something out of her pocket.

"Oh — I almost forgot." She handed me a flyer. "My boss is sponsoring a design contest. I thought you might want to enter. You're the best glassblower I know."

I chuckled. "The only one you know?"

She grinned. "Still the best. And the prize is pretty impressive."

That sure piqued my interest. "How impressive?"

Stacy was about to answer, but I yelped when I spotted it on the flyer.

"Twenty-five thousand dollars?"

She lit up with a proud glow. "Yep. Business is good, and my boss is very generous."

Clearly, Stacy had a thing for her boss. From what I'd gathered, she hadn't found Mr. Right to swap vials with — yet — but it was obvious she was keeping that option open for the day her boss finally took notice of her. Then he would sweep her off her feet, share his vast wealth in a marriage of true love that had no need for a prenuptial agreement, and they would live happily ever after.

How likely that was, I didn't know. But, heck. We all had our secret fantasies.

Meanwhile, visions of greenbacks filled my mind. Make that, visions of me strolling along the canals of Venice, then hopping a ferry to Murano, a mecca of glassmaking since the Middle Ages. Twenty-five thousand dollars could not only get me there, but also allow me to enroll in a course taught by one of the famous masters — and still have plenty left over.

Now, that would be a dream, and a win wouldn't hurt my résumé either.

I tucked the flyer away in my pocket. I would definitely be poring over that later.

"Thanks so much for thinking of me."

"You're welcome. I'll see you next week!" With that, the bubbly redhead picked up the box and headed for the door.

The teenage boy scurried over to open it for her. Either he had good manners, or pretty redheads were his type.

"Aw, thank you." Stacy flashed him a smile.

His dopey grin confirmed my second theory.

Stacy's elbow bumped the door frame as she departed, and the vials in the box clinked softly.

The storefront windows afforded a view of a big SUV idling at the curb. The hatch popped open, and Stacy loaded the box, then walked around the vehicle to slide into the back seat. The driver — barely a silhouette through those dark, tinted windows — eased away, heading down the road.

"Blood vials, huh?" the girl murmured, gazing after Stacy.

I was tempted to point out the sets we sold retail, but the mother shot me a hard look that said, *Don't you dare give her any ideas.*

I pointed in the opposite direction. "These dream catchers are really popular."

"Wow! I bet none of your friends has one of those." The mom towed her daughter over.

Outside, a Jeep rolled into the spot vacated by Stacy's ride. The driver hesitated, then parked and hurried toward the shop entrance. The door burst open and—

Joyful butterflies fluttered in my belly, and an angels' chorus filled the cathedral of my mind. The doorway was too packed with hot-blooded man for me to see much sky, but I wouldn't have been surprised to find a rainbow there.

Ingo, my heart sighed, as it always did whenever he made an entrance. Because Ingo didn't simply enter a room. He owned it the moment he stepped over the threshold.

A moment later, my Hallmark-card moment shattered. He was just another guy now. Nothing special about him. No siree. Not even with those midnight eyes that lit up when he saw me or that raven hair I used to run my fingers through.

He paused at the door, eyes bright, cheeks pink, stuck in a time warp a moment longer than I. Clearly, he remembered what we used to have too.

Then his expression hardened, and he bustled in, six-foot-two inches of broody man muscle fit for the cover of a calendar of *Hot Firefighters* or *Ripped Ranchers*.

Or, more fittingly, *Sexy Secret Agents*. Not that that was public knowledge.

The teenaged daughter gaped. So did her mother. Even the son did a double take at the way Ingo's biceps stretched the sleeves of his dark T-shirt.

"Welcome to Sedona Glass," I said, as if we hadn't once dreamed of a happily-ever-after.

He shot me one of those looks that ignited my girl parts, and I swear, the space between us sizzled.

"Uh, we'll come back later." The mother hustled her kids out of the shop.

Smart lady. Ingo exuded a *something's about to go down* intensity that made folks scan the street for drug dealers and mafia hit men.

"But, Mom—" her daughter protested.

The door slammed behind them, and the bell rang merrily.

Long after the sound died, Ingo and I gazed at each other in silence.

Finally, I pointed at the fleeing family. "That was a sure sale you just chased away."

Either Ingo didn't hear me, or he ignored my words. Both were equally possible. The guy was that focused. So focused, his gaze didn't so much as dart to the beautiful glass art all around him. The glass art I had poured heart and soul into.

Reason number one we were no longer together.

He stomped over to the front window and peered out at an angle. "What did she come for?"

I rolled my eyes. This again?

This was reason number two. An unhealthy obsession with work — his, not mine.

He gazed in Stacy's direction, but I refused to indulge him.

I pointed to the mother. "She wanted a dream catcher. You know, a dream catcher? Because some people have happy dreams, not just obsessions."

"I have happy dreams," he grumbled in that gritty, dragging steel over gravel voice that used to make my toes curl.

Operative term: *used to.* I was older and wiser now. This man no longer affected me.

Well, barely.

"Happy dreams aren't about catching bad guys. They're about good times with nice people," I lectured. "They're about success in goals you didn't even know you had." I narrowed my eyes and leaned in. "Some happy dreams are about sex. Like the best sex you ever had, only better."

His nostrils flared, and his eyes dropped to my lips, then lower.

My throat bobbed, but I held my ground. Yes, all my *best sex* dreams featured Ingo. And they weren't just dreams. They were memories.

His lips twitched, and several silent seconds ticked by as we stared at each other.

Then Ingo gave himself a shake and jerked a thumb toward the street. "I meant her."

"Stacy?" I asked, though I already knew.

The question was, why? Stacy was sweet, friendly, and genuine. There was no way she was involved in anything iffy.

Ingo, on the other hand, was broody and mistrustful. Borderline paranoid, at least when it came to the safety of others. Even his buddy Nash worried about him.

And, yikes. That was saying something. Nash was great, but he'd been one to worry about until he'd met my sister. For him to point the finger at Ingo. . .

The tragic thing was, Ingo used to laugh, dance, and joke around like any other person. Now, he wore the weary look of a World War II hero — a guy who'd just crawled over a beach, scaled a cliff, and seized an impenetrable fortification, all under intense enemy fire. A guy who no longer had time for fun, games, or laughter. Not enough time for me either, because there was always one more foe to vanquish, one more battle, one more front in the never-ending war of good versus evil.

"Stacy, huh? Last name?"

I shrugged. "I don't know."

He tapped the window, still fixated on Stacy. "I need to know what she came for. *Who* she came for — the company's name and address."

I crossed my arms. "Get me a warrant, and I'll give you the address."

He stuck his hand in his back pocket, wiggling his wallet free.

I anchored my hands in my own pockets, ordering myself not to help him with that, no matter how tempting the prospect.

With a look of triumph, he flashed his ID.

I leaned in to scrutinize it. "Department of Agriculture?"

He snapped it shut. "That's my cover story."

"Still doesn't make it a warrant."

His black-on-black eyes flashed twin bolts of lightning. "It's important, Pippa."

I snorted. "My dad does that too."

Ingo frowned. "Does what?"

"Using my name when he really, really wants something."

And, oops. Somehow, my voice had gone all sultry and suggestive. So I had only myself to blame that Ingo's gaze raked over my body.

I crossed my arms before my nipples peaked, but I couldn't stop heat from coloring my cheeks.

Not what I meant, I wanted to growl, though it was only half true.

Ingo jerked his eyes back to chin level. "Like I said, it's important."

"So is business, and I don't need you to jeopardize our relationship with an important client."

A good thing pride held me back from detailing how I wished for another kind of relationship — or how badly we needed the business. Not just Sedona Glass, but me personally, along with my family.

He leaned closer and, dang. There it was, that heady scent of wild rivers and thick forests, underpinned by a teensy-tiny whiff of canine.

"She could be in danger," he rumbled.

I worked in a glass shop — a warm, cheery place full of possibilities. Ingo worked in a top-secret branch of law enforcement. His world was one of danger and intrigue.

"She is in trouble if she's got a wolf shifter prowling around after her," I pointed out.

His eyes flashed, and he glanced around the shop. The empty shop, because I wasn't dumb enough to reveal his big secret in public.

Make that, one of his secrets.

"Dammit, Pippa..." He clenched his fists.

I clenched mine back. "Yes?"

He stepped closer, telegraphing something like, *This is important.*

Yeah, well. Everything was important to Ingo.

Everything but me.

I crossed my arms, staring him down.

We got so mired in our little standoff that we forgot what happened when our bodies passed an unmarked border into the danger zone. Gradually, the heat and proximity took me to a different time and place, and my anger ebbed, giving way to something much more pleasant.

Ingo's eyelids drooped, and his lips parted. I found my arms drifting to his waist. Time and place drifted too, until we were no longer in the hot shop. We were beside a mountain stream, years ago, sliding into our first kiss. The space around our bodies tingled as our lips brushed, then pressed together in a bolder, needier motion. Again and again until we were barely breathing, barely thinking. Just *doing.*

My mind filled in all the sensual details, and my nipples hardened. When my eyes fluttered open, Ingo was cupping my cheek, and his eyes were soft and loving, just as they had been in the split second before our first kiss.

My heart thumped in happy anticipation. But good sense used bad timing to throw up a red flag at exactly that moment.

"You're doing it to me again," I murmured, catching his arms to keep us an inch apart.

"Doing what?" he whispered, equally dazed.

"This." I waved between us. "Making it impossible *not* to touch you."

His eyes stayed at half-mast. "Maybe it's you doing it to me."

In truth, we both knew destiny was to blame. But we'd agreed not to be its puppets a long time ago.

I pushed him gently away. "Go, before I kiss you."

Ingo flashed a tiny, sentimental smile, but there was sorrow in his eyes too. "Would it be that bad?"

I shook my head. "It would be great. That's the problem."

We'd broken up for good reason, and we had to keep it that way.

He took a deep breath, then nodded. God, I hated it when he agreed with me.

I could practically read his mind. Kissing me was nice — great, even — but somewhere out there, someone or something needed saving, and he was the only one who heard their cries for justice.

With a deep, steadying breath, he stepped back and turned slowly away. Then he stopped, glancing down at the shop counter.

"Um..."

I stuck my hands on my hips. Did he really think I was going to give him the address he wanted?

A terrible idea, but I had to get rid of him before the love bug called in reinforcements and swarmed us with renewed energy. I could already hear the approaching buzz as its force field nudged us closer...closer...

I could see it now: him flipping the *Open* sign to *Closed*, then rushing back to me. We would end up half naked and doing it on the counter... and he would still get that address in the end.

At least if I gave it to him quickly — the address, not my aching, overheated body — and got him out of there, my heart wouldn't end up broken.

"Here. One look," I grumbled, holding up the invoice.

His throat bobbed, and he tore his eyes away from mine. I watched his lips move as he memorized the address. Bad idea, because my libido grabbed that little motion and inserted it into an entirely new, R-rated context.

"Go. And be careful." I crossed my arms so I couldn't reach out to stop him.

He nodded, then paused with one hand on the knob.

"Pippa..." he whispered, begging me to understand.

I did, but I didn't. Saving the world was a worthy cause, but it tended to be a job you did solo. Yet the sacrifices made were shared by everyone — the hero and anyone who loved him.

And sadly, my goals were nowhere near as lofty.

"Nice seeing you," I sighed.

His eyes filled with hope and longing. But a moment later, he went all hard again.

"Be careful, Pippa."

Out the door he went, a man on a mission.

"You too," I started, but the door slammed before I finished.

The bell chimed, but the sound failed to cheer me.

Chapter Two

INGO

I threw my Jeep into gear and sped off down the road in pursuit of the SUV.

Grabbing my phone, I recorded the address Pippa had shown me. "TTC Limited, 3020 North Baseline Road, Park City, Utah."

There'd been a six-digit office number too, but I wasn't sure I'd gotten it right. One-two-eight, then a dash, and three more numbers. Not an address I recognized, but I would call it in soon.

I like 422 Forest Road better, my wolf growled the address of Pippa's glass shop into my mind.

Every cell in my body screamed for me to turn around and race back to her, because she was all that counted. I could explain everything and patch things up between us. We could figure things out and get back on track to that happily-ever-after that had seemed like such a sure thing eight long years ago.

But how could I explain things to her if I could barely explain to myself?

I tightened my grip on the steering wheel and continued in the direction the beige SUV had gone. The one with Utah plates and tinted windows.

Suspicious as hell, if you ask me, an inner voice declared.

Yes and no. Tinted windows could mean a lot of things. Some legit, some not so legit.

My money was on *not* legit, but I couldn't explain why.

I knew what Pippa would say to that. *Chill out. You don't need to suspect everyone.*

Words she'd uttered about a hundred times before we'd broken up.

Which was for the best. Pippa deserved a guy who not only put her on a pedestal, but also remembered not to leave her stranded there while he went off chasing windmills.

My wolf growled continuously, and I hesitated at the next corner — the perfect place to make a U-turn and race back to where I belonged. To Pippa, the only woman I'd ever met who combined the gumption of a tomboy with the grace of a supermodel.

On the other hand, the SUV was heading away quickly. Something about the driver — a bear shifter I'd caught a whiff of at a gas station a few minutes earlier — seemed off. It was my job to keep an eye on supernaturals in Sedona, so I'd decided to observe from a discreet distance, just in case. When they'd stopped at Pippa's glass shop, every alarm in my body had started clanging.

I gripped the steering wheel harder and drove through the intersection, following my hunch instead of my heart.

I scanned the side streets as I drove, then pulled into the parking lot of a strip mall. And, bingo. One beige Chevy Tahoe, and one redhead heading into the drugstore.

I studied the parked vehicle, not that I could see much through those deeply tinted windows. I dialed a contact on my phone while scanning every detail. The vehicle had a ding in the front bumper, but it was clean as hell, not caked with dust — or mud from the storm that passed last week. No Forest Service parking tag, no bumper stickers, no dealer sticker.

When a voice came over the line I'd called, I replied with a little swell of pride. "Agent Kemper, Sedona office. I need Records & Tracing, please."

Dozens of agents had applied for the job, but I'd been the one to get it. Taking a brand-new, one-man post was a great opportunity to set my own priorities and demonstrate initiative, which would help me work my way up the ladder. It didn't hurt that my friend Nash had just moved to Sedona or that the place was beautiful. All those red rocks, all that space to roam on two feet or four.

And Pippa, my wolf had eagerly reasoned at the time.

I'd ignored it, imagining I could be around Pippa without being haunted by what could have been.

But, ha. Sedona could build me a statue and call it *wishful thinking.*

Apparently, I wasn't smarter now than I'd been at twenty-two, but then again, we'd been different people and truly perfect for each other back then.

We're still perfect for each other, my wolf insisted.

Maybe. Probably. But a guy didn't hunt vampires by day — or night — and lead a white-picket-fence life with a sweet, peppy woman on the side. It was just too much to risk — especially when that sweet, peppy woman didn't understand the meaning of the word *risk.* Pippa was trusting. Optimistic. Unguarded. In the normal world, those were all positive traits.

In my world, they could get her killed.

Just then, I spotted Stacy exiting the drugstore, pausing to hold the door open for the next person with a bright smile.

In some ways, she was a lot like Pippa. All the ways that could get her killed.

"Records & Tracing. This is Agent Heller," a voice came over the phone.

I snapped back to focus. "I'd like you to run a license plate number, please."

I gave him the number, listened, then nodded. "Later today would be fine. Thank you."

I hung up, still watching Stacy. She placed her purchases in the vehicle, then walked to a coffee shop and disappeared inside.

Stacy who? From where? Doing what, for whom, and why?

And what about her hulking driver who barely showed himself? He wasn't a bodyguard or her employee, because he never emerged to open the door or help her. That suggested two employees of similar rank. But employees for whom or what company?

My radio squawked with an APB.

"All units. Report of a 10-54 at Gunnery Point. Repeat, possible 10-54 at Gunnery Point."

I frowned. A 10-54 was a dead body. I listened in as two police units called in. Both were dispatched to the scene.

I glanced at the SUV, then the radio, torn. The 10-54 could be anything or anyone, and I could read the police report later. But two units — and the urgency in the dispatcher's tone — suggested a case of special interest. And as good as the local police were, they were mere humans and thus likely to overlook any hints of supernatural activity.

Stacy emerged from the coffee shop, looking as carefree as ever. Meanwhile, a police car drove down the main road, followed closely by a second one. Neither had their lights on, but they were clearly in a hurry.

I threw a last glance at Stacy, then threw the Jeep into gear. Right now, the police call took priority.

I pulled out onto the main road, following the squad cars.

∞∞∞∞

Gunnery Point, as it turned out, was an overlook five miles north of town and another two miles down a rough trail. Two pink Jeeps stood there with about a dozen tourists milling around, some peering downward, others turned away in horror. Several hugged or shed tears, while others held hands, looking morose.

The police waved me away at first but let me through a moment later.

"Ah, Agent Kemper," the first officer, an olive-skinned woman, sighed with a note of resignation.

City police officers didn't know what agency I worked for, but they knew I was cleared to observe all local investigations. I'd overheard rumors claiming I was everything from FBI to a top-secret NSA unit specializing in extraterrestrial activity.

Close enough, I supposed, to my actual employer — the Agency for the Detection and Monitoring of Supernatural Activity, or ADMSA.

"Officer Jimenez." I nodded my greetings and strode over toward the heart of the action, where a police officer and one of the Jeep drivers had started herding the tourists away to a safe distance. Another two officers peered over the edge of the cliff as the second driver and a pair of tourists explained how they'd made their discovery.

"...taking pictures, and that's when we spotted her," one of the tourists was saying.

I stepped up, exchanging silent nods of greeting with the officers.

"We wanted to go down and check in case there was any hope," the other tourist said. "But Jim here said it was too late."

I glanced over the cliff, grimacing. Definitely too late for the woman sprawled over the rocks below, her limbs askew, eyes wide in unblinking shock and fear.

I jutted my jaw, reminded of another place, another young woman, another senseless death. Another case where I'd arrived too late.

I sucked in a lungful of clean mountain air, then exhaled slowly.

My mind jumped to Stacy. Worse, it jumped to Pippa next, and my breath broke sharply. Beautiful, bubbly Pippa with her bright-blue eyes, smattering of freckles, and long, wavy hair the color of sunshine. It was impossible to think of all that life, all that beauty, getting cut off far too soon. But not impossible enough.

One of the officers patted me on the back. "You never get used to it, do you?"

I shook my head. His thoughts weren't where mine were, but the sentiment still rang true.

"Never seen nothing like it," Jim, the tour driver, lamented. "Never wanted to."

"How long do you think she's been down there?" one of the tourists asked.

"Too early to tell," one of the officers said, ushering them away.

I stepped back, leaving the investigative perimeter the police started to mark. Any tracks on the ground had been obliterated by the tour vehicles and dozens of footprints, so I didn't hold much hope of visual clues. Instead, I closed my eyes and sniffed.

Pine. . . oak. . . a few drops of oil. . . My wolf side dissected and identified latent odors one by one. *Sweat. . .*

Then my nose wrinkled, and I froze. *Shifter. Bear shifter.* At least two, in animal form, not human, judging by the intensity of the scent.

I moved around, sniffing here and there and studying the ground. No clear bear marks, and only a few other Jeep tracks, but nothing recent. The dead woman seemed to have arrived here on foot.

"A hiker, I suppose," I heard the tourists speculate. "Or one of those trail runners?"

I shook my head quietly. Not in that frilly shirt and sandals of hers.

I pictured Pippa getting dressed in the morning, checking in the mirror that everything matched and looked good. The dead woman had probably taken the same care, this morning or last night, never suspecting it would be her last.

"Maybe she went too close to the edge to take a picture?" another tried.

Officer Jimenez and I exchanged doubtful looks. It happened, but you'd have to have your eyes closed to miss a drop-off that obvious.

"Suicide?" someone else tried.

"Why come all the way out here to do that?" another asked.

I pursued my lips. Why, indeed?

"Maybe she was afraid of something — or someone," another person suggested.

That was my bet, though any telltale paw prints would have been erased by the tour group. Still, it wasn't hard to picture a couple of bears charging after that poor young woman, who would have been running for her life.

I frowned at the cliff. Life just sucked sometimes. Death, even more so, especially when it hit far too soon.

I stepped left, then right, painting a grim picture in my mind. A couple of bear shifters had chased the woman over the edge, then prowled back and forth several times, making sure she was dead before they lumbered away.

The scenario was all too easy to picture but harder to explain. Who were those bears? Why did they want the woman dead?

Again, my mind went to Stacy — and the bear shifter who drove that SUV.

"God, I hate these cases," one of the officers muttered. A guy old enough to have a daughter about the victim's age.

"Even figuring out what happened doesn't help the family," Jimenez lamented.

The police would do their best, but I doubted they would find any evidence that suggested foul play. Even if they did find bear prints, they would conclude a wild animal was involved. And I couldn't exactly say, *It was a shifter. Shifters, actually. I can smell them all over the place.*

I kicked the ground, silently agreeing with the officer. *Yeah, I hate these cases too.*

Chapter Three

PIPPA

It had been a hell of a day at the glass shop — and that was before reports of a death zipped through the grapevine. A young woman, apparently killed in a hiking accident not far north of town.

Terrible, my friend Amy had written, followed by a crying emoji.

Her next message, sent seconds later, was an abrupt change of gears. *Want to meet for dancing tonight?*

I winced. Tact, anyone?

On the other hand. . . that would cheer me up, and I'd been promising myself a night out for a week now.

Wrapping up work, I held a solitary vigil for the dead woman, lighting one of the shop's candles and closing my eyes to think of who she might have been and who she had left behind. Then, with a sad sigh, I blew out the candle and headed for a quick shower in the shared facilities behind Sedona Glass.

Afterward, I drove to Buffalo Bill's — the place my sisters and I preferred, thanks to its mostly local, low-key crowd. The evening was crisp, cool, and revitalizing after all those hunched, sweaty hours in the hot shop.

The death was a hot topic in the bar, but life went on, especially since the woman was an out-of-towner nobody knew. Plus, Wednesday was Oldies Night — though half the regulars objected to the label — making it impossible to be morose.

I danced my way inside to the tune of Pat Benatar's "Hit Me with Your Best Shot." In no time, I'd downed half a non-alcoholic beer — I would be driving home later — and was rocking my moves on what passed for a dance floor. At Buffalo Bill's, it didn't matter whether you danced alone, with someone else, or everyone. I was perfectly happy with *alone*, but that rarely worked out, because the guys inevitably found their way over to me.

The first of the night was Hank, a sweet, fun trucker twice my age, which was fine, because *sweet* and *fun* were my top two criteria. Also, he kept his hands away from the danger zones, which was good. I would hate to ruin a guy's night by kneeing him in the balls.

By the next song — Journey's "Any Way You Want It" — Hank had been edged out by Ryder, an all-American, ex-football hunk/construction worker/wannabee rodeo ace. His looks were a ten. As far as brains went, he was also a ten — on the IQ scale, give or take.

Either way, Ryder met my criteria on points one, two, three, *and* four, with fun, sweet, handsome *and* well-built on his résumé. That was about the extent of his résumé, but heck. He kept his hands away from the danger zones too.

Yes, I liked to dance, preferably with a platonic partner. A placeholder, almost, that my imagination could fill in with Ingo — er, with Mr. Right, whom I would someday find and live happily ever after with.

Dancing was as far as I took things, however. A placeholder was just a placeholder, and no one had ever come along who felt right.

No one like Ingo.

I danced on, not paying much attention to who came or went, but maybe I should have. Because a few notes into the third song — Boston's "More Than a Feeling," appropriately — an itchy sensation registered on my back. I swiped at the spot a couple of times before losing the beat and turning slowly.

"Dammit, Ingo..." I muttered.

There he was, taking up way too much of a dim corner booth all by himself.

I cursed the day Ingo had been introduced to Buffalo Bill's by Nash, my sister Erin's flame. Literally. Nash was a dragon shifter. And, yikes. My sister now was too.

My sisters Erin and Abby went out a lot less often than I, but when they did, they came here.

"You know that guy?" Ryder growled.

I went back to dancing. "Yes."

"What is he — a hit man or something?"

I laughed out loud. "Guess again."

A nervous tic set in at the corner of Ryder's eye. "FBI agent with a license to kill?"

I laughed again. So much for Ingo keeping a low profile.

"You got something to hide?" I teased.

When he winced, I stuck up a hand. "Forget I asked."

It was all too easy to imagine Ryder carrying a friend's bag over the Mexican border after a weekend trip with the boys or some such thing. He was perfectly capable of committing a crime by mistake, ignorance, or sheer stupidity, though he wouldn't consciously do something that could hurt anyone. His mom — treasurer of the local Rotary club — would kill him if he did.

I nudged him to dance on. I was here for a good time, dammit.

But Ryder backed away by the end of the song, mumbling something about a knee injury. All the other guys did too, leaving me dancing with Amy, who'd finally shown up, and Lauren, another friend. But even they were more focused on Ingo than the song.

"God, he's hot," Amy murmured as we bopped to "Sultans of Swing" by Dire Straits.

Yeah, maybe, but so were most wolf shifters. It came with the territory.

"Hot but unapproachable," Lauren added.

Ha. That summed up Ingo perfectly.

And this was him in off-duty mode. Or as close as he got.

On-duty Ingo had blazing eyes and a stiff jaw that put deep creases in his cheeks. Creases I wanted to lick my way through en route to other places. Off-duty Ingo was slightly more approachable than the on-duty version — on a good day. Both were a feast for the senses.

A crying shame that there was more on-duty Ingo than *off* these days.

"He's staring at us," Amy observed.

Lauren shook her head. "He's staring at Pippa."

I grimaced. "Just ignore him, all right?"

I could practically see their antennas perk and rotate.

"You know him?" both asked at the same time.

I sighed. Yes. Intimately. Or did knowing someone have an expiration date? Enough time had passed — and Ingo had veered so far over to one side of his personality — that I wondered if I could still claim to know him.

"Sort of. He's a friend of Nash's," I admitted. "New subject, okay?"

Amy and Lauren exchanged looks and went on dancing.

A third friend joined us — Lucille, from the yoga studio — but not to dance.

"Hey, Pippa. Is it true? Are you really selling the ranch?"

I stopped in my tracks. Huh?

"No!" I barked. "Never!"

Lucille stuck her hands up. "I didn't think so. It's just what I heard."

"From?"

She shrugged. "A friend of a friend said Bob was getting ready to list it." She pointed to a pudgy man in a booth near the front.

I glared at the guy. Bob Hardy of Red Rock Vistas Real Estate. The guy had pestered my aunt to sell for years, and after she'd sold the property to us for a song, he'd hounded us just as persistently.

Normally, we ignored the jerk. But I didn't like the smug *I know something she doesn't know* way he chuckled at the guy beside him.

"Yeah, well. It's not for sale — and never will be."

"I guess I heard wrong." Lucille flipped her hair, then tilted her head the other way. "Also, there's a completely hot guy checking you out."

I followed her eyes to Ingo and sighed. *Checking out* came in welcome and unwelcome versions. Ingo's was both, somehow.

"I Want You to Want Me" came over the speakers next, but there was no way I was dancing to that now. Instead, I blew out my cheeks, excused myself, and stomped over to Ingo.

"Oh, he's busted," Amy whisper-hissed.

"Twenty bucks says Pippa whips his ass," Lauren threw in before the lyrics drowned her out.

Sensing dozens of eyes on me, I glanced around. Everyone jerked away, suddenly intent on the candles on their tables. Candles which flared suddenly.

Oops.

I marched over to Ingo, then stopped and jammed my hands on my hips.

He pointed around. "Better watch yourself. You don't want to burn the place down."

God, I hated men who knew me better than I knew myself.

"It would help if you weren't staring," I said.

"I wasn't staring."

His words came in a low, rumbly growl that suggested all kinds of wonderful things he could do to me if I gave him free rein.

I did my best to loom over him, which only worked when he was seated. As kids, I'd always been the taller one. Then he'd hit a growth spurt and put on a full foot of height between turning sixteen and seventeen. Not fair, but such was life.

"You were staring, and it's ruining my night."

He snorted. "As if those guys are worth your time."

"Like I'm such a catch."

His firm gaze said he disagreed, and the little smile that ghosted over his lips when the next song started — "Every Little Thing She Does Is Magic" — implied he agreed with Sting.

I shook my head, exasperated. We both knew we were perfect — er, no good — for each other. But that was easy to forget when we got close.

I stood there a minute longer, then slid into his booth before I caused a scene.

Ingo wrapped his lips around the beer bottle and gulped a few times. And damn, was the rippling motion of his throat mesmerizing.

I dragged my eyes away before he noticed, and neither of us spoke.

Ever since Ingo had come to town a few weeks ago, I'd been mentally composing a lecture for him. One about how this was different from the other times destiny had brought us together over the years, when we could defy that meddlesome force by heading in opposite directions as quickly as possible. Sedona was home, so I couldn't pick up and leave. That was up to Ingo to do, and it was time to tell him that in no uncertain terms.

But now that we were face-to-face, all those clever lines vanished from my mind, and I couldn't get out a word.

Besides, Hank was coming up just then. He'd rustled up three other men, and they approached in a nervous huddle.

"Is this guy bothering you, Pippa?"

Yes. No. Maybe?

Their concern touched my heart, though. How sweet.

"It's fine. Thanks, guys. Ingo and I go way back."

Still, they did their best to hold their ground under Ingo's withering glare.

"It really is fine. Thank you so much," I repeated. "We just need a few minutes to catch up."

Hank shot Ingo a doubtful look. "Well, holler if you need help."

The posse shuffled back to their table and sat stiffly, keeping their eyes on us.

I sighed. "You attract a hell of a lot of attention for an uncover agent. What are you doing here anyway?"

He swished his beer bottle. Non-alcoholic, of course. "I'm here to unwind."

Ha. Only Ingo could make a night off look like a stakeout.

"Unwind. Right." I shook my head in exasperation. "How long are you planning to stay in town again?"

"Driving you crazy already?"

"Yes. And not in a good way."

His lips quirked, and while he didn't answer, he held up his beer in a question. Against my better judgment, I nodded, because we really did need to talk — if only so we could figure out how to foil destiny and go our separate ways.

He signaled to the waitress for another beer, and she hurried over with it seconds later, practically undressing him with her eyes.

"Anything else I can get you?"

"Bacon cheeseburger, please." Ingo turned to me, waiting, and a moment later, I caved, echoing his order.

"Sure thing, honey," the waitress said — to Ingo, not me. Then she wandered away, strutting her considerable assets.

To his credit, Ingo didn't follow her swaying hips. Instead, he went back to glaring at Hank and the others.

I snapped my fingers in front of his face. "Stop that. They'll file for a restraining order if you keep that up."

His jaw clicked, and his expression went grim.

I froze, studying him. "Wait. Those guys actually have a restraining order against you?"

"Of course not."

But someone else did, I realized.

"Who?" I pressed on. "Stacy?"

He looked hurt. "I'm not after Stacy. I want to protect her."

That Ingo had a protective streak a mile wide wasn't news to me. But that someone had filed a restraining order against him... Wow.

"Who, then?" I demanded.

Ingo kept his lips sealed.

"Someone you once investigated?"

Ingo's lips tightened, and a second storm joined the one that permanently brewed in his eyes.

Aha. So, it was a former suspect.

"A mafia boss?"

A tic set in next to his eye.

Okay, I was getting closer. But, jeez. How long was I supposed to keep up this game of charades?

I stirred the air with my hand. "Who, Ingo?"

He glared at the table, then grunted. "A guy tangentially involved in an arson case I investigated a while back."

I kept stirring, and oops. The candle on the table echoed the motion, swirling into a tiny whirlwind.

I laid my hand flat on the table. A good thing Ingo was too distracted to notice.

"Victor Jananovich," he finally said. "Ring a bell?"

I let out a dry laugh. Ingo was the one who read FBI reports. I skimmed through back issues of *Arizona Highways.*

"The rodeo pro?" I said, just to get under his skin.

Ingo bought it for a moment, then made a face when he realized I'd made that up. "Victor Jananovich, the *vampire*," he hissed.

I leaned back. Wow. A vampire with a restraining order against a wolf shifter?

"Since when do vampires go to the police to file for restraining orders?"

"They don't. But Jananovich went to the *agency* for a restraining order."

My eyes went wide. "Wow. What did you do?"

Ingo gripped his glass so hard, it was a wonder it didn't shatter.

Tempered or laminated? my professional side wondered, and I tapped mine. Tempered.

"He's the criminal, not me," Ingo insisted.

"And yet, you're the one with the restraining order."

"Yeah, well. The world can be a fucked-up place."

"I guess so," I murmured, chewing that over for a while.

Our legs touched, but I didn't have the brain space to move away.

"Did you have evidence?" I finally asked.

Ingo made a face. "He's slippery as hell, but everything pointed to Jananovich."

"Pointed to or actually proved?"

"I was in the process of collecting that proof when I was called off the case."

"Did you ever consider that you were wrong? That he isn't a criminal?"

"And risk another innocent person dying?"

Another? I stared. What had gone wrong? And, shoot. Did Ingo blame himself for that particular tragedy — whatever it was?

"Two bacon cheeseburgers." The waitress plunked a plate in front of each of us while batting giant, furry caterpillars — er, fake eyelashes — at Ingo. "Can I get you anything else? Another drink? Extra ketchup?"

Me, naked? her dancing eyes added.

Ingo stuck up his hands. "We're fine, thank you."

She moved away, disappointed.

I pressed down on my burger, bringing it closer to mouth-size.

"Where were we?" Ingo asked.

"Vampires," I murmured, chomping down.

And, yum, was it good. Juicy *and* cheesy — so much that a little escaped the corner of my mouth and dripped down my arm.

Ingo reached over to dab it with a napkin before it reached my sleeve.

"Yes, vampires," he grumbled, as if the burger proved my point.

I chewed, swallowed, and wiped my mouth. "So, this Victor Jananowhiz—"

"Jananovich."

"Where is he? California?" That was Ingo's last posting, I knew.

Ingo looked at me, his expression perfectly flat and devoid of emotion — except that little vein that pulsed by his eye.

Then it hit me. "He's here?"

Ingo looked at the door as if a Transylvanian with fangs and a cape might come through at any moment. "He might be."

Might be, my ass. Either the vampire was already here, or Ingo had reason to believe the guy was on his way.

Wherever he is, I'll find out, his eyes swore.

I shook my head, tempted to take his hand and talk some sense into him. Yes, there were a lot of bad guys — and gals

— in the world. That didn't mean Ingo had to personally hunt down every one.

But I'd have more luck explaining that to my burger, so I didn't try.

I did have a question, though. "Hang on. If this Jananovich guy has a restraining order against you, why did the agency assign you to his case?"

Ingo stared at the candle, not meeting my eyes.

Uh-oh. I leaned closer. "They didn't assign you?"

"Not exactly."

I thought it over a moment longer. "Is there even a case?"

"Not officially, no."

Oh boy. Ingo was way out in the middle of a thinly iced-over lake, and he knew it.

"And yet the agency gave you the Sedona job."

He nodded. "They didn't know Jananovich had his eyes on Sedona. No one knew."

As I stared into his eyes, the last puzzle piece fell into place. "No one except you."

Ingo's nostrils flared on a deep inhale, and he nodded faintly.

Wow. It really was personal, wasn't it?

And a little disappointing, because part of me wanted to believe Ingo had come to Sedona for... Well, for me.

Kind of an ego-killer, I had to say.

"So, you're here to put the bad guy away? And that's why you've been following Stacy — to keep her safe?"

Ingo waited, as if willing me to figure out something I'd missed. But for the life of me, I couldn't.

"I want to keep *everyone* safe from Jananovich." He stared deep into my eyes.

I stared back. What was I not getting?

A long minute later, he looked away, disappointed.

All in all, the conversation summarized our fundamental problem. Ingo wanted to save the world. I wanted to make beautiful glass objects. Two objectives with nothing in common except they were both awfully fragile.

I looked at him, struck with sorrow. My sweet, loyal child-hood buddy. My gentle, generous ex-lover. My dear, sorely missed friend.

We hadn't broken up over one big thing. It had been all the little things that had slowly done us in. His work hours. The nights I stayed up worrying about him. Him missing small but important occasions, like one of my art shows. *All* my art shows, actually. Little, forgivable things that were nothing if you took them one at a time, but they added up to a lot. Too much — at least for me.

Part of me must have been holding out hope for a happily-ever-after, but at that moment, I accepted the truth. We weren't ever going to make this work. Never. Our love was a train that had long since chugged into a dead-end station, and it would never make a comeback. Wisps of steam from the engine were all that remained, but soon, those would fade away with the rest of my sweet memories.

I put my burger down. It would never make it past the lump in my throat anyway.

By then, the candle on our table was close to drowning in its own pool of wax, but I couldn't find it in me to pep it up a bit.

Then the next song came over the speakers, and I couldn't help humming the opening notes. Ingo's eyes met mine, and we both flashed thin smiles.

I took a deep breath, then stood and stuck out a hand.

Ingo cocked his head at my abrupt change in gears. "You're asking me to dance?"

Yes, I was. Because as Kenny Rogers put it, Ingo did something to me that I couldn't explain.

I nodded slowly. "Against my better judgment..."

Ingo's grin was a thing of beauty. He stood, took my hand, and followed me to the dance floor.

One last time, I told myself. *One last time.*

Chapter Four

INGO

I forced myself to leave the bar before Pippa did, because otherwise, I would have been tempted to follow her home, which just wouldn't do. It didn't matter how much I loved her or that she loved me back, as evidenced by the slow dance we shared.

Yes, a slow dance. A terrible idea, but neither of us could resist. "Islands in the Stream" had come on, and that football-jock Pippa had danced with earlier was making eyes at her like that might be his chance, when it was absolutely not. Especially not that song — the one Pippa and I used to call ours back when life was simpler.

"Against my better judgment..." she'd murmured, offering her hand.

The candle on our table had flared, burning brightly.

Against my better judgment too, though that didn't stop me from following her to the dance floor and easing into old, familiar moves. Close moves, with her chin snuggled against my shoulder and our chests touching. Much like the many mornings-after we'd once shared, with no one in between, just like the song said.

You'd think the daughter of a pyromancer and a dragon shifter might carry the scent of smoke or ash, but Pippa's was more like lavender incense. Every breath calmed and centered me — enough to make me wonder how I got by without her.

All day, I'd been agonizing over the mystery of the dead "hiker." But even that faded away when I was with Pippa, and I could believe in good things, at least for a while.

Too bad the next song — Michael Jackson's "Thriller" — ripped us out of the mood. I'd left Pippa with a peck on the cheek instead of the full-on, *Gone with the Wind*, bent-over-backward kiss I'd been dreaming of. Then I'd hurried out to my car, where I'd spent five minutes waiting for my heart rate to settle down. Finally, I cranked up the engine and drove into the night.

Janet Sullivan, I reminded myself. The dead hiker. My office wasn't far. I could easily drive over, log in to the agency database, and do some more investigating.

But I'd been digging through that rabbit warren all day, and my wolf was howling for a change.

Well, howling for Pippa. But a run would be good too.

So, I drove "home" to the cabin I was renting, having taken over the lease from Nash. It was way out of town, down a dirt road, on a property owned by an older guy named Henry.

As the dragon flies, it was only about three miles west of Pippa's ranch. As the wolf trots, it was more like five miles. I knew, because I'd been drawn in that direction night after night. Drawn by what, I wasn't sure. By Pippa? Destiny? By my own foolish hopes and desires?

That night, like every night, I told myself I wouldn't go. But that night, like every night, I went anyway.

Just a little run, my inner wolf begged. *Just to get out and move. We don't even have to head in her direction.*

The same lie I let myself fall for every time.

I only entered the cabin long enough to drop my car keys and jacket. Then I stepped outside again, stripping layers as I went. Sweater, shirt, pants, boots, socks. Henry was a perfect neighbor as far as that went — plenty distant and lights out by nine, due to his early starting time with the hot air balloon company he owned. So I was all alone.

April nights in Sedona were as chilly as the days were warm, so I shifted as I walked. The tiny hairs on my skin thickened and grew. Color drained out of my eyesight, while scents flooded my nose. I hadn't been in Arizona long enough to name each of the flowers I whiffed, but there was an astonishing array — everything from prickly cacti to the sticky-sweet blossoms hummingbirds buzzed around.

I dropped to all fours, curling my hands, hunching my back. My body ached and burned. Then, once every bone, muscle, and sinew snapped into place, the usual adrenaline rush hit me, and I took off at a sprint.

I'd been able to shift from the age of seventeen, but the sense of freedom never failed to thrill. All day, I was bound by a thousand human rules: where to drive and how fast (or how slow), when to wait (always too long), what to say (and what not to). Now, I could do anything, from rolling in the dirt to howling at the moon. I could scratch an ear with my rear leg without being told it wasn't polite, and I didn't have to fuss with clothes. Wherever instinct led me, I could go without thinking about how or why. In fact, without having to think at all.

Which was how I found myself panting under the stars on a ridgeline overlooking a familiar cluster of buildings and barns. Painted Rock Ranch, where Pippa and her sisters lived. Nash, too, though my nose wasn't pointed in the direction of the cabin he shared with Erin, nor the main house where the younger sister, Abby, lived with her daughter, Claire.

No, my nose was pointed at Pippa's home, a converted barn at the far edge of the ranch.

The entire property lay under a protective spell none of the sisters could — or would — explain, so it was blurry at first. If an ordinary human had stumbled across my viewpoint, their eyes would only register another expanse of dirt, scrub, and ochre-tinted rock. But if you knew where to look and you concentrated hard enough, the buildings and paddocks took shape, as they did to me now.

Pippa's car was parked in its usual spot beside the barn and the fire pit. No fire, though a couple of embers glowed. I perked my ears, half hoping Pippa would step out, wave, and invite me in.

There you are, my love. I imagined her calling. *Come on in and make yourself at home.*

That didn't happen, of course. Not in the first five minutes I spent waiting, wishing, hoping. Not in the next few minutes that ticked by even more slowly. Gradually, my wagging tail went limp. My ears drooped, and I sat on the cold ground, trying to digest the truth. We were destined for each other, but my job kept driving us apart. Pippa was right about work becoming an obsession. But how could I live with myself if I quit?

A howl built in my throat, but I held it in until I was halfway back to my place. Pippa didn't need to see — or hear — me in such a state.

It was only when I reached a faraway, lonely patch of desert that I stopped for a good, long howl.

Well, a long howl, at least. *Good* didn't apply when the emotions tore your own heart to shreds. The long, sorrowful notes hung in the chill night air, and the stars winked, trying to cheer me up. They didn't, but I did take solace in the fact that Pippa was home safe. She must have left the bar shortly after I had instead of staying on to drink or dance. So maybe there was still hope. Maybe she was in bed now, yearning for me the way I yearned for her.

I listened to my last, warbly note fade into the night, then made my way home. Outside the cabin, I shifted wearily, then headed to bed. There were bad guys to catch — really, really bad guys ready to harm, steal, and kill. If I didn't stop them, who would?

∞∞∞∞

Sleep did about as much for me as howling did, so the sunny day I woke to didn't shine all the way into my soul. On the drive into town, I cursed every delivery truck and monster motorhome crawling along the roads. I stopped in at my office — a back room of the local Department of Agriculture office, in line with my cover story — then headed out again. No new leads in the hiker case, not that I'd had much hope in official channels anyway.

But I did have a lead on a bear shifter, whether he was involved in the hiker case or not. So, I decided to start there. That meant staking out the strip mall in hopes of picking up the trail of Stacy's SUV — and driver — there.

Sure enough, the Chevy Tahoe with tinted windows appeared, dropping Stacy off at the coffee shop. All I could see of the driver was a faint profile.

My mind drifted as I waited, taking me to a different place and time. A different case — my one big failure. I'd been taking my time, building my case against Jananovich... Too long, at least for the woman who'd come forward with a tip. She'd been afraid for her life, and rightly so.

Her name was Bridget, and she was only twenty-five when she died.

A death I might have prevented, if I hadn't waited as long as I had.

So, yeah. I overdid it sometimes, and the price I paid was my own relationships. But I'd made my peace with that.

Well, mostly.

When a car pulled into the space beside me, I glanced over, then back at Stacy's SUV. Then I drew in a long breath. It was time to build a case or forever drop it. Either way, I would have to live with the consequences.

My wolf growled, and I went with option A. Building a case.

I drew in a long breath, puffed it out again, then dialed the agency.

"Agent Kemper calling for Records & Tracing," I said when the operator replied.

I waited, tapping my fingers on the dash, then frowning at the reply.

"Unable to process my request? Why?" I asked the guy at the end of the line.

He had no idea, but he promised to look into it.

As I hung up, miffed, Stacy emerged from the coffee shop with a steaming cup and slid back into the vehicle. I started my Jeep to follow it, then hit the brakes as my nostrils flared.

Pippa! my inner wolf crooned.

I whipped my head around just in time to see her screech into a parking spot, leap out of her car, and storm toward a storefront. I threw on the handbrake and left my car, racing after her. Clearly, something was wrong. But what?

I burst into the office she'd entered just in time to see her slap a newspaper on the desk of a bald, pudgy guy.

She didn't pick him up by the collar, but she did growl. "What the hell is this, dammit?"

My eyes jumped to the nameplate on his desk. *Robert Hardy, Red Rock Vistas Real Estate.*

The man stuck his hands up. "Now, Ms. Martin—"

So, he knew her — well enough to maneuver his rolling chair to a safer distance.

"Don't you Ms. Martin me." She smacked the paper. "What the hell is this?"

"Um, the latest listings?" He sounded guilty already.

Pippa glanced at me with a *What are you doing here?* look, then turned back to Hardy.

"I mean this." She stabbed a finger at the center of the page.

"Um...a listing?"

Amazing how a grown man could look like a kid with one hand in the cookie jar.

Pippa snatched up the paper and read. *"Seventy-eight stunning acres of secluded property along Painted Rock Creek, perfect for your own private getaway or development into subdivisions..."*

"That could be any property," he tried.

"Who else owns seventy-eight acres along Painted Rock Creek?" She scoffed, smacking the paper back down. "How many times have we told you? Our property is not for sale, and it never will be."

"I only want what's best for you, your sisters, and Sedona."

"Ha. You want what's best for you. So, stop pestering us or...or..." She cast around for something to threaten him with, then glanced at me and lit up. "Or we'll get a restraining order."

Ouch.

Hardy tapped the tiny print at the bottom of the listing. "See this? It says we can't be held responsible for inaccuracies or changes."

"I'll show you being held responsible—" Pippa hissed.

I caught her hand before she did something rash.

Hardy threw a wild-eyed look at the only other person in the office — Louise Bartly, according to her nameplate — who reached for her phone, eyeing the numbers nine, one, and one.

I flashed my government ID, then stuck it away before they noticed the Department of Agriculture part. "All right, everyone. Settle down."

Hardy pointed at Pippa. "Tell her that."

She crossed her arms. "No, you tell *me* why my property is listed when it's not for sale."

He stuttered a few times. "As I said, I only want the best for you and your sisters. And if your circumstances were to change..."

"What circumstances?"

A satisfied look flashed behind the fear in Hardy's eyes.

"Say, a property reassessment or a tax increase you're unable to meet..."

Pippa's brows pinched. "Tax increase?"

Hardy shuffled through some papers, then turned one around. Pippa opened her mouth to yell, then stopped, stunned. Her eyes ran over the text again and again.

I frowned. Now what?

She grabbed the paper to inspect it more closely. "What are you doing with an assessment of my property?"

Hardy went from terrified to smug. "Property assessments are a matter of public record. And that there document says yours has been undervalued for years."

Pippa reread the paper, muttering, "Harlon fucking Greene. He's behind this, isn't he?"

My ears perked at that mention of the warlock who'd recently been intercepted by the agency. I hadn't been involved in the case, but it had led to the establishment of a new agency post in Sedona — the post I now filled.

I leaned in to read over Pippa's shoulder. Harlon Greene's illegal business deals had been brought to light by Pippa, her sisters, and Nash. Now, it appeared the warlock was wreaking his revenge, perhaps through an anonymous tip to the tax authorities.

"Property in Sedona is worth a hundred times what it was in your great-aunt's day," Hardy pointed out.

I narrowed my eyes. It seemed Hardy had had the ranch in his sights for years.

"Maybe, but twenty-six million?" Pippa shook her head.

Hardy pulled out a calculator and made a show of working out the math. "That's…let me see… Yes. It comes to a tax increase of about ten thousand dollars."

"Ten thousand?" Pippa screeched.

"Per year." Hardy placed his glasses on the desk with glee. "And seeing as such assessments can be backdated three years…"

Pippa's eyes went wide. Mine too. There was no way she or her sisters could come up with that kind of money.

"Thirty thousand." Hardy tut-tutted. "Quite a burden, I know."

Pippa slapped the document back onto his desk and leaned in, looking dangerous as hell. "You seem to know an awful lot about all this, Bob."

The wheels of his chair squeaked as he edged away.

"You think I don't see through this?" Pippa went on.

I touched her shoulder, but she smacked my hand away.

"You've been after our property for years, and you know it," Pippa raged. "I bet you already have the plans all sketched out. Subdivisions, McMansions, a golf course…"

My nose twitched, and I glanced around. What was that acrid smell?

"Let me guess," Pippa continued. "You even have the marketing planned. What will you call the place? Painted Rock Gated Community? Painted Rock Ruined Subplots?"

"Is something burning?" Louise Bartly asked.

Pippa didn't seem to hear. "Painted Rock Cooker-Cutter Mansions? Painted Rock Starter Castles, each with their own Garage Mahal?"

My eyes fell to the desk and, crap. The real estate listing was going black around the edges. The pages curled, and a thin wisp of smoke rose.

I grabbed Pippa's shoulder while Hardy smacked at the flames.

"Fire! Fire! Stop!" he grunted, as if the fire might obey.

It didn't. Not until I squeezed Pippa's shoulder — hard. She blinked a few times, then glanced down with a sour look.

"Holy crap..." Hardy continued smacking at the flames, and finally, they extinguished. "Where did that come from?"

Pippa crossed her arms and glared.

I pulled her away while pointing to his glasses. "Looks like the angle was just right for a magnifying glass effect."

Hardy snatched up his glasses and peered at the lenses, then the sunlight streaming through the window. "Huh. That's never happened before..."

No shit. I towed Pippa toward the door.

"Maybe you should be more careful," she snipped.

"With your glasses," I hurried to add. "Goodbye."

The moment I shoved the door open, the heat of the day hit us like a wall. I thrust Pippa through it and out onto the sidewalk.

She glared at Hardy, then at me. "Whose side are you on anyway?"

"Yours." I towed her away before Hardy figured out what had set off that fire. "You want to be charged for assault and arson?"

She jerked her arm free. "Hitting a desk with a piece of paper isn't assault."

"And what about the fire?"

"What about it?"

I pinned her with a stern look and towed her toward her car. A glance back showed me she was tearing up, but it wasn't until we reached the car that she let them flow.

"I can kiss Venice goodbye," she mumbled through her tears.

I bent closer. Venice?

"Even worse, I might have to kiss the ranch goodbye," she went on miserably. Then she balled her fists and banged on the car roof. "I have to win that contest. I have to."

"What contest?"

Her answer was so garbled, I settled for rubbing her back softly.

"It will be okay."

I wished someone could rub my back, though. I knew exactly what set off that fire in Hardy's office. And as an agent of the ADMSA, I was duty bound to report it — and any other supernatural activity that qualified as harassment or assault. But I was also madly in love with Pippa, and I would always, always stand on her side. But one of these days...

I wrapped my arms around Pippa and tucked my head over hers, wondering where this would all lead. Bitter disappointment, no doubt. For her, for me, and for our foolish hearts.

Chapter Five

PIPPA

I took a deep breath, then blew, keeping a close eye on the glowing mass at the end of the rod as it slowly expanded. When I ran out of breath, I capped the end of the blowpipe with my thumb and started swinging the rod. A little too forcefully maybe, because my mind was still on what had happened the previous day.

Damn that Bob Hardy! Damn property assessments and taxes!

I'd shared the news with my sisters, who were just as furious — and just as cash-strapped — as me. We'd stayed up late discussing the problem, but every idea we'd come up with would take time. The first step was checking if the property assessment really had increased, and if so, how to appeal it. I'd volunteered to stop by city hall to inquire, but my sisters had nixed the idea once they found out about my teensy-tiny, totally insignificant fire-setting mishap.

So the task of visiting city hall fell to Abby, and all I could do was glance at my phone every few minutes, hoping for news.

In the meantime, I did my best to turn my anger into determination. I had to win that contest!

My mind was brimming with ideas, but I had to finish other projects first. The owners of Sedona Glass were happy for me to use the shop for private projects, but only after I'd worked down their job list. So, there I was, working on yet another project for yet another client.

I switched to the bench and did my best to focus. An upscale resort on the outskirts of town had ordered multiple sets of matching glasses — water, wine, brandy, and so on — so I had to keep moving. The sooner I finished those, the sooner I could get to work on my contest entry. The $25,000 prize was a long shot, but it would come in awfully handy.

Make that, crucial.

By noon, two tidy rows of glasses filled the annealer — a damn good start. Then the bell jingled, and Stacy entered with a cheery wave.

"Hi, Pippa. How are you?"

I pulled off my work gloves and stepped toward the counter. "Great, and you?"

"Great!" Stacy chirped.

We were both lying. Well, I sure was, and Stacy didn't look great herself. On the other hand, that could have been the light, her makeup, or just a bad night's sleep.

Or a vampire sucking her blood, I couldn't help thinking after what Ingo had said.

Still, I doubted Stacy was the type to get mixed up with any kind of criminal, let alone criminal vampires. And frankly, I wasn't looking my best either, with my frazzled hair and messy work clothes. At least Stacy was nicely styled, with matching colors, makeup, the works.

I pointed to the colorful Monet-flower-print fabric around her neck. "Wow. You always have such beautiful scarves. You must have a whole collection."

She froze. Oops. Had I said the wrong thing?

She recovered quickly, though, flipping one end of the scarf over her shoulder like a 1930s movie star. "Why, thank you, darling."

We both laughed.

"I got your order, but it said Tuesday, so it's not done yet," I said, moving on to business. "Is that okay?"

Stacy nodded. "Totally. I'm just here for a gift for a friend."

I put my hand on my heart, truly touched. "Aw, thanks for thinking of us. I hope you find something you like."

She chuckled. "The only problem will be choosing between everything I love."

My cheeks warmed. If only every customer were as sweet and easy as her.

The door opened on a young couple — Stacy's polar opposites, at least in terms of style. Both were clad in head-to-toe black. Their skin was punctured by a dozen piercings and covered in a web of heavy tattoos. But, hey. Whatever made them happy.

"Hi." The twentysomething woman stepped to the counter and shaped the air with her hands. "We're looking for a couple of those love vials."

The guy nodded, making the skeleton tattoo on his throat ripple. "Two of them."

The girl chuckled and bumped his arm. "That's what a couple is, dummy. Like us."

He grinned, just as dopey with love. A slightly offbeat, ghoulish kind of love, but hey. I'd take a *happy Goth* couple over *groomed but grouchy* any day.

I opened a drawer and pulled out some samples. "We have a few different types..."

They leaned in, inspecting the vials.

"What do you think of these?" the guy asked.

"Nice," his girlfriend decided.

I forced a polite smile, though I disagreed. There were so many ways of expressing love. Why carry around a vial of blood?

Stacy, on the other hand, touched her vial with a genuine smile. But worry gnawed at the corners of her lips, and she shot a furtive look at the SUV parked outside.

"Ha. They're about half the size of a shot glass," the guy joked, making a knock-it-back motion.

Ugh. The vials were for holding blood, not sipping it.

Then I froze, thinking of the vampire Ingo had mentioned. Victor Janano-something. I glanced toward the binder where we filed our invoices. What was the name of the company Stacy worked for? TTC Limited, I recalled. No mention of a Victor or vampires. Then again, a company called TTC could belong to anyone.

Or any*thing*. A shiver went down my spine.

But that was way, way circumstantial. Ridiculous, actually. I pushed the thought away and focused on business. The sooner I helped these customers, the sooner they'd move on, and the sooner I could create my contest entry.

The tattooed woman held the vials up to the light and turned them this way and that. "I guess you have to cut yourself and funnel the blood in there?"

Ugh. That probably appealed to some but was a bile-burner for others. Like me.

I opened my mouth, then closed it as imaginary headlines flashed through my mind. *Glass artist under investigation for role in tragic bloodletting accident.*

I kept my lips sealed. This was not one of those things I was qualified to dispense advice on.

Luckily, the young woman went on without waiting for an answer. "And how do you seal them? I mean, what if they leaked?"

The guy tapped one chewed-to-the-quick fingernail against the glass. "I'd say there's more risk of the blood drying up in there."

Another reason I found the whole concept gross. But it was my job to sell, so sell I did.

"They come with this kit." I pointed to a shrink-wrapped bag containing a cap and a tube of anticoagulant. "I hear it's pretty easy, and I've never heard of one leaking."

Stacy looked up behind them, and I half expected her to chime in. But she sealed her lips and went back to browsing candlesticks.

The couple inspected the instructions.

"Crazy glue?" the woman murmured. "Isn't there a better way to seal them — like those?" She pointed at a display of glass tubes sealed at both ends.

Those were our cheesiest souvenirs, some declaring *Take home the clean Sedona air* and others, *Genuine Sedona Sand — collected from Sedona's strongest vortexes!* We didn't sell many, but the profit margin was huge.

"I guess you could..." I mused. "But you'd need the right tools..."

The woman waved at the workbench behind me. "Like those?"

Stacy looked up, openly curious.

"Technically, yes. But we're not certified to deal with bio-hazards."

I was making that up, because I really, really didn't want to handle someone else's blood.

For the briefest of moments, I second-guessed myself. Maybe if they offered a hell of a lot of money...

But, yikes. I wasn't *that* desperate. Yet.

"Too bad," the woman sighed.

"I'm pretty good with a blowtorch," the guy said. "Could you show me what to do?"

Wow. When his woman wanted something, he found a way. A keeper, for sure.

The woman beamed.

"Well..." I shot a look at the clock. I really had to finish my current project.

The guy rooted around in a deep pocket, produced a wallet secured to his low-hanging jeans by a heavy chain, and pulled out a twenty-dollar bill.

"Would that be enough?"

I stared. Oh. I hadn't been hinting at a tip or bribe, but heck. Now that he was offering...

It wasn't twenty grand but, heck. Twenty bucks for a two-minute demo wasn't bad.

I nearly said yes, then caught myself. You didn't mess with young love, and you certainly didn't make a quick buck off it.

"Not necessary," I said. "I'm happy to show you — but you didn't see me show you, if you know what I mean."

He grinned, putting his wallet away. "Show us what?"

Good. I was happy to keep this our little secret.

I got to work, setting the materials on the counter: a blow-torch and a couple of pieces of cast-off glass tubing.

"Basically, you hold the tip of the vial to another piece of glass in the heat of the blowtorch. Once they start to fuse, you rotate them like this..."

He watched closely as I demonstrated, as did his girlfriend and Stacy, who peered over their shoulders.

"When you pull them apart slowly, it seals both ends..." I stretched the glass until it was as thin as a thread. It separated on its own, leaving me with two pinched-off tubes. I tapped the molten ends on a steel plate, then rolled them gently. "Then you do this to give it a smooth finish. That's it." I held up the sealed tube. "Easy."

The man lit up like a child at Christmas, and his girlfriend beamed. "That's awesome! We'll have to tell all our friends!"

God, I hoped not. We would end up inundated with requests for the real deal, which would be hard to explain to my boss. Or worse, my boss might embrace the idea and advertise it to pull in a whole new revenue stream. I'd be sealing blood vials for the rest of my life.

"That's really cool." Stacy fingered her own vial quietly.

It did beat the crazy glue solution, but *cool* was not how I would describe blood vials. More like *creepy*.

"It's super cool. Thanks," the couple gushed.

In the end, they bought three sets of vials — one for themselves, two for friends — and headed for the door. The guy had vertebrae tattooed on the back of his neck, and that was my last view of him. That and the arm slung tenderly around his girlfriend.

Ah, love. It came in all shapes and sizes.

Stacy watched as I cleared the impromptu workshop from the counter.

"Did you find something you liked?" I asked.

She jerked up with another insta-smile, then went back to the candlestick display. "They're all so beautiful. It's hard to decide."

"Take your time."

She did. A long, long time, punctuated by furtive glances outside.

She sure didn't seem in a rush to get back in that fancy SUV today.

I came around the counter to join her. "Anything else I can help you with?" I spoke softly, tilting my head toward the car.

"Oh no, thank you. I'm fine." Her laugh was a nervous whinny.

I kept my eyes on the items before us and whispered, "Seriously, Stacy. Is everything okay?"

She didn't say anything, which set off alarms in my mind. Then she flashed a huge smile and chirped, "Everything's great! Just trying to decide."

My eyes wandered to the pinboard by the door. It was filled with flyers for local events, artists, yoga instructors...and a hotline for battered women.

"Maybe I can help you decide?" I aimed my gaze at that flyer.

Her eyes followed mine, and her hand went to her neck. "Thanks," she whispered, "but I have to figure this out on my own." Then she flashed that fake smile and waved at the candlesticks. "The hard part is deciding."

Yes, it was. As in, deciding where the line between *concerned citizen* and *minding my own business* lay. Because something was one hundred percent, totally, definitely wrong here.

Stacy touched my arm, smiling more genuinely now. "I'm fine, thanks. Really. I just need a minute."

I was sure she needed a lot more than that, but I couldn't exactly call the hotline for her.

I wandered back behind the counter. "I'm right here when you need me. Anytime." I emphasized the last word.

She nodded that sweet smile of hers, and I couldn't help thinking of Ingo, vampires, and his hushed warnings.

I want to keep everyone safe from Jananovich.

If Jananovich was, in fact, in Sedona, and if he was who Stacy worked for. Two big ifs.

I mulled that over while keeping myself busy for a minute or two, then looked up. Stacy was holding two candlesticks, but her eyes were unfocused, her thoughts elsewhere.

I burned to ask her the name of her boss and what TTC Limited did, but that would be out of line in a client-customer relationship. Besides, if I pried, she might stop coming to me entirely, and what help would I be to her then?

"If you like, you can test the candlesticks with those sample candles," I said gently. "That might help you decide."

She sniffed one of the candles, but clearly, her mind was elsewhere.

"The vanilla one is really soothing," I suggested.

Stacy found it and struck a match from the box we kept there. But her hands were shaking — not much, but just enough — and it went out. She tried another, then another—

I narrowed my eyes on the third match and wiggled my fingers, giving her a helping hand. And, oops. It flared so bright, she nearly dropped it.

"Whoa. Okay, here we go," she murmured as the candle caught, filling the shop with its sweet aroma.

I stretched my fingers, then formed a fist silently.

"Oh, it does smell nice," she said, closing her eyes.

Now, if only we had garlic-scented candles I could send her home with. . .

Stacy sniffed a moment longer, looking slightly more at peace. Then the driver honked outside, and she whipped her head around.

"Oh, I'd better go," she yelped.

I thought fast. Normally, I jumped at the chance to make a sale. But candlesticks weren't what mattered here.

"Why don't you take time to think it over?" I suggested. "You can decide when you come back to pick up your order." I gave the flyer another pointed look.

Her head bowed for a moment, and I nearly blurted, *Or I can lock the door, draw the shades, and call that number for you right now. We can have the police here, lickety-split, too. Or better yet, my ex and his buddy. They're BDSM agents, you know.*

It occurred to me that BDSM didn't sound right, but whatever.

Stacy took a deep breath, then mournfully blew out the candle she'd lit. But when she turned to me, she worked up another smile.

You don't have to pretend, I wanted to tell her. *I'm on your side. I can help.*

Her eyes had a hollow, *No one can help me* look.

"I'll think it over and let you know when I come back," she finally said. Then her smile grew warmer, and a little sass came back into her voice. "So much to do, so little time," she quipped, tossing the scarf over her shoulder.

We both laughed, and the bell over the door jingled as she left.

"See you soon," I called, watching her go.

For a long time afterward, I thought of her. Her and her scarf and those vials.

Chapter Six

PIPPA

At seven o'clock the next morning, my phone rang its Ragtime tune. I glared at it. Who called at such an hour?

I was consuming breakfast — and the previous day's news, courtesy of a paper Erin had brought home.

Sad news. The dead hiker had been identified as Janet Sullivan of Denver, just twenty-four years old. Police hadn't yet determined the cause of death, but they seemed to be leaning toward an accident.

I could picture Ingo's scowl as he read that.

Meanwhile, the jaunty Ragtime tune of my phone went into its fourth repetition.

"Will you get that already?" Abby said while rushing around the kitchen to get Claire's school lunch ready. Claire was upstairs, changing into yet another different outfit.

On the ranch, we sisters each had our own little area. Erin shared a cozy cabin with Nash, while Abby and Claire had the upstairs of the main house, and I lived in the converted barn. The conversion wasn't quite finished — okay, barely even started — so I ate most meals at the main house, where the ground floor was shared territory.

I made a sour face, showing the phone my displeasure before answering it.

"Hello?"

"Hi, Pippa. It's me," Erin said, sounding breathless.

Uh-oh.

I steeled myself. My sisters and I lived within shouting distance, and we saw plenty of one another. We could also

51

mind-talk, as most related supernaturals could. We only really used a phone if we needed something right away — and Erin's tone was urgent.

"Hi," I stretched the word out warily.

She came right to the point. "I need a favor."

"I figured."

Erin broke into a long, complicated story about a tear in a basket at Desert Skies Balloon Adventures.

"We need to fix it by tomorrow. And the parts we need are in Phoenix..."

Subtext: almost two hours away, each way.

"...and it will take a couple of hours to actually weave the wicker..."

I rolled my hand in the air. "What do you need, Erin?"

She dropped the overly careful tone. "Nash promised to show a friend around the back roads of Sedona, but I need his help on the repair. So we need someone to show his friend around."

That didn't sound so bad.

Then it hit me. Nash wasn't exactly a gregarious, *I'm off to meet my dozens of friends* kind of guy. In fact, I only knew of one friend of his.

"What friend?" I growled.

Abby looked up from cutting apple slices.

"Ingo," Erin admitted, rushing right into, "Please!"

I'd never told my sisters about how serious Ingo and I had been, way back when, and I hadn't talked to them about my conflicting feelings now either. But my sisters could read me like a book — one they'd already read cover to cover many times, like *Black Beauty* — or, more recently, *Fifty Shades of Grey.*

I shook my head. "Nope. Can't do it."

Won't do it was closer to the truth, but hey. The less time Ingo and I spent together, the better.

"Please, Pippa. I need you to do this."

I balled my hands so tightly, my fingernails cut into my palms.

"It's just for a few hours," she went on.

Plenty of time for my body to betray me. And as for Ingo...
He liked to give the impression of zen-like master of self-control,
but I knew better.

"I don't have time. I'm behind in the shop..."

I looked at Abby, who shook her head in a vehement, *Whatever it is, I don't have the time for it* motion.

Which was totally legit. Abby worked long days at the
metal shop, stopping only for a quick lunch and to pick up
Claire from school. Even after that, the two of them headed
back to the shop for another few hours until dinnertime.

"Please, Pippa," Erin pleaded. "If the basket's not fixed,
we'll have to cancel the guests who booked for tomorrow."

Subtext: money neither she nor the balloon company could
afford to lose.

"What time were you supposed to meet Ingo?" I asked.

"Four."

I made a quick calculation. "You could make it to Phoenix
and back and still have a couple hours for the repairs."

"If we break every speed limit, yes." She waited a beat,
then went on. "But if we're down in Phoenix anyway, we could
run some other errands. And Nash and I could finally try that
pizza place everyone is talking about."

Aha. Now her ulterior motives were clear.

I sighed. My sister's courtship with Nash had consisted of
meeting at work, hating each other for a while, fighting off a
criminal warlock and a ruthless vampire, and surviving several
near-death experiences. A sure formula for a happily-ever-
after.

My thoughts strayed to Ingo, but I yanked them back. Not
going there.

I was happy for Erin — really, really happy — and for
Nash. They'd both needed someone to put a little spark into
their lives.

Sparks. I chuckled at my own pun. Both were dragon
shifters, and boy, did they spark. Not just in the flames they
could spit — only slightly jealous, I swear — but also when
their mojo got up and demanded a little bow chick a wow
wow. And believe me, a dragon shifter's mojo got up *a lot.*

Again…only slightly jealous.

Anyway, I truly wished them the best, and they definitely deserved a mini date, even if it was just pizza between errands. But the last time Ingo and I had gone exploring in a Jeep, we'd ended up *exploring* in the back seat. And that was one trip down memory lane I really didn't want to take.

"Just tell Ingo you have to reschedule," I said.

"We already have. Twice. And Nash says it's really important."

Ha. Birds of a feather, those two agents. Okay, former agent, in Nash's case — one who'd finally settled down into a quieter, happier life.

If only Ingo had it in him to do the same.

And as for important… I didn't doubt it. Law enforcement was a crucial and often thankless job, and I was grateful to the people who did it. I just preferred that not to be the man I loved. I knew all too well what that meant, having a firefighter father.

All those nights I'd spent as a kid, praying he and his crew would make it home safely after another raging forest fire. All the holidays interrupted by sirens signaling the next big emergency my father had to rush away to, often for days at a time…

I loved that my father was a hero. But that didn't mean I wanted to spend the rest of my life with another one.

I sighed. Selfish, I know. But at least I was honest.

"Please, Pippa," Erin pleaded. "I could help you in the shop later this week to make up for it."

I snorted. Erin had helped me once, and I had the shattered glass to show for it. Little known fact: even a badass balloon pilot/dragon shifter/wind whisperer did not necessarily make a useful assistant in a glass shop.

"That's almost worse than being in a Jeep with Ingo," I muttered.

"Hey! I did my best…"

Still, I stuck to my guns. "Really, it's not a good idea for me to take Ingo."

Spending time with him wasn't just a threat to my heart. It risked my secrets too.

Erin, Abby, and I had decided to keep our little...um...vortex *experience* to ourselves. Even with Nash, we downplayed it. No one needed to know exactly what had happened the day we'd channeled the power of our ranch's secret vortex to repel a warlock's attack.

Hell, *I* wasn't sure what had happened — or why I'd felt a little different since then.

As a wolf shifter, Ingo knew all about the supernatural. He also knew that I possessed very minor magic abilities, despite having two powerful supernatural parents.

But that was all he knew, and I was happy to keep it that way. Especially if we weren't going to spend the rest of our lives together and thus share *all* our secrets.

My chest squeezed.

"Besides, Ingo is hot." Erin's voice dropped. "And you two have crazy chemistry."

Exactly the problem. Could she not understand that?

"I've seen you look at him..." she continued.

Oh, I'd done a lot more than look, once upon a time. The point was, I had to move on. We both did.

I gulped away the lump in my throat. "Enough, Erin."

"Okay, okay. Not my business. But I'd really appreciate your help. Just this once..."

My head said *no*. My heart said *yes* — to Ingo and to helping Erin. Did that count as two against one?

Claire came downstairs and twirled around, showing off her pink pegasus shirt and purple tutu. "How does this look, Mommy?"

Abby, to her credit, bit back her skepticism. The apple had fallen about as far from the tree as possible, at least when it came to fashion choices.

"Very colorful," Abby said. "And I love the pegasus."

I gave Claire a thumbs-up while Erin's broken record skipped again and again.

"Please..."

No was on the tip of my tongue, but guilt held it back.

"What does Auntie Erin need, Mommy?" Claire asked, proving how loud Erin was. And I didn't even have the speaker on.

Abby shrugged. "Some kind of favor."

Claire brightened, eager as always. "Can we help?"

Abby shot me a pointed look.

Even as kids, we sisters had vowed to stick together, especially with three different fathers and *without* a devoted mother acting as the glue in the family. When Abby had faced becoming a single mother, Erin and I had renewed that vow, and all three of us had promised to model those values for Claire.

I gritted my teeth and forced a smile. "No need to, sweetie. I can do it."

"You'll do it?" Erin cried over the phone. "You're the best! Thank you! He'll be at the Desert Skies office at four o'clock today. Okay?"

"Okay, okay," I sighed, already lecturing myself.

I was a grown woman. I could spend a couple of businesslike hours in Ingo's company without jumping his bones. I might even be able to convince him Sedona wasn't brimming with evil vampires at the same time.

"Four o'clock," Erin repeated. "Don't forget."

"All right, already. I have to go." Before I clicked the phone off, I threw in, "But you owe me. Nash does too."

"We do owe you," Erin agreed. "Thank you."

"Bye," I mumbled, ignoring the alarms ringing in my mind.

"Ready to go?" Abby asked her daughter as I hung up.

Claire rushed to the door. "I just have to say goodbye to the horses."

Abby looked at the clock. "Three minutes. And don't let them slobber on your nice new shirt."

Claire hurried off, cheery as ever. Another example of the apple falling from the tree and rolling far, far away. She did have Abby's creative mind, though.

"Okay, Mommy! Meet you at the car in a minute!"

Abby sat with a sigh and bit into her toast.

I went back to the paper, checking the sports section on the back page.

"Sad about that hiker, huh?" Abby murmured, skim-reading the front side.

I nodded absently, then stopped and peered over the edge of the paper. Abby was staring at an article on the front page, somewhere near the bottom. I half turned it for a peek. Something about a mining accident in Nevada.

Uh-oh. I narrowed my eyes on Abby. Was she worried about her father?

Not a *What if he was hurt in the accident?* kind of worry. More like, *What if he'd caused it?*

Erin and I had lucked out with amazing, doting dads, but Abby had never been on good terms with her father. I'd met him twice, and he didn't seem like a bad guy. Just a bit overzealous about his "job" as an eco-warrior.

I sighed, thinking of Ingo. At least the mission he devoted himself to didn't land him in the slammer every few years. But he would probably end up being just as much of an absentee father, and I refused to subject my kids to that.

Kids I would never have, if I couldn't have them with Ingo.

I bit my lip, thinking, then looked back at Abby.

"Everything okay?" I asked her.

She pursed her lips, then shrugged. "What can I say? I hope so."

Chapter Seven

INGO

I tapped my fingers on the steering wheel of the government-issued Jeep, then checked my watch. It wasn't like Nash to be late. What was keeping him?

I'd checked and rechecked my messages, but nothing. Of course, reception was spotty out where Nash lived, and work took him to equally out-of-the-way places, so his messages had a way of pinging through hours after he sent them.

I was in the supermarket parking lot, not far from the Y intersection that had become the center of my compass rose for Sedona. People skittered in and out of sight in my rearview mirror, pushing empty shopping carts into the store and full ones out. The coffee shop Stacy frequented was over to my right, just a few doors down from Red Rock Vistas Real Estate.

I scowled at both places, then glanced back at the office of Desert Skies Balloon Adventures.

Five minutes passed, and still no Nash.

I called in to the agency, following up on the license plate trace. I'd never had one take this long or been put on hold so many times.

"Sorry for the wait," the woman at the agency finally came back on the line. "I've been told to direct your inquiry to Captain Edwards."

I frowned. Edwards was way up the chain of command. Why him?

"Um, did I do something wrong?" I asked, only half joking.

The woman's laugh straddled the same line. "Ask Edwards. Do you want me to put you through?"

A dusty orange Subaru pulled up beside me. I glanced over, did a double take, and hastily ended my call.

"I'll call back, thanks." I put down the phone and stared at the new arrival.

Not Nash.

Pippa.

Joy and hope swept through me, as they did every time we met. My mind went blissfully blank, and my inner wolf bayed as I slid out of the Jeep.

"Hi." Pippa's greeting was flat, but that didn't stop my inner wolf from wagging its tail.

"Pippa," I murmured, then glanced at the office. "Here to book another flight?"

A few weeks ago, I'd taken a balloon flight to get an overview of the area for my initial risk assessment report. I hadn't accomplished as much as I'd hoped, because Pippa had joined the same flight, and my mind had been too busy filling in a totally different risk assessment — the one estimating the chances of us ever reconciling.

She glanced at the balloon office with a dry chuckle. "Another flight? If I could afford it, I would."

Had it not been for recent events, I would have laughed. Instead, I positioned myself between Pippa and the real estate office before she got it in her head to go stomping back in there and set the place on fire. Pippa was a kind, loving soul, but once you got on her bad side...

The wind pushed her lavender scent toward me, and my throat went so dry with longing, it ached. My heart ached too.

"Are you here to meet Erin?" I asked.

"Nope. I'm here for you."

Words that had featured a thousand times in my dreams over the last too-many years.

"Erin said you needed someone to show you the back roads," Pippa said in a carefully neutral tone.

I cleared my throat, but the words still came out all husky. "I did."

She looked at her watch. "Well, we'd better get started. I have an hour and a half, tops."

A fib, and I knew it. Pippa calculated time by the sun, not by a clock. But she was right. This was about business, and I had a schedule to keep too.

Still, my wolf did a happy dance as I motioned to the vehicle. "Well, then. We'd better go."

She hopped into my Jeep, and I followed suit.

"What exactly did you want to see?" she asked, all businesslike.

My wolf nearly made me blurt a totally inappropriate answer. Something like, *you, asleep, with your arms around me.*

Pippa was a beautiful sleeper. Well, a beautiful everything, but beautiful sleeper was high on the list.

But I doubted that was what she meant.

"I've been to all the main vortexes." I pointed toward the stunning rocky outcrops around town. "Cathedral Rock, Airport Mesa, Bell Rock, and Boynton Canyon. I didn't feel a thing, but I've been there."

Pippa chuckled. "Not everyone can feel them."

Well, a bunch of New Age types I'd found beating drums at Bell Rock had insisted they could. I was skeptical, though. Most humans couldn't tell a vampire from a turnip. Were the vortexes they claimed to sense wishful thinking or the real thing?

I fired up the Jeep and headed for the parking lot exit, watching Pippa out of the corner of my eye. "Can you feel them?"

Her eyes got a cagey look I'd rarely seen.

"Sometimes. When they're going, at least. They seem to slumber more than they fire off, though." She tilted her head. "Do you want to check one now?"

"No. I want to get out around the back roads. Not the ones they follow." I pointed to a passing Jeep tour. "Quiet back roads that might be used by someone looking to keep a low profile."

She gave me one of those looks that said, *There you go again, suspecting everyone.* "You mean, the kind locals use to keep away from tourists?"

I nodded. "And maybe a couple of overlook points, so I get a sense of how things fit together around here."

The light turned green, and I waited, looking at Pippa. Her nose wrinkled a little as she thought — one of her many irresistible quirks. Then she pointed left. "Okay, turn here, then go right at the Y."

Lots of *lefts* and *rights* followed over the next few miles, which brought us to a fancy development called *Cactus Point Manor.*

Not a cactus in sight — we were at way too high-altitude — and definitely no manor, just a bunch of faux-adobe Mc-Mansions.

"Um..." I started.

"Be patient," she assured me. "Not far now."

She reached back, resting her arms on the back of the seat, roughly where her foot would have been that time we'd had sex in the back of a similar vehicle, almost a decade ago.

My foot went a little heavy on the gas, and the engine revved.

"Whoa, boy," Pippa chuckled.

Which only made my jeans feel tighter. Same joke as back then, *totally* different context.

I gulped, shifting in my seat.

Seconds later, she pointed. "We're coming to the turnoff. Right...about...here." She indicated a narrow, overgrown trail.

I hit the brakes. "That's private property."

She shook her head. "The folks who live around here do their best to give that impression, but it's a public right of way. It was grandfathered in to protect access to Dead Man's Creek. Go ahead."

I hid a grin. This was exactly the kind of local knowledge I'd hoped to tap into. And the fact that the *local* was Pippa was icing on the cake.

A hundred yards down the rough track, we came to a steep gully, and I stopped again.

"You want me to go down this?"

That was the thing about being with Pippa. It came with joy, heartache, and massive leaps of faith.

She patted the doorframe. "This is a Jeep, you know."

Ah, just like old times, with her daring me and me taking the bait every time.

I put the Jeep in four-wheel-drive mode and eased over the edge, thrilled and a little scared — which also fit everything I did with Pippa. Including falling in love.

My hands tightened over the steering wheel as we careened down what felt like a vertical drop. Pippa whooped in glee.

Then, *splash!* We hit the puddle at the bottom, ground over a couple of rocks, and rounded a turn on a steep incline with no hint of what lay ahead.

"You sure about this?" I hollered over the creak of the chassis and grind of the engine.

Her hands were thrust up against the dashboard, but her smile was a mile wide. "Trust me, baby. Trust me."

Ninety-nine out of a hundred times, Pippa was right. It was that leftover *one* I was wary of... But, whew. The moment we rounded the blind corner, the Jeep track was no lumpier or steeper than any of the popular trails around town. The only difference was, we had it all to ourselves.

"My aunt used to take us to an old cliff dwelling up here," Pippa explained.

I'd never met the aunt, but I had the feeling she was a lot like Pippa. Coming all the way out here with three little girls... I tipped an imaginary hat to the woman.

"So, it winds around for a while..." Pippa narrated the route for the next fifteen minutes, pointing in the jerky way the vehicle's movement dictated. "If you went down that way, you'd come to a dead end. An hour's walk brings you to the cliff dwelling..."

An hour. The aunt's idea of a good time, I figured. No wonder Pippa had a thirst for adventure.

"And if you took that track, you'd have to be real careful, because it got washed out, and you're likely to roll most of the way down." Pippa pointed left casually.

I hugged the right side of the trail and continued climbing. Hairpin after hairpin, with gravel grinding under the tires and scrub oak scratching the sides of the Jeep.

"Now turn left..." Pippa pointed.

I stared. Maybe on a mountain bike. There wasn't enough space for a Jeep.

"Oh, come on," she goaded. "You wanted a lookout point, right?"

"I also want to make it back to town alive."

Pippa chuckled, smacking my knee. "That's a good one."

Little, er — neutrons? Protons? Something very small but packed with a ton of energy — zipped through my body, and my wolf side sighed.

My mate...

I abandoned my last scrap of good sense and revved onto that side track. It was narrow and bumpy as hell, but Pippa was right. We could get through.

Which brought me one step closer to hitting that one out of a hundred times Pippa was wrong. I made a mental note.

"Is there a place to turn around?"

She shook her head, not at all perturbed. "You have to back out." She narrowed her eyes at my double take. "I can drive if you want."

I clutched the gear stick possessively. Pippa drove the way she did everything else: leap, then look.

"Not necessary," I grunted.

Five minutes of driving later, we'd thoroughly tested the suspension and started ascending to heaven, or so it seemed. The track angled upward, and all I saw was sky. More and more of it as the shrubs around us thinned out.

"Keep going... Keep going... Stop!" Pippa threw an arm across my chest when we reached the crest of the trail.

I hit the brakes, pitching us both forward.

Pippa unbuckled her seat belt and slid out of the car, casual as can be. "There's a drop-off."

As in, the five-hundred-foot cliff I was staring down now.

I followed her slowly, inching around the Jeep until we met at the front bumper, where we had about three feet of safe space before the cliff fell away. I kept my right hand open behind Pippa, ready to grab if she took one more step.

She didn't, thank goodness. She just led me into the scrub until we emerged at a ledge.

"There's another vortex over here. Hardly anyone knows about it, though."

Over here was up a narrow, iffy trail that would make a mountain goat pause.

Pippa charged ahead.

I glanced down the precipice on our left, wondering if she had more dragon shifter in her than she realized.

"Pippa..." I warned.

"We're almost there."

Famous last words?

"It's not worth it," I said, hanging back.

"Oh, of course it is. It's for your *job*."

And oh, the subtext.

I followed slowly and eventually found her in an open slot between two jutting rocks high on the hill. The drive up had been shady, but now, the late-afternoon sunlight bathed Pippa from behind, casting her shadow out over the lower slope of the mountain.

"So, there's the Y intersection... Cathedral Rock... The road to Slide Rock..." Her finger tapped the air here and there. "The ranch is way back there..."

The ranch was *her* ranch, a place she'd raved about as long as I'd known her. Losing it would destroy her.

She went on to indicate other points of interest, such as a spot with a hidden sinkhole — a portal to the underworld, according to some indigenous cultures. Then there was a mountainside that had burned in an alleged act of arson, and the location of the vet who checked on Roscoe and the other ranch dogs.

She must have noticed my consternation at that last one, because she thumped me on the arm. "What? It's important. Besides, you're a canine too."

Yeah, but way, way, way above Roscoe's line in the evolutionary hierarchy.

"Oh, don't be so snooty," Pippa chided.

There she went again, reading my mind, as fated mates and closely associated supernaturals were capable of. The question was, what category did we belong in?

She edged forward. The rock we stood on ended in a diving-board-sized ledge that stuck out into nothingness, and that was where Pippa went.

"Here it is. The vortex." She tapped a foot.

My pulse went through the roof as I imagined the ledge collapsing. Plus, if that was a vortex, it didn't seem like a good idea to stand right on it. What if thousands of volts of energy suddenly came jetting out?

"Um, I take it it's not on right now?" I asked as neutrally as I could.

"Oh, it's on," she said. "Just not very powerfully."

Like that made me feel better.

I inched out beside her. "What do you feel?"

She looked at me askance. "You can't feel it?"

I shrugged. "What am I supposed to feel?"

"It's an upflow vortex with a light, pulsing sensation." She held my hand over the middle of the rock.

I felt her hand, which was nice, but no vortex.

"Oh, wait." She stepped to the safe end of the ledge. Whew. "It's more powerful here."

She felt around with her eyes closed, hovering her free hand over different parts of the ledge.

"Oh. Wow," she murmured.

I peeked sideways. Was she serious?

Yes, because her eyes were half closed, and her expression was that of a person listening to a symphony.

For fear of sounding like an idiot, I said nothing. I did keep hold of her hand, though. For research purposes.

"Yep. Much more powerful here," she murmured.

A raven flew overhead, cawing.

Pippa frowned, felt around for another minute, then sighed. "Now it's off again. They tend to come and go."

Her tone was as casual as if she were talking about fashion trends or Texan tourists. Then she smiled and pointed. "Look. Our shadows."

Good old Pippa. She had the ability to find wonder in anything. Flowers. Scampering puppies. Even her own shadow.

I had to agree this was especially cool, though. The sun cast a shadow of the rocky outcrop onto the landscape, and nestled in the slot between the two jutting rocks were two small figures. Us.

Pippa waved, and her shadow waved back.

"You have to wave too!" she said.

I did as I was told, and my shadow waved back just as obediently.

A bittersweet feeling snuck up on me as I looked down at our two shadows. The two of us together — that's how we belonged. And with nothing but our silhouettes down there, you could almost buy into the fantasy. A happy young couple, looking at a promising future together.

A thick, lumpy feeling registered in my chest, like it always did when I thought about Pippa.

She started forming letters with her arms and singing like The Village People. "Y-M-C-A..."

I chuckled.

She tried the Macarena next, but that didn't show up in her shadow.

"Oh, here! Make a star!" She slipped in front of me, holding her arms to the sides.

Like a loyal dog intent on pleasing its master, I stuck mine up at forty-five-degree angles.

"Is this appropriate behavior around a vortex?" I scolded.

"Well, seeing as the vortex is off..." She went on trying other shapes.

Eventually, though, she slowed down and simply gazed over the landscape.

"So beautiful here..." Her chest lifted and fell.

Mine too, because we'd ended up pretty close, and my hands had landed on her shoulders.

"Beautiful..." I whispered.

"That's the thing about Sedona," Pippa murmured. "Even if you close your eyes, it's beautiful."

I tried it. Yep. Still beautiful.

"The wind...the clean air..." Pippa murmured.

My mate in my arms, my wolf side whispered.

My thoughts blurred. A pleasant buzz tickled my skin.

Pippa swayed gently, moving with the breeze or the vortex or whatever it was she was tuned in to.

It was like a slow dance, but out in nature instead of on a dance floor. Every beat of my heart brought me closer to peace...and closer to Pippa.

Chapter Eight

INGO

I closed my eyes, inhaling Pippa's scent. Maybe there was something to that vortex stuff. Even my arms were tingling. Tingling their way right down to Pippa's waist, before I even realized it.

Pippa didn't seem to realize either, because she hummed and went on swaying.

"Mmm. Nice..."

She'd said something about the vortex having an upflow, but I could have sworn it was more of a slow squeeze, bringing our bodies closer together.

My arms slid around her waist, but not on any conscious command from me. Pippa echoed the movement, putting her arms over mine in a back-to-front hug.

The breeze played with her hair, and it tickled my cheek. Or maybe that was the vortex?

Whichever it was, I didn't care. I was too lost in the moment. Too lost in our kiss...

Yes, a kiss. One I pressed to her neck, ever so gently. Another side effect of that pesky vortex.

"Mmm," Pippa mumbled, setting off a dozen flashbacks of long, lazy mornings in bed.

For once, the memories were more like blueprints than painful lessons of the past, and I reconstructed every one. The slide-kiss that started at her collarbone and ended in the notch of her neck. The long kiss that swept along the edge of her jaw, ending near her lips. Best of all, the kiss that met those lips exactly as Pippa turned in my arms.

Call it a vortex kiss.

And, oh. The vortex must have jumped to full flow, because Pippa cupped my face in her hands and hung on.

My research on vortexes described them as swirling centers of energy that fostered meditation, healing, and self-exploration. So...

Meditation — *check*, because I'd never been more focused on the present.

Healing — check plus, because the ragged edges of my heart stopped hurting.

Self-exploration, though, was a stretch. More like exploring Pippa.

And boy, did I explore. From the coast of her lips to the bays of her cheekbones and the home port of her mouth.

Pippa tugged me closer and kissed harder. Harder...

Then, *Caw! Caw!* That damn raven flew by again.

Pippa opened her eyes and pulled back slowly.

My lips puckered up as she did, stretching the kiss. Then I was blinking too, though my arms didn't release their grip.

"That's some vortex," I murmured.

Pippa nodded, and her eyes glowed like a shifter's.

"You know how it is," she breathed. "They tend to come and go."

My vote was for *come*, and I leaned forward, eager for more.

But a loud hum sounded over the landscape, and I couldn't help but look up.

Pippa did the same, shielding the sun with her hand.

We watched as a helicopter chop-chop-chopped its way over from the airport, heading our way. About to slice through our shadows, in fact. A growl built in my throat.

But, no. Seconds later, its course became clear — it was heading slightly north of us, to a lumpy structure as high in elevation as our spot and a good mile away.

I cocked my head. "What's that?"

Pippa shrugged. "La Puebla."

As I studied the spaceship-style structure, a bad feeling set into my gut.

"La what?" I attempted a measured, not-at-all-loaded tone.

"La Puebla. Kind of a commune slash art studio built by hippies in the sixties."

"Commune, huh?"

Even from this distance, I could make out a security checkpoint bristling with cameras and antennas. Here and there, the sun glinted off a tall steel fence — the kind that guaranteed the owner had something to hide.

"It was neglected for years, until someone tried converting it into an exclusive resort," Pippa went on. "From what I know, that fell through, but someone recently bought it to use as some kind of a private club."

"How do you get there?"

"You mean, if your helicopter is in the shop? You drive up Old River Road, then branch off." She traced a line over the mountain. "Not that they let just anyone in. My friend Ryder was on the landscaping crew, and he said they got frisked every time they entered the grounds."

At some point, I would have to drive over for a closer look. But not with the Jeep, and not in this body. No search warrant either.

My inner wolf grinned, showing its teeth.

I ran my tongue over them, though I kept the beast locked away — for now. I couldn't rush in there without a plan. And certainly not with Pippa at my side.

Out of nowhere, all my old fantasies reared up. The ones where Pippa could turn into a wolf like me and trot along at my side just for the joy of it.

Sedona would be perfect for that. All those mesas, mountains, and open miles of land. Warm days, cooler nights. Perfect for a couple of wolves out for an innocent romp.

The helicopter grew closer and louder, drowning out my fantasy. I watched it swoop toward the compound, then descend and disappear behind the buildings.

"La Puebla, huh?" I murmured.

Pippa nodded, then froze. "Wait a minute. You're not suspecting them of something?" She stared at me, then sighed. "Of course you do. You suspect everyone."

Ouch. That hurt. Doubly so because it was true.

I clenched my fists, already formulating a plan for sneaking in for a closer look. Sure, I ought to go by the books and do more investigating first — the kind that might turn up something I could use to make this case official. Things like tracking down delivery firms, interviewing employees, and scouring agency records. But all that took time.

Too much time, my wolf side warned.

I thought of Stacy. Of Pippa. Of all the other nice young men and women who would never hurt anyone, so they never suspected someone might hurt them.

People like Bridget.

My heart beat harder. "Who bought it?"

Pippa shrugged. "Someone very rich and a little loony, I guess. Who else would spend seven million on a place like that?"

Rich. Loony. That certainly rang a bell.

"You don't know who?" I held my breath.

"Nope. But if you've seen one rich guy, you've seen them all."

"Which you know from knowing so many rich guys?"

She gave me a haughty look. "I've worked in catering, mister. I've seen them all."

And clearly, she wasn't impressed.

Which was good, in a way. I wasn't dirt poor, but I definitely wasn't rich. So, I had that going for me in the unlikely event that I would someday bring every single criminal to justice and find myself with nothing to do. Unlikely, but hell, a man could dream.

"Harlon was a rich guy," I pointed out. "And dangerous as hell."

"Well, we showed him."

Yes, Pippa, her sisters, and Nash had definitely given that warlock what he'd deserved. But it could have gone either way, and she knew it.

"What else do you know about La Puebla?"

She studied my face all too closely. "Let me guess. You think a diabolical warlock has moved in and is currently plotting to eradicate all of humankind."

No, I suspected a diabolical *vampire* had moved in and was currently plotting something bad. Possibly even to eradicate all of humankind.

"Just tell me what you know," I said in as neutral a tone as I could.

Pippa made a face, but she did indulge me.

"Some superrich guy from Illinois. Wait. Indiana. Or maybe Ohio..."

It was all I could do not to nod at *Indiana*, where Victor Jananovich hailed from.

"Anyway, somewhere over there." She motioned vaguely, like those states were right behind Schnebly Hill. "I've heard he comes and stays for a few weeks, then leaves it empty for a while, then comes back. A snowbird warlock, you could say, if that's what he is." She chuckled at her own joke.

Snowbird vampire, my wolf muttered.

"Anyway, he brings guests with him. Paying guests," she continued. "So, it's like a club, I guess. A super-exclusive one."

"How exclusive?"

"By-invitation-only exclusive. They must have done a hell of a renovation..." Then she stopped. "Uh-oh. You have those cunning wolf eyes."

Oops. A shifter's eyes tended to heat with their emotions, each showing in a different fiery hue. Love. Fear. Passion. Hatred.

I blinked hard, trying to dim the fire in my eyes. "Well, I am a wolf."

"And you are cunning."

"I'll take that as a compliment."

We both broke into grins at that echo of an old line of ours from way back when.

The helicopter lifted off again, and the whirr of the blades echoed off the hills. The sound moved with the helicopter, fading slowly as it returned to the airport.

"Well, there you have it," Pippa murmured. "That's how exclusive it is."

"And what do those exclusive guests do there?"

"Well, it sure ain't golf," Pippa quipped, indicating the steep property. "Probably some kind of wellness place, where you can relax and rejuvenate."

A shiver went down my spine. Rejuvenation for a vampire called for blood. A lot of it, and fresh as can be.

And, oops. Pippa must have caught my reaction.

"Wait. What are you thinking?"

After weighing it up for a moment, I decided to show my cards. Some of them anyway.

"That woman who was found dead at Gunnery Point..."

"The accident," she filled in.

I shook my head slowly. "The pawprints were erased by the time the police arrived, but the scent of bear shifter was all over the place."

Her mouth formed a surprised *Oh*. Then she nodded for me to go on.

"Stacy's chauffeur is a bear shifter," I continued.

Pippa narrowed her eyes. "Same bear shifter or different bear shifter?"

"Not sure."

She threw up her hands. "That's as bad as racial profiling!"

I stuck up my hands. "I'm not assuming it's the same guy, but it's the only lead I have."

"Not really a lead, though, is it? Just a baseless accusation."

"I'm not accusing anyone. But it's all I have to go on right now. Do you know anything about him?"

Her expression went grim. "No. Only that he drives — and the last time Stacy came by the shop, she wasn't eager to leave."

That didn't sound good.

"Can't you trace the car or the company? I did show you the address."

"I'm trying, but it takes time. And there's a thin line between waiting for enough evidence to protect a suspect's rights and waiting so long that you risk an innocent person's life."

Pippa frowned, and I knew she was thinking of Stacy. Hell, I was thinking of her too, along with the vow I'd made to myself — and to a murder victim named Bridget.

Just then, the security gate rolled aside, and an SUV exited the grounds of La Puebla. The same color and model driven by the bear shifter, with the same ding in the front bumper. I could tell by the way the sun glinted off it.

"Baseless, huh?" I murmured.

Pippa stared at it. "Could be another one that looks the same."

I jutted my jaw. Right down to the dinged bumper?

Pippa squinted. "Too far to see the license plate..."

We watched silently as it rolled down the road and disappeared around a bend.

Pippa shivered, rubbing her arms. "Now you're making me paranoid too."

I didn't reply.

After a few quiet, pensive moments, Pippa shook her head wearily. "Either way, we need to get going."

I looked around. The sun would set soon, and we had a long way to go back down the mountain.

Pippa headed back toward the Jeep, then pointed a finger at me. "And don't forget, you owe me."

My inner wolf wagged its tail. *Anything.*

"I do. You have something in mind?" I asked, following her through the scrubby bushes.

She didn't turn around, but I could hear the mischief in her voice. "You know the old saying about a bull in a china shop?"

"Yes..." I replied, curious.

"Something like that, maybe."

I had no idea what she meant, but I was intrigued. And to be honest, even a little hopeful, because any time with my true love — especially at a time like now, when darkness crowded out light in my soul — was time well spent.

Dangerously hopeful, one might say.

Chapter Nine

PIPPA

"Well, thanks for the ride," I said, sliding out of Ingo's Jeep in my best fake-casual way.

And, woo-hoo for me. I'd managed two hours in a confined space with Ingo, and I hadn't even slept with him.

Just those couple of kisses we pretended didn't happen. Side effects of the vortex and all that.

Never mind that my heart was still tap-dancing and my nerves fluttering, dammit.

"Thanks for showing me around," Ingo murmured.

His pupils were still dilated, and that woodsy scent he got when his wolf inched closer to the surface clung to him.

Roscoe rushed out of the house, jumping at me in greeting. Calvin and Hobbes weren't far behind, and they all swarmed Ingo in glee. Wolf shifters were the canine equivalent of rock stars, and it showed.

"All right, all right," Ingo laughed, motioning for them to sit.

All three obeyed instantly, butts glued to the ground, tails wagging at warp speed.

Claire emerged next and called from the porch. "Hi, Auntie Pippa! Hi, Ingo!"

Ingo waved. "Heya, kiddo. Heya, Hopper."

Claire made her stuffed animal rabbit wave an ear back, and whatever genes I possessed that judged men as potential mate material registered a solid ten for Ingo.

Stupid genes.

"Mommy and I drove home in your car," Claire told me.

"We did. Thanks for loaning it to us," Abby said.

Her car had broken down — again — so she'd picked up my car and driven it home; hence Ingo giving me a ride.

"Are you staying for dinner?" Claire asked him.

He shook his head quickly. "Not tonight, kiddo. Another time, though, okay?"

A split second later, his nostrils flared, and he whipped his head around.

I did the same, as did Abby and Roscoe. A short distance away, Erin and Nash shot out onto the porch of their cabin. Everyone was still tense after our recent tangle with Harlon Greene, the warlock.

My ears registered the hum of a truck. Or, wait. A motorcycle. A truck *and* a motorcycle?

Erin and Nash started moving toward us, on high alert. We didn't get casual visitors at the ranch — not with the entrance protected by a cloaking spell that worked on humans and most shifters.

Abby moved in front of Claire in a protective stance. I stepped clear of Ingo's Jeep. He slid out quickly and stood beside me, hair bristling as if he was defending home turf.

Evolution poked at those genes of mine and added another ten points to Ingo's scorecard. Definitely mate material.

A motorcycle appeared on a steep rise, followed by a pickup. The driver of the motorcycle waved, and the driver of the truck — a vintage Grand Wagoneer — tooted the horn merrily.

I cheered, as did Erin, Abby, and Claire. Ingo and Nash, slower to recognize the occupants, continued bristling until the vehicles reached the house.

"It's Grandpa and Grandpa!" Claire exclaimed.

I trotted over to the Wagoneer as my father slid out and opened his arms wide.

"Dad!" I threw my arms around him.

"Sweetheart!" He wrapped his arms around me and rocked a little.

As a kid, I'd considered my dad a giant, and his hugs made me feel invincible. Nowadays, they still did, even though I was almost as tall as him.

My dad was one of Claire's "grandpas." Erin's father was the other. Neither she nor Abby was related to either of them, but they treated both like their own flesh and blood.

Dad released me to tousle my hair, and I echoed the gesture. Good old dad. His youthful, Richard Gere looks were going a little gray around the edges, but he was as fit as ever. Firefighter fit, he liked to call it.

Erin's dad, Mike, gave his motorcycle a last, loud rev, then killed the engine. His worn leather jacket creaked as he stood in time to catch Claire in a hug.

"There's my girl!" he cheered, spinning her around in a huge circle, then setting her down gently.

I stepped aside as Claire sprinted toward my father, who repeated the procedure.

All in all, my father and Erin's went a long way toward making up for our mother. She'd hooked up with Erin's father just long enough to get knocked up — Mom's term, not his — and have Erin, only to abandon them a short time later. It hadn't taken her long to hook up with Abby's father afterward, and mine two years later. Each time, it was pretty much the same procedure. *Slam, bam, thank you, man — oh, and good luck raising our daughter.*

Erin's dad and mine had done a great job. Abby's... not so much. Another reason our dads doted on little Claire the way they did.

"Let me fix your beard, Grandpa." Claire ran her fingers over Mike's thick handlebar mustache.

"Thank you, sweetheart." He tapped her nose, then set her down and marveled. "You get bigger every time I see you!"

Claire stood Roscoe up on his hind legs to show off. "I'm taller than Roscoe now."

Roscoe wagged his tail weakly. Unlike Claire, he knew two powerful supernaturals when he sniffed them.

Erin was the next to hug her father warmly. Nash followed with a stiff handshake.

"Hello, Mike," Nash said evenly.

"Nash," Mike grumbled.

Poor Nash. It was hard when your true love's father was a tough-talking, spell-weaving, overprotective warlock and leader of a motorcycle gang — er, club.

And poor Mike. He loved Erin, so he tried to tolerate Nash. But I had the feeling Mike wouldn't have minded if his "little girl" had remained single — and a virgin — forever.

My dad, on the other hand…

He stuck out a hand and caught Ingo in one of those three-part manshakes followed by a hug.

"Greg!" Ingo might as well have been embracing his own father.

"Ingo!" My dad greeted him just as warmly.

Yeah, my dad had a lot fewer hang-ups than Mike. Also, he'd spent the last twenty-five years working on a wildland fire crew with Ingo's father, his close buddy. Ingo had joined the same crew before a couple of arson cases had set him off on a new career path in law enforcement.

Second *also*, my dad thought Ingo and I were perfect for each other. He hadn't even blinked the time he'd discovered seventeen-year-old Ingo and me in bed together.

Yeah, I figured, was all he'd said. *Just don't get pregnant, okay?*

Thank goodness for laid-back fathers.

Except, of course, when they couldn't get their idea of your perfect partner out of their heads.

"Some coincidence that you got a job in Sedona, hey?" my father chuckled at Ingo.

Ingo glanced at me, and his throat bobbed. "Yeah. Funny coincidence."

My dad half coughed, half muttered, "Can't fight destiny."

Yeah, well. I fully intended to.

"Abby!" my father called, hugging her next.

Mike greeted her just as warmly.

Abby closed her eyes with each hug, and my heart swelled when I saw her arms firmly around their shoulders. Erin liked to say we had the world's most functional dysfunctional family. Me, I was grateful for having two out of three blue-ribbon fathers.

And two hot ones, too. I could see why Mom had been attracted to them. Hell, if they were total strangers and twenty years younger, I would have a hard time choosing between them.

But then my eye caught on Ingo, and a voice deep inside me whispered, *Easy choice. Ingo, Ingo, Ingo.*

I'd known him my entire life, and even as a child, I'd known he was the only one for me.

I scuffed the ground. Too bad things hadn't worked out that way.

"How are things, honey?" Mike asked.

"All good, all good," Erin assured him.

"No more trouble around here?"

"No, Dad. All fine. Thanks."

"And... you know. Finances. Everything okay there?" Mike went on.

"The usual," Erin bluffed.

Not the usual, but we were too proud to admit it. We'd received official notice of the new property assessment and back taxes to the tune of $30,000 — all due within thirty days.

Thousands we didn't have, not even when we scraped every cent together.

I did my best not to exchange worried looks with my sisters. We could lose the ranch. Even more than a home, it was our keystone — the thing cementing the fragile construction we called family.

Abby's eyes bored into mine, and she spoke into my mind and Erin's. *We'll never let that happen. Never!*

There was something even more significant about the ranch. The part we never mentioned out loud.

Magic.

Magic was rooted in the earth here, in the rocks, the earth, the sky. I could feel it in every wrinkle of the cliffs and every meander of the creek. Being here drew out the weak powers I'd inherited from my much more powerful parents. And ever since the vortex incident... well, those powers were becoming more and more evident.

"It's great to see you both," Erin said. "What's the occasion?"

She glanced at me, then Abby, speaking into our minds. *They're checking on us, aren't they?*

Her father folded his arms, making his muscles bulge. "Do we need a reason to visit the four best girls in the universe?"

He left Nash out of the equation, but I suppose it was better than saying, *the four best girls and that guy I'm forced to tolerate.*

Definitely checking on us, Abby sighed into our minds.

"We just wanted to say hi — and to treat you all to a barbecue," Mike added. "It's been too long."

"A barbecue *and* a bonfire." When my father rubbed his hands in anticipation, sparks flew off the tips of his fingers.

"Careful, Grandpa," Claire giggled.

He winked. "Oops. Sorry."

Nash's eyes went wide, but he was the only one who expressed surprise.

My father, like Erin's, was a warlock — but while Mike specialized in wind and weather, my dad's talents related to fire.

I could see Erin mouthing to Nash now. *Pyromancer, remember?*

A really, really powerful one — one of the few who could kindle fire from nothing, rather than manipulating an existing one.

Nash considered my dad, then me. I looked away just in time, holding my head high despite the harsh truth. *My father is a powerful pyromancer, and my mother is a badass dragon shifter, but I'm fine with not having any of their powers.*

Totally fine with that. Really.

Okay, so I knew a few small tricks that came in handy in the hot shop. But none of the cool stuff: changing into a mighty beast or flying. No conjuring, directing, or extinguishing flames at will either.

"Barbecue, bonfire, *and* stargazing," Mike added.

Nash looked up and around. "It might be too overcast for stargazing."

Mike flashed a smug grin. "Oh, I'm sure it will clear up in time." Then he clapped once. "Come and help unload, everyone. We brought everything we need."

"*I* brought everything we need," my dad corrected him, motioning toward his truck.

Ingo pitched in, then waved goodbye and moved toward his vehicle.

"Now, wait a second there, son." My father stopped him. "You can't leave before the party starts!"

I shot my dad a pained look and made a chopping motion with my arms.

"Um..." Ingo stalled.

"Ingo has a lot of work," I threw in. "He's *very* dedicated to his job."

"All the more reason for him to take a little time off. You know what they say about all work and no play."

Usually, I would be on board with that plan. But I'd just spent two hours with Ingo and barely managed to keep my hands off him. (The kiss didn't count. He started it.) Spending an evening under the stars together would be way too much like old times.

"Also, it's a conflict of interest," I tried. "With his line of work and everything."

My dad cackled and smacked him on the shoulder. "Nah. You'll keep this off the books, right, kid? You're family."

"Thanks, but..." Ingo started.

"You can't go now," Erin admonished.

I glared at my sister. Of course he could.

But he didn't.

And so it was that I found myself running around with firewood, sausages, drinks — everything a girl needed for an evening around a bonfire with her crazy family *and* her ex-lover.

Chapter Ten

PIPPA

"And then he said, 'How long have you two been together?'"
Erin's father hooted as he delivered the punch line to his story.

We'd been around the bonfire for several hours by then, all
full from a delicious dinner, and Mike was telling us about the
time he and my dad had taken Claire to town for ice cream.
A friendly cashier, hearing them go by Grandpa and Grandpa,
had assumed they were a couple.

"I just about died," my dad admitted.

Mike leaned over and planted a loud smooch on his cheek.
"Happy couple. That's us, baby."

My dad rolled his eyes. "One inch closer and you're toast,
buddy."

Ah, pyromancer humor.

"I mean, really," my dad huffed. "I would have much better
taste than this yo-yo."

Mike hit back with weathermonger humor — making play-
thunder rumble in the distance.

I stood, clearing the last of the barbecue utensils away.
"Marshmallows, anyone?"

"Me! Me!" Claire hopped up and down. "And then story
time!"

Bonfire story time was a tradition handed down from my
dad's side of the family. A tradition he continued when he
visited Arizona — ostensibly for Claire, but really, for all of
us.

My dad rubbed his hands eagerly. "Definitely story time.
Right after those marshmallows."

The timing was perfect, because the sun was setting, and by the time we finished marshmallows, stars dotted the spring sky. Mike looked up, then shot a smug glance at Nash.

Most of us were in jackets or wrapped in blankets by then, though the fire kept us warm.

Ingo, who knew what to expect, gestured for Nash to scooch back.

"For story time?" Nash asked.

"You'll see," Ingo murmured.

Smart man, because story time with a pyromancer was truly something to behold.

Claire sat nestled in Mike's lap, right beside my father, who turned to her.

"All right, young lady. Where does the story begin?"

"On Painted Rock Ranch," Claire said immediately.

I grinned. All of Claire's stories started on the ranch, but my dad had a way of thinking big.

He thought for a moment, then pulled back his sleeves, raised his hands, and started.

"Once upon a time, there was a girl named Claire..."

Mike patted her on the head, and she grinned.

"Claire lived on Painted Rock Ranch with the best mom in the world..."

Abby's eyes danced. She hadn't had a lot of positive feedback as a kid, but my father and Erin's did their best to make up for that. And, hey. Dad was right. Abby might have some issues, but she was a doting, loving mother to a great kid.

"Claire had a dog named Roscoe, two supersmart aunts, and the world's best grandpas..." my father continued.

"And a new uncle," Claire threw in. "Nash."

Nash grinned, as did Erin. Mike fought to maintain a neutral expression.

"And an uncle and lots of horses and other great things," my father continued. "But there was one thing Claire didn't have, so one day, she galloped off on her horse, Star, to find it."

Up until that point, the bonfire had been snapping and crackling in the usual way, with a thick, central blaze and smaller flames swirling up toward the stars from there. But then...

My father wiggled his fingers. "Claire galloped fast and far, following the creek for miles and miles..."

The fire burned lower and wider, and a meandering shape formed in the center. A river of flames, you could say, snaking this way and that.

"She galloped over the desert and into the mountains..."

The flames bunched and reformed, throwing up flat-topped mesas and jagged peaks.

"She galloped so fast and so far, she ended up in medieval times..."

I chuckled. A slight jump in logic, but hey. Pyromancers had a way of getting away with whatever ignited their fancy.

One side of the fire flared, forming a castle — an entire castle, right down to tiny flaming flags that danced at the corners of the towers.

Claire clapped, while my sisters and I oohed and aahed. Nash's jaw hung open.

"Show-off," Mike grumbled.

Any pyromancer could control fire, but only the most skilled could do so with such precision. So skilled, there was a special name for them: Fire Dancer.

"Oh, hush. You'll get your part soon," my dad stage-whispered, then went back to his story. "Now, where was I? Oh, yes. As it turns out, Claire was a princess in medieval times. A princess and a brave knight, all in one."

The flames died down briefly, then reformed.

"Whoa," Nash murmured as a ghostly horse and rider galloped through the heart of the blaze, kicking up a wake of swirling flames.

"Claire traveled far and wide, looking for the one thing she lacked. But she and Star faced some hardships too. A snowstorm..."

My father nudged Mike, who grumbled, "Finally," and clasped Claire's hands, moving them in tandem with his.

Something cold and damp hit my ear, then my nose.

Ingo chuckled, cupping his hands to catch the snowflakes that wafted by.

"Then a windstorm..."

Mike nodded at Erin, who held her palm up and puffed gently.

My hair blew from over my shoulder to my chest, and a tumbleweed rolled by.

Abby clapped in delight. Erin looked just as happy. She hadn't been able to command magic until recently, when true love and a deadly threat had combined to bring her powers she never knew she had. Every time Mike visited, he taught her a few new tricks.

I held up my hands in silent applause. Erin blushed proudly.

Maybe too soon, because the dust blew harder, making the fire blaze.

"Whoa, there." Mike made a catching motion, snuffing the storm out.

Oops, Erin's expression lamented.

My father went on, barely noticing. "Claire and Star galloped from town to town, scaring away bad guys along the way..."

At a flick of his fingers, swords flashed and fiery arrows shot through the flames.

Ingo leaned forward like this was his favorite part. Hell, it probably was. He knew my father that well, and my father loved him like a son.

I sighed. If I ever succeeded in finding a man to share my life with, Ingo would still be a part of it. Talk about awkward.

Almost as awkward as the thought of sharing my life with anyone but Ingo.

But seeing him beside my father reminded me of all the reasons we couldn't be together. All the nights I'd stayed up worrying... All the nightmares... All the interrupted holidays...

Heroes were...well, heroic, and I revered every one. But the idea of a nice, normal guy who worked a safe job and spent weekends on comparatively selfish hobbies had a lot of appeal.

Except it didn't, because I still loved Ingo.

I hugged my knees and stared into the fire.

Meanwhile, my father continued his story.

"Claire banished an ogre and a nasty squirrel shifter and a rampaging boar..."

The fire morphed, taking the shape of each beast.

Habit had me subtly mimicking my father's gestures. As a kid, I thought I could control fire. It wasn't until later that I'd accepted the bitter truth. Anything other than the most elementary tricks were beyond my meager abilities. But it was still fun to play along with him.

"Then along came a griffin and a two-headed serpent..." My dad continued his parade of medieval monsters.

The only creatures he didn't mention were dragons. No need to remind Claire of her conspicuously absent grandmother on this *one big happy family* occasion.

"One day, Claire heard cries for help, and she raced to the local castle to see what was going on. There, she found a dastardly prince who was claiming the most beautiful horse in the land for himself. Claire tried to stop him, but the dastardly prince had dozens of troops, and before long, Claire was surrounded."

"Uh-oh," Mike said, hugging her tightly.

She patted his hands. "It's okay, Grandpa. My magic friend will help me." She looked at my father as if to cue him.

The thing was, Dad looked a little blank. Claire had gone through a long string of imaginary friends, and it was hard to keep track.

"Right," my dad bluffed, then threw both hands wide.

I mimicked the gesture, trying to send him a hint.

A unicorn appeared in the fire, tossing its mane and a spiraling, ivory horn.

Close, but no cigar, I wanted to hiss.

Claire shook her head. "Not that one."

I changed the shape of my hands, trying to signal him, but Dad didn't see.

"Oh, sorry," he murmured. "*This* magic friend."

Whoosh! A tornado whirled in the heart of the fire, and Diana, goddess of the hunt, appeared at its core. An old friend from Claire's Greek mythology stage.

"No, not that one." Claire chuckled as if he was deliberately teasing her.

Oblivious to my hints, my dad tried an elf, a mermaid, and a phoenix — all recent visitors to Claire's imagination. But not the one she'd been obsessed with for the past few weeks.

I motioned even more vigorously, demanding his attention while my own mind jumped to Stacy, with that pretty pendant she wore next to that awful blood vial.

"That one!" Claire cheered, pointing into the fire.

A smoky horse galloped through the flames, coming right at us. But instead of disappearing at the edge of the fire or plowing right through us, it leaped into the air on huge, fire-laced wings.

"Pegasus!" Claire clapped.

Everyone watched in awe as the pegasus reared and snorted. Then, with a mighty heave of its feathered wings, it thundered toward the stars. The fire blazed as high as the house, following it. Then, bit by bit, the pegasus faded, though brilliant orange embers marked its outline against the indigo sky. Then they, too, extinguished, and the pegasus became one with the stars.

Claire clapped, thrilled. So did the others, and everyone looked stunned. . . including my father.

I stared at my hands. They were pointed at the sky, and little sparks played around them. In a flash, I dropped them to my lap and shook them out.

"Wow, Greg," Abby breathed. "That was your best show ever."

My father looked at his hands, puzzled. He shot Mike a quick look, but Mike appeared just as surprised as the others.

Me too. *Super* surprised, and a little frightened. What had just happened?

I flicked my fingers a few times, trying to get rid of that odd tingle.

And, oops. A trio of tiny sparks rose into the air before I clamped my hands into fists.

Ingo's midnight eyes locked on mine, and he cocked his head.

I gulped. Um, fireflies, maybe?

"Wow. That really was amazing," Erin agreed.

My father shot me a side-eyed look. I kept my eyes down and my fingers folded tightly.

Dad cleared his throat and replied very quietly, "Sometimes, I even surprise myself."

Again, his eyes sought mine. Again, I avoided them. Because, whoa. The tingling went from my fingers to my lungs, and my body felt lighter, as if part of it had galloped into the sky with that pegasus.

"Fire Dancer..." Nash whispered in awe.

And, shoot. Now Ingo was really staring at me.

"Keep going, keep going!" Claire begged.

I kept my fingers tightly folded.

My father cleared his throat. "Actually, that's the end of the story. Thanks to the pegasus, Claire was able to save the beautiful horse and take it home with her. And when the pegasus flew to the stars afterward, he wasn't flying away. He was flying across time, all the way to Arizona, where he joined Claire on the ranch and they all lived happily ever after."

I swear Claire would have taken off to check the stables if Mike hadn't been hugging her.

Abby and Erin clapped, helping wrap up the story. I joined in a split second later, though my heart was still hammering.

"Lucky girl," Erin told Claire. "You get the best stories."

Abby stood and tousled Claire's golden hair. "I know Grandpa could hug you forever, but now, it really is bedtime."

"No!" Claire retreated into Mike's powerful arms.

"I'm afraid so, sweetheart." Graceful as a cat, he got to his feet, still holding Claire. Then he set her down and sent her off with a pat on the back. "But I'll tell you what. If you get yourself ready and tucked in quickly, I'll come up and read you one last bedtime story."

"You're not leaving tonight, are you?" Claire latched on to his leg and looked up with big, irresistible eyes.

And just like that, the big, tough, leather-clad motorcycle rider melted.

"I can stay tonight and tomorrow — if you're good, and if your mom and aunts say so."

Erin gave a thumbs-up, and Abby grinned. Nash stuck on a stiff smile.

"Of course you can stay," Abby said.

"Yay! Can I ride Grandpa's motorcycle tomorrow?"

Ha. That Claire. The world's cutest, sweetest opportunist.

"We'll discuss that tomorrow," Abby announced firmly. "Now, off to bed. Then Grandpa can read you that new book Auntie Pippa got you."

"Let me guess. The one about a pegasus." Ingo pinned me with a hard look.

As a matter of fact, it was. But I kept my lips sealed.

Chapter Eleven

INGO

I'd borne witness to lots of Greg's bonfires, but that was truly a doozy. Especially since I had the feeling Greg wasn't the only one orchestrating the show.

Pippa had refused to meet my eyes afterward, and she'd hung back when the time came for me to go.

"You come back soon, son." Greg had left me with a fond smack on the back.

Pippa, meanwhile, was still staring into the last embers of the fire.

I'd driven home, then gone for a good, long run through the desert in wolf form. Which led me — again — to the viewpoint over the ranch.

I gazed at Pippa's barn for a while, then circled around three times and settled down right there on the mesa, my nose nestled between my paws and aimed at the ranch. As if Pippa might come out and call to me, as I always dreamed she would.

She didn't.

My night watch only lasted an hour or so, because nights at this altitude were cold, even with thick wolf fur protecting me. Eventually, I shot a last, longing gaze at Pippa's house, then headed back to my cabin.

I woke up cranky, with a whirlwind of thoughts competing for my attention. A double helix, actually, with one strand made up of Pippa and all the emotions that brought, and the other occupied by the case of the young woman found at Gunnery Point.

By nine a.m., I was in my office in town and calling the police for an update.

"We got confirmation on the initial ID," Jimenez reported. I heard her flip through a few sheets of paper. "Janet Sullivan, aged twenty-six. According to the coroner, there were no drugs in her system and no signs of foul play. None at the scene either."

None except the bear scent all over the area.

"So, all indications point to an accidental death," she concluded. When I snorted, she sighed. "My thought exactly. But we'll be pursuing it until we have a clearer picture."

I hung up on that call, then steeled myself for the one I'd been putting off.

"Captain Edwards, please," I told the agency operator.

Soothing music played while I was put on hold. Then came a click, and the phone practically exploded in my ear.

"What the hell are you doing putting a trace on Jananovich's car?" my boss hollered.

I winced, holding the phone away from my ear. "Putting a trace on what?"

"Don't you play games with me," he blustered.

My mind spun but remained blank. Nada. Nothing. Zilch.

Then it hit me. "The Utah plate I called in is registered to Jananovich?"

"Don't play dumb with me, Kemper," Edwards barked. "And if I find out you took the Sedona position because you somehow anticipated Jananovich moving there..."

"He's here?" I sputtered.

Wow. It was one thing to have a gut feeling, but another to have it confirmed.

Edwards snorted again, then took a different tack. "His whereabouts are no business of yours. Restraining order, remember?" He sighed, then muttered more to himself than me. "I should never have assigned you the Sedona office." The line went silent as he thought it over. "All right. I'll give you the benefit of the doubt this time. But stay away from Jananovich and any of his holdings."

My mind stuttered. Did that mean TTC Limited, the company name on the invoice I'd seen?

"I had enough of him and his lawyers last time," Edwards grumbled.

I grimaced. *Last time,* three young women had been found dead, plus a fourth who might have survived if only I had acted faster. But my hands had been tied, as Edward liked to put it.

"My hands are tied, kid."

I rolled my eyes. Yep. I'd heard that before.

"Focus on what you've been assigned to do," he continued in a more measured tone.

Like detecting and monitoring supernatural activity? I nearly shot back. *Like the suspicious bear shifter driving that car? Like the bear shifter scent at the scene of the crime? Like possible links to Jananovich?*

"We opened an office in Sedona to investigate reports of witchcraft, and that's where your focus should lie," Edwards continued.

I'd covered those bases in my first week in town, but the only witchcraft in town was so amateurish, it was laughable.

Totally laughable... except Pippa and her sisters. But technically, they lived outside city limits, right?

Yeah, I might have a minor conflict of interest. One I didn't plan to mention to Edwards.

"You know as well as I do that our resources are limited," Edwards lectured. "So don't go wasting your time on what will only cause you grief in the end."

I bit back a comment about the grief caused by senseless, preventable deaths.

"It's just not possible to investigate all supernatural activity in every area, and unnecessary too. Just the activity that causes concern or harm."

Like bear shifter scent in the vicinity of the dead woman at Gunnery Point? I wanted to yell.

"And it's certainly not our mission to harass law-abiding citizens without reasonable suspicion. Operative word — reasonable," Edwards emphasized. "So you will cease and desist from anything involving Jananovich, even remotely, starting yesterday. Is that clear?"

I kicked the chair opposite mine, and it skidded over the cool tile floor.

"I said, is that clear?" he growled over the phone.

"Yes, sir," I forced myself to say.

∞∞∞∞

I did some serious soul-searching — and chair-kicking — over the next few hours. But I didn't truly calm down until about an hour into my visit to the glass shop that afternoon.

"Grab that and hold it still," Pippa instructed, intent on her work. "A little higher... higher... right there."

Minutes earlier, that mass had been a brown lump. Now, it was shaping up to be a beautiful wineglass.

"Higher," she prompted, her brow knitted into parallel furrows.

I was making good on my promise to pay her back for her time, though she'd been reluctant to accept. But she was crunched for time — or better put, *desperate*, considering the pace she worked at — so she'd agreed.

Even so, I found the work calming. Or maybe that came from working beside Pippa and inhaling her sweet, soothing scent.

Nothing like being home, my father liked to say, slowly settling down after days away with his job — one dominated by gritty, life-and-death days in the middle of a burning forest.

He would come home, shower, eat, and settle down, keeping my mother close like *she* was home, and that would calm him right down.

Home, my wolf sighed when Pippa's leg bumped mine.

"Hold it there," Pippa murmured.

My leg or the glass? I decided to keep both where they were.

Apparently, the owner of Sedona Glass let Pippa work on her own projects when she was finished any outstanding orders — like now. That meant she had a window of opportunity to

96

work on her entry for a glass contest with a $25,000 prize. Which sounded like a long shot, but with Pippa, you never knew.

That window was short, though — a single afternoon — because she'd previously committed to help a friend with a catering job later on. Typical Pippa — helping a friend even when her ranch was in serious jeopardy.

So, time was at a premium. I did my best to help, though it didn't feel like much.

"Closer..." Pippa murmured. A drop of sweat fell from her forehead.

Outside, people were bundled in warm jackets. In the hot shop, I was down to a T-shirt and sweating up a storm, even with the back door propped open and a fan blasting. Moist fabric clung to my skin, and salt stung my eyes.

"Get me that pad, please," she asked.

When I did, our hands brushed, and my wolf side hummed.

"Okay. I'm going to tap the glass here so it breaks from the stem, and I need you to catch it. Ready?"

I pulled on oven mitts that would fit an elephant — if an elephant needed oven mitts — and waited.

"On three," Pippa said.

I held out my hands, sweating buckets, and not just from the heat. Pippa had spent ages on that wineglass. If I dropped it now...

I swear, I would have been less anxious if I'd had to catch a premature baby.

"One...two...three!"

Pippa tapped, and, *ping!* The wineglass separated from the rest of the rod. I caught it — thank goodness — but disaster still lurked, because now I had to rush it across the hot shop to the annealer.

"Watch the bench," Pippa warned, racing ahead to push things out of my way.

Why the shop hadn't been designed with the annealer next to the workbench, I didn't know. But I was definitely ready to suggest it.

The annealer looked like a giant cooler, where the temperature of worked glass was gradually reduced to prevent it from shattering. And that was just one way Pippa's delicate work could break. My mental notepad was full of dire warnings, all bold and underlined.

The moment Pippa opened the door to the annealer, I lowered the glass gingerly, then stepped back so she could close the door. Whew. One piece down. How many more to go?

She high-fived me. "Good job."

My inner beast wagged its tail joyously, less wolf than golden retriever at that moment.

She pulled two cold drinks from a tiny fridge, handed me one, and held the other against her forehead, rolling it slowly back and forth. Her head was tipped back, her chin up, and her golden hair stirred in the breeze of the fan.

I gulped my drink, desperate to cool down in more ways than one.

"Did you make that?" I asked, motioning to a vase on a shelf.

"No, it walked in off the street." She shot me a rueful look, then went on. "Yes, I made it. I made that, too. And that and that and that. Everything on those four shelves."

I looked them over, struck by the colors, the delicacy, the smooth, light-catching shapes — everything from vases to flowers and vibrant hummingbirds. There was even a whimsical piece in the shape of a prickly pear cactus, but my favorite — so far — was a globe filled with fire. *Glass* fire.

"Wow. My mind is officially blown," I murmured.

Pippa chuckled. "No pun intended, I hope."

I gave her a look, then went back to admiring her projects.

All those years she'd devoted to making glass, I'd only ever pictured bowls and vases, because glass was just glass. But these were works of art, full of skill and passion, and every piece exuded movement and life.

I have an exhibit coming up on Friday... I remembered Pippa telling me with bright, hopeful eyes, way back when in Colorado.

A fire in the Sangre de Cristo Mountains had made me miss that one — her very first show. Yet another fire had made me miss the next one — her first solo show. And the next one, and the next one...

I raked through every corner of my memory, but I couldn't unearth a single occasion I'd made the time to see Pippa's work. And it really was work, not just a hobby or an *anybody can do it* handicraft.

Another thing about her work struck me. Every piece was cheery, colorful, and upbeat. Not at all like real life.

But when I glanced out the shop window, the sun shone, and the red-tinted cliffs practically glowed. A young couple walked by, pushing a baby in a stroller. A singer-songwriter strummed her guitar on the corner, and a couple of people sang along.

I took a deep breath. My job might plunge me into the darkest, meanest pockets of society, but that didn't mean I couldn't pop up and see the bright side of things too.

A lump formed in my throat — for what I had become, and for what might have been.

Pippa glanced at the clock, re-clipped her hair, and strode over to the supply closet.

"Okay, next one..."

I straightened quickly, following her like a faithful mutt.

Faithful mate, my beast side whispered.

Half an hour later, Pippa was well into the next piece for her project.

She stuck out a hand. "Calipers."

I handed it to her, channeling *assisting nurse* at an open-heart surgery.

"Paddles," Pippa murmured.

I whipped out a couple of chunky cork things.

Ha. I was getting good at this.

When Pippa had said she was making a wine decanter set, I'd nodded gravely. Eventually, I figured out that meant wineglasses with a matching pitcher. Really, really nice ones with a fishnet design that took an incredible number of steps to make. Pippa mentioned something about the technique dating way back to the Middle Ages in...um...Florence? Venice? Something like that. Tiny air bubbles appeared in each "hole" in that fishnet, though I had no idea how she managed that.

Magic, maybe?

I'd been watching closely for signs, but there was a fine line between skill, talent, and magic. In this case, I was willing to give skill and talent the credit.

Last night, on the other hand...

I was still reeling from the sight of a fiery pegasus galloping into the sky — and I bet Pippa's father was too. I was sure he hadn't conjured it. Pippa had. Pippa, who'd always bemoaned the fact that she had no supernatural powers.

How could I be sure? Other than Greg's shocked expression was the fact that I'd been by to see Nash on the ranch a week earlier, and Claire had run over to show us her new pegasus book.

"Wow. Pegasus, huh? With wings and everything?" Nash asked, suitably impressed.

Well, duh. Wings kind of defined a pegasus, right?

But he wasn't playing dumb. He was giving Claire the excuse to set off on an enthusiastic ten-minute lecture about winged creatures.

Yes, an eight-year-old lecturing a dragon shifter on flying.

Key point: all that had taken place last week. There was no way Pippa's father could have known about Claire's latest infatuation.

But Pippa did.

So many questions. Did Greg's presence awaken or amplify his daughter's hidden magic? Was Pippa a Fire Dancer like him? Was last night a first? And, how was it possible for her to smell so good?

That was my wolf side, chiming in with that last question.

I watched her closely in the shop, but it was hard to know. Glassblowing seemed to be part art, part science... Part magic too?

She stuck out a hand. "Blowtorch."

I pressed it into her hand, and she sent flames licking over the glass. Although she kept the blowtorch centered, the flames had a way of reaching exactly the place she needed at exactly the right intensity. A little hotter on the left, where the glass had warped a tiny bit, a little shorter on the right, where the glass didn't need adjusting.

When she handed the blowtorch back, I turned away and gave the trigger a quick squeeze. The flames were a fraction of what they'd been for Pippa and far less pinpointed.

The agency classified witches and warlocks into five levels, and what I'd just witnessed was about a class-four on the pyromancer scale — low, in other words. But the fiery pegasus was the work of at least a class-two pyromancer, with one being the highest rating.

So, Pippa was all over the scale.

Witches and warlocks, like shapeshifters, typically come into their skills in puberty, I remembered the agency lecturer saying, way back when I'd first joined. *But their skills often emerge in fits and starts...*

Pippa had been a late bloomer in terms of developing...er, girl parts. But, boy. She was a super late bloomer if her supernatural powers were only coming out now.

That, or something, had suddenly accelerated the process. Maybe that recent run-in with Harlon Greene? The sisters had been pretty tight-lipped about how they'd defended themselves against a powerful warlock, but I'd overheard hushed references to tapping into a nearby vortex.

Could that have been the catalyst that finally made Pippa's powers start to emerge? And, hell. How far did they still have to go?

Chapter Twelve

INGO

Pippa dove right back into work, gesturing with her elbow a moment later. "I need pressure here."

I grabbed a steel plate and held it up to the rim of her glass.

"A little more..." Pippa said.

I had to lean way in to do that. So far, my chin brushed her head.

"Closer..."

The hot shop smelled mildly of beeswax and sweat, but getting close to Pippa gave me a whiff of her lavender scent.

"Okay, now the calipers..."

I nearly hummed in pleasure. God, it was nice to have her close.

Then an elbow nudged my ribs, and Pippa spoke louder.

"Ingo — calipers."

I straightened quickly. Oh. Right.

The glass looked perfect to me, but Pippa kept at it, checking this and that.

She'd pulled her hair back with a clip, but a lock escaped, and she blew up at it.

"Dammit..."

I caught it with a finger and smoothed it behind her ear.

"Thanks," she murmured without so much as a glance.

I celebrated and mourned at the same time. It was nice, this quiet, together time. But Pippa was so deep in the tunnel vision of work that I doubted she noticed me.

Then I pursed my lips, because she wasn't the only one guilty of tunnel vision sometimes.

Okay, a lot of times, in my case.

"Get ready to catch," Pippa said a few minutes later.

I grabbed the oven mitts and held them out, holding my breath.

"Ready?" she asked, preparing to tap the decanter free of the rod. "One...two...three!"

She tapped, and the decanter dropped lightly into my hands.

I raced for the annealer and set it in carefully, then backed away for Pippa to close the door.

We stood over it, sweating bullets but grinning a mile wide.

"High five," she announced, sticking a hand up.

The moment I smacked it, she turned back to the workbench, ready for the next piece. Three seconds later, she turned back to me, her eyes wide. "Oh my gosh. That was the last piece. We did it!"

I laughed. "You did it."

She held her arms high like a runner crossing a finish line, then threw them around me. "I can't believe I'm done." When she pulled back a little, her eyes were alight with pride. "And you know what? I think they're going to come out really well."

"I know they will," I assured her.

Pippa fell back into the hug, basking in her little victory, and letting me bask too. I held her close, happy to have been part of it, even in a small way.

The longer I held her, the happier I felt, and the less I remembered why. It didn't seem to matter much any more, only that we were together, and everything was good. Really good, in a way I hadn't felt for a long time.

My breaths slowed. My heart thumped. My eyes closed.

Happy. Together. Good.

Over the next few seconds, I didn't move, speak, or even think. Neither did Pippa. But something must have changed, because the hug went from being the punctuation mark at the end of one thing to the beginning of something new. Something very warm, comfortable...even sensual.

Pippa sighed, sliding her hands a little lower down my back.

I inhaled, tempted to let mine slide up. My skin tingled, and my thoughts blurred.

The next thing I knew, we were kissing. Touching. Wanting. Getting...

Pippa's lips parted, and the kiss went from gentle to raging, as if we'd turned the blowtorch on ourselves. Our hands roamed boldly, and our breaths turned into pants.

My body burned, and my jeans grew uncomfortably tight.

"So good," Pippa whispered, dragging her body against mine.

My mind grew more and more hazy. Sex became more and more inevitable. Undeniable, actually, because it had been too long.

Much too long, my wolf hummed greedily.

Pippa eased up onto the workbench, keeping her knees wide. I stepped closer, hissing in need when our hips meshed.

"Yes..." Pippa breathed, leaning back. The angle shoved her core against mine, and I went from *tight* to *hard.*

Angling farther and farther back, she pulled my shirt up, then fumbled with the button of my jeans.

Ring-ring! The bell over the shop door sang merrily, and we froze.

Pippa's hand stayed on my back, and I nearly roared at whomever that was.

The shop was dead quiet for an instant, other than the sound of our panting breaths.

"Oh. Hello. Am I interrupting?" the brunette at the door asked, more snide than amused.

I nearly let my wolf fangs out to snap at her, but then I caught myself. Really caught myself. Whoa. What had just happened?

Pippa's lips moved as she blinked at me. Slowly, grudgingly, we fought our way out of that all-consuming magic spell woven by... love? Lust? Fate?

Pippa straightened her shirt and stepped away from me, making my wolf howl.

"Can I help you?" she asked, snippier than I'd ever heard her.

Good to know I wasn't the only one mourning the end of that kiss.

The woman thumped a paper on the counter and tapped it with a long, manicured nail. Her crimson nail polish matched the color of her pouty lips.

"I'm here to pick up the order for TTC Limited."

Most folks in Sedona wore clothing suitable for scaling cliffs or zipping over mountain bike trails, whether they actually set off on such adventures or not. This woman had more of the casual-yet-carefully-curated yoga retreat look, though maintaining balance with those artificially enhanced boobs would be quite a trick. Her white down jacket was wide open and pushed aside to show off her shoulders. Underneath, a skimpy purple leotard struggled to contain those fake boobs. It was cut so high in the thigh that skin showed above the hem of her designer sweatpants.

Pippa went perfectly still. "Oh. You mean the vials?"

"Yes, I mean the vials," the bitch — er, woman — shot back. "Is something wrong?"

I hated her already, and I was pretty sure Pippa did too.

Pippa gave herself a little shake. "No. Sorry. I guess I was expecting Stacy."

"Mm," the woman said, conveying no meaning at all.

I did a double take. Stacy? The Stacy I'd been following?

Pippa didn't exactly demand an explanation, but her posture sure did.

"She couldn't make it today," the woman said with a sharp look.

Pippa considered for a long minute, then let out her own cryptic, "Mm." She turned back to the workshop. "Just a second, please."

The few times I'd been in the shop, Pippa had practically jumped to help customers. Now, she took her sweet time turning off the oven and checking the annealer settings.

Click, click, click. The customer tapped her long nails on the glass counter.

I spotted a big beige SUV with tinted windows parked outside. Stacy's ride.

Every muscle in my body coiled.

I turned away before the glance became a stare and busied myself tidying Pippa's workbench, though my ears remained perked.

I sniffed the air, but the fan was blowing the woman's scent away from, not toward me.

Click, click, click.

Pippa disappeared into the back then emerged with a huge box. When she thumped it on the counter, lots of small *somethings* clinked. Pippa opened the box and started riffling through it, counting out loud.

"Two...four...six...eight..."

I couldn't see the contents. Lots of small glass items was my guess.

Small glass items headed for TTC Limited — one of many shell companies in a long, dirty chain my gut saw leading to Victor Jananovich, though I had no evidence to prove that.

Yet.

Click, click, click.

"Twenty-two...twenty-four..."

"I'm sure it's fine," the woman snipped.

Pippa kept going, counting silently, then pulled out a sheet of paper. "Sign here, please."

The woman pinched the pen between her claws — er, long fingernails — and scribbled away with an annoyed air.

I looked at the box, then at the SUV. A golden opportunity, so I jumped.

"Can I carry that for you?" I offered.

The woman's feral eyes traveled over my body and lit up.

I plucked the sweaty fabric of my white T-shirt from my chest.

"Yes, please," she purred with a lick of her too-red lips.

Pippa shot me a sharp look.

I lifted the box onto my shoulder and headed for the door, where I paused.

Little Miss Clicky paused too, waiting for me to hold the door open for her. Never mind that my hands were full and hers were not.

I balanced the box with one hand and opened the door with the other, letting Clicky march through. And, whoa. Did she bathe in Chanel No. 5? The odor was so intense, I nearly sneezed.

Pippa stuck her hands on her hips, but I didn't have time to explain.

The driver must have hit a button, because the trunk opened. I leaned as far in as I dared, keeping my face behind the box. The musky scent of bear shifter enveloped me, along with pine cleaner, and I nearly sneezed. Bear shifter, pine cleaner, and something else... but it was hard to smell anything over the reek of Clicky's perfume.

There was nothing else in that squeaky-clean trunk. The tires and underbody were just as spotless, but whoever had scrubbed it had missed a spot of orange dust by the rear light. Dust like the ground around Gunnery Point?

I peeked at the driver out of the corner of my eye. He was a big guy — weight-lifter big, but so were most bear shifters — with a buzz cut and a dark suit. I could feel his eyes on me via the rearview mirror.

The woman hadn't lifted a finger the whole time, but now, she stuck a hand on the raised hatch and canted her hips to show off her curves.

Her voice was an inviting purr. "Nice of you to help, Mr...."

"Anytime." I forced a tight smile and opened the back door for her, keeping my back to the driver while I scanned the interior. Nothing there apart from a couple of shopping bags — the luxury kind with fancy handles and embossed print.

I held the door a little wider to prevent Miss Clicky from brushing against me on the way in. I wasn't sure whether she was going for a cheap thrill or if she'd been trained to take away a hint of my scent, but I wasn't keen on either.

Once seated, she opened her mouth to speak, but I slammed the door before she could and marched back into the shop.

Outside, the SUV rolled away as silently — and ominously — as it had come.

I kept my back turned for five full seconds, then went to the window to check the license plate.

Yep. Same plate, same SUV. Same driver, I would bet. So, where was Stacy?

"Did you have to be so helpful?" Pippa grumbled.

"Believe me, it was just an excuse to have a look at the car."

"Oh," Pippa said, deflating. "And?"

"It's the same vehicle Stacy rode in. Same driver. Same vehicle we saw exiting La Puebla, too."

She nodded, uneasy.

I stepped to her side, and together, we studied the invoice the woman had signed.

Pippa turned it this way and that, but the scribble might as well have been secret code.

"Deirdre somebody," Pippa tried.

At least the rest had been preprinted on the invoice. *TTC Limited.*

I looked at the order section of the invoice. "Fifty vials? What kind of vials?"

Pippa rooted in a drawer and held up two small tubes. "Love vials. Couples get them to fill with..." She trailed off, going pale.

I frowned. "Filled with what?"

Her throat bobbed, and she looked in the direction the SUV had gone. "Blood."

Every alarm in my mind began to whoop.

"Blood?"

She nodded slowly. "Not my thing, but some people like to carry around a little of their true love's blood."

I grimaced. "Seriously?"

She crossed her arms again, but not in defiance. More like hugging herself. "Yep. Totally gross, if you ask me."

"And these are what Stacy was picking up?" I asked. "Every time?"

"Yes. Fifty. Every week, more or less."

My mind spun. Fifty vials meant twenty-five couples. What use did Jananovich have for that?

"Half a shot glass..." Pippa murmured. "Vampires..."

I cocked my head, letting her think.

"Vampire couples?" she mused.

I couldn't make sense of it either, but I was definitely on red alert.

"When was the last time you saw Stacy?" I asked.

Pippa's lips wobbled. "Yesterday. No, wait. The day before."

"Did she say anything about picking up this order?"

"Indirectly. She's always been the one who picks up the order. Always."

"Did she say anything else?"

"Nothing specific. But she did look nervous."

She stared at me, then rummaged in her bag for her phone. I watched as she pressed a few buttons, waited, then spoke into voice mail.

"Hi, Stacy. It's Pippa. I was just—"

I made a cutting motion in the air, prepared to grab the phone out of her hand.

Pippa stared, then caught on. Stacy might not be the only person who heard those messages.

Pippa gulped and considered her words before finishing. "I'm just calling to say I hope you're happy with the latest order. Please let me know when you have a chance, okay? Thank you." Then she paused again, stuck. "I'll... I'll see you soon, I hope."

She hung up, staring at me with wide, pleading eyes. Then she turned briskly to the workshop, as if she didn't want an answer to her unspoken question.

"I'm sure everything is fine..."

I wasn't so sure. I hoped she'd see Stacy soon too. But my gut feared the worst.

"Damn," Pippa cursed, catching a glimpse of the clock. "I have to get going."

Right, the catering job. I watched her race around, closing the shop down, but my mind was elsewhere. Pippa's too, no doubt.

Twenty minutes later, Pippa hustled me out the back door and locked it behind us.

"See you soon?" she said when I'd walked her to her car.

I frowned at the echo of her message to Stacy. I took her hands and squeezed.

"Be careful. I mean it," I said before she could protest. "The moment anything feels off, call me." I shook her hands a little. "Promise, okay?"

Her lips wobbled a little. I hated to spook her, but she had to understand this was serious.

"I promise." She looked at me for a minute, and I braced myself for a *but*.

Instead, she rocked on her heels, then threw her arms around me and held me tight.

The contact was the best feeling, but the scariest too. Something was up, and we both knew it.

I closed my eyes, soaking in the positive part of the feeling. Then I leaned away, because it was time to go.

Pippa searched my eyes for a long, silent moment. I wavered too, then gave in and kissed her. Hard and long, on the lips, letting her know how much I loved her. How much I'd missed her. How much I regretted.

Pippa sighed, and her body relaxed against mine. Everything but the lips, which kept massaging mine.

My inner wolf howled in joy and relief.

But a passing car tooted, and someone cheered, making us break apart.

"Asshole," Pippa muttered. Then her eyes went wide. "Him, I mean! Not you."

My lips curled. "Does that mean I might get another kiss later?"

She chuckled, all coy. "Maybe."

A smile stretched my cheeks — the biggest I'd managed in years, it seemed like.

She closed her eyes briefly, warring with herself. "I have to go..."

The way she said it — all sad and regretful — gave me hope.

I popped a goodbye kiss on her lips.

"See you soon," I said, biting back another, *Be careful.*

"Soon," she promised, patting me on the chest.

I watched her go, then blew out a deep breath. My mind filled with multiple trains of thought — many more than tracks to organize them with. But another deep breath narrowed my focus to the one that took priority.

I pulled out my phone and dialed a number. Not the agency. Captain Edwards had made it perfectly clear I couldn't count on agency support regarding Jananovich. Which didn't leave me with many aboveboard options.

But that didn't mean I didn't have other resources. And the agency wasn't the only force to be reckoned with when it came to supernatural activity in this area.

The phone rang. Once…twice…three times.

Finally, my contact picked up. "Williams here."

I turned away from the street and kept my voice low. "This is Kemper." I hesitated, knowing full well I was risking my career. "We need to meet. It's urgent."

The man on the other end of the line processed that for a moment before answering. "Meeting in an official capacity?"

I shook my head. "Not exactly."

The ensuing pause was so long, I worried he'd hung up. But then he spoke. "When?"

"As soon as possible. With you and, ideally, your boss."

Another excruciating wait. Then, finally, a reply. "I'll see what I can do. But no guarantees."

My laugh was dry. Nothing was guaranteed in my line of work.

"Call me back in an hour," he finished.

Then the line went dead.

Chapter Thirteen

PIPPA

I left the hot shop with mixed feelings. On the one hand, I was jubilant at finishing my contest entry — and still tingling from kissing Ingo. On the other hand, I worried about Stacy. But there were a dozen reasonable explanations for her absence, and only one off-the-deep-end, paranoid one to worry about. The odds didn't add up.

That didn't stop me from checking my phone for messages at every red light, though.

Twenty minutes and a few miles of back roads later, I pulled into the parking lot of the Kokopelli Spa and Resort.

"Thanks so much for coming!" My friend Nancy hugged me when I found her inside.

I smiled. "Happy to help."

I was — truly — but the money didn't hurt either. Even half a day of catering work paid well at pricey resorts like this. And unlike that glass contest, the payoff was a sure thing.

"So, what do we have today?" I asked, pulling on an apron.

She motioned to a glass pavilion beside the resort kitchen. "Late lunch for a group of fifteen. They've booked the entire resort."

I whistled. The resort had space for five times that number.

Nancy shrugged at the question in my eyes. "I guess they really wanted their privacy."

That total lack of curiosity — aka discretion — made Nancy's small company one of the most sought-after caterers in Sedona. That, and her award-winning food.

"Kind of late for lunch, though, huh?"

She shrugged. "From what I understand, they slept in and had a late brunch."

I peeked out the door for a first impression. My eyes roved around, then I stopped for a low, "Wow."

Nancy chuckled. "Do you mean the guy closest to the door or the one over by the pool?"

I'd meant the first one, but now that I'd spotted number two...

I whistled. "Wow again. Is this like the Olympic volleyball team?"

Nancy laughed. "Nope. The women are too short. My guess was an elite dance or cheerleading squad, but they mentioned something about being consultants."

Ha. That was a lot like *artist* — an occupation that could mean anything. And, heck. What would those gorgeous twentysomethings lounging by the pool be qualified to advise anyone on? Beauty products? Exercise programs?

I tightened my apron and looked around the kitchen. "You want me to start with drinks?"

Nancy nodded. "You know the drill."

I did, because I'd moonlighted for her catering company lots of times. Some of them memorable, like the time I'd first encountered Harlon Greene and Angelina Saint James. Some less so, like that conference of dental assistants...or had they been safety inspectors?

I picked up a tray of glasses and headed into the adjoining pavilion — one of those giant glass structures that conveyed an outdoors feel even in nippy winter weather. This one was big enough to enclose the entire pool and a deck with thirty or so lounge chairs, only half of which were occupied.

I poured a dozen orange juices and started making the rounds.

"Juice?" I asked the nearest woman, a stunning redhead in a bathrobe.

"God, yes. Please."

I set it down beside her water bottle and moved on.

"Juice?" I asked the next guy — a muscled football player type.

"Yes, please." He helped himself to two and downed each in a single long gulp, then placed the glasses back on the tray.

Next came a dark-haired, dark-eyed beauty who could have starred in a Bollywood movie, then a serious — and seriously buff — young man of Asian heritage.

All in all, a United-Colors-of-Benetton-meets-Olympic-team kind of bunch: they represented every race, creed, and color, including two plus-sized beauties.

Same deal each time. Everyone gladly took a juice — or two.

Not so noteworthy, but that was in addition to the liter-sized water bottles each person kept at hand, and most of those were down to the last drop.

Apparently, consulting was a very thirsty business.

By way of experiment, I poured a dozen cranberry juices, and those went just as quickly. So, huh. Thirsty, indeed, because cranberry juice never went fast. Not a picky bunch, these Benetton Olympians.

Meanwhile, I was starting to reassess the dance troop/cheerleader/athlete hypothesis, because all those things took energy. This gang was as lethargic as sloths at high noon. Maybe they ate a high-fiber diet that was really, really hard to digest.

Some were snoozing, while others just stared off into space. One woman leaned back, turning blind, cucumber-clad eyes to the sky.

Definitely a laid-back group.

All except for two big, hawkeyed men who stood at opposite corners of the pavilion. They wore suits and sunglasses and kept their hands at their sides. Their necks were as thick as my waist, and their gazes roved the area continuously. When I approached them with drinks, they shook their heads and looked over my head, like I was just another patch of empty space.

Nancy, over at the kitchen door, shook her head, indicating *Not those two.*

Interesting. What cheerleaders — er, consultants — came with a security detail? And, wait a second. The security guys seemed to spend more time facing the consultants than the outer perimeter. Were they keeping people in or out?

They hadn't asked for ID or checked me in any way, but maybe Nancy had had me precleared.

Anyway, the young people barely acknowledged the existence of the security guys. So, huh. Maybe they were some kind of pop stars who used security to keep fans at bay while they enjoyed the peace of this remote resort.

For the next few minutes, I imagined a dozen different glamorous and scintillating scenarios, each blessing these men and women with lives far more exciting than my own.

"God, I love this part of my workweek," one of them quipped. "The recovery stage."

The others chuckled.

Recovery, huh? Maybe they were athletes after all. That would explain the sweatbands most of them wore around their wrists. So, maybe they were athletes who had just returned from a very taxing competition in a different time zone. I made a mental note to look up what events I'd recently missed.

When I circulated with my third load of drinks, a peppy, outgoing blonde named Kelly followed me, dispensing pills. Big ones, fit for a horse.

"One for you, and one for you..."

She was behind me, but I didn't hear a single *No, thanks.*

"Gotta keep up your iron," she chirped.

Enough iron to stick to a magnet, judging by the size of those pills. Maybe they had other stuff in them too. Stuff a lowly caterer like me had no business asking about.

I threw another glance at the security guys, then looked away.

The guests didn't rush forward when we set up a table with food — not even the football player. So, I piled some hors d'oeuvres on a tray and made the rounds again. Which wasn't really in my own self-interest since Nancy generally let me take leftovers home. But, heck. If those poor dears were so low in iron and hydration, they probably lacked other nutrients too.

That worked, though most guests treated food as an afterthought. They treated me the same way, and conversations that had been hushed during my first few rounds now continued without missing a beat.

"Vic...not my favorite. Henry is much gentler," one of the guys said to another.

Masseurs, maybe? Physical therapists?

"I kind of wish I'd get Svea, though," the other said, and they both chuckled.

I pictured a buxom Swede trained in the art of healing.

The next woman I walked by — gorgeous, with coffee-colored skin and beautifully arranged cornrows — winced and rubbed her thigh, murmuring something to a blonde. Cornrows wore sweatpants, and Blondie, a robe.

Blondie nodded sympathetically. "I know how you feel. But think of it this way — another six weeks of this and you'll have enough for that down payment."

I couldn't help but speculate. Down payment on a house? A car? A monthly gym membership? What income bracket were these people in?

"True. Especially with free housing," Cornrows agreed.

"Best view of Chimney Rock in Sedona," Blondie quipped.

I froze. Stacy had once said the exact same thing.

Over in the far corner sat a strawberry-blonde, the only restless member of the squad. A newbie, it seemed, judging by the amount of advice the others doled out.

"No need to worry, Delaney. You'll do great," Kelly assured her. "It's always scary the first time."

"Not scared," Delaney insisted, wringing her hands. "Just excited, I guess."

About as excited as Roscoe on a visit to the vet, if you asked me. Not that they did.

"Exciting is right," Kelly agreed. "I heard the boss say he's expecting a full house on Friday."

I made a mental note to ask Nancy about that. Had she been hired to cater that event too?

"The best thing you can do now is drink. Lots," Miss Bollywood advised Delaney.

Hydration, hydration, hydration. Maybe that's what they consulted people on.

"Lots of meat, too," another added.

A good thing Nancy already had steaks sizzling on the grill.

The guests roused themselves for those, sitting four to a table with panoramic views of Deer Mountain and Boynton Canyon. Whoever was paying for this gig sure was generous to their staff. And, hey. Maybe these were incredibly skilled and successful consultants who deserved every last perk for whatever exhausting work they did.

"Delicious," one gushed over a bite of steak.

"I feel better already," another decided.

"How many other people get to work three days on, four off?" another crowed.

Lucky people, that was for sure. Though their work certainly seemed exhausting.

"High-priced escorts," Wendy, Nancy's other helper, whispered, half serious, half in jest. "I bet you anything that's what they are."

I couldn't decide whether to chuckle or frown because, huh. That did fit.

Nancy tut-tutted. "What some people will do for money."

I tsked too, but then it hit me. How far would I go? Say, when it came to saving my ranch?

Suddenly, I wasn't half as judgmental.

Still, the gears in my mind ticked over. As I made my next rounds, I studied the guests even more closely. And, oh. A whole new, horrible scenario dawned on me.

I went over the factors, wishing I could come to a totally different conclusion. But I couldn't.

Gorgeous young people. Check.

Well-paying jobs. Check.

Long hours on weekends, lots of time off during the week. Pampered conditions in their downtime, with a couple of security-types keeping an eye on them even then.

Check, check, check.

High-priced escorts, for sure. But who did they work for?

I had a hunch, but it made me sick.

Up until then, I'd been casually curious. Now, I really was actively curious in one of those *I want to know, but I don't want to know* states.

None of your business, I reminded myself.

Still, I kept snooping away.

And, bingo. The third time I passed Delaney, a tiny detail registered. Not about how she picked at her food or how young she looked or how out of place she seemed. Something else. The tiniest, faintest detail I hadn't noticed before.

Her scent.

My step hitched, but I managed not to gawk.

She had the same fresh, woodsy, mountains-in-springtime scent as someone I knew well. Ingo.

The same woodsy scent, in fact, as Ingo's father and mother and my dad's friend Howie, too.

Wolf shifter scent.

How did I know? I just did.

Maybe my mother's dragon shifter genes made me sensitive to such things. Maybe it came from growing up around a mixed group of supernaturals, from warlocks like my father to the wolves of Ingo's family. I could even identify vampires, though I hadn't been around many, and I really hoped to keep it that way.

In Delaney's case, the scent was faint. Barely there, in fact, unless I really piqued my senses.

Relic, the back of my mind said. A person with very diluted shifter — or other supernatural — blood, with no special powers other than a few faint hints. In some cases, that meant fierce loyalty, the way wolves were loyal to their packs. In others, it meant keen eyesight or sharp sense of smell or especially fleet feet. Other relics had no special abilities at all — truly zilch. All they got were a few leftover identifiers that highlighted how painfully ordinary they were.

Kind of like me.

Well, not entirely, because my supernatural blood wasn't generations old. It just hadn't bothered carrying over one measly generation to me.

At least, that's what I'd thought my whole life. Recent events had made me wonder, though.

I blinked a few times, pushing the thought away. I could figure myself out later — or, more likely, never. Now was the time to figure out what was going on here.

Delaney was a relic. Was she the only one?

No, I decided a few minutes later. Saanvi — of Bollywood fame, at least in my mind — had a hint of shifter in her too, though I couldn't identify what kind. And possibly Rob too — the big, handsome football player. Lion shifter, maybe, judging by his smooth, easy gait.

But what about Becca, the plus-sized beauty who spent most of her time in the hot tub? Her eyes were a striking, luminous green.

I worked my way closer to her. When I sniffed her scent, I thought of seashells, sand, and the ocean.

And, whoa. I turned away before she spotted my surprise.

A mermaid relic? I'd never met one, but my dad had, and she sure matched his description.

So, huh. Three or four relics in a pool of fifteen — at least as far as my senses could ascertain. I could be wrong. In fact, I was almost guaranteed to be wrong, because I was me. Still, this was way, way out of proportion to a random, everyday sample — even in Sedona, a place that attracted all kinds of supernaturals and relics.

Which led to my next question. Were those four here by design or coincidence?

I glanced at the security guys, then did another round of the tables. Having finished eating, the guests drifted back to the lounge chairs, where they collapsed in weary, sated bliss. I stacked plates and collected silverware, brought them into the kitchen, then headed out for more.

Kelly stood and made space for me to clear her table with a friendly smile.

"Thank you. That was delicious," she said.

"I'll let my boss know. Thanks."

Then my eye caught on a detail, and my stomach lurched.

Kelly tilted her head. "Everything okay?"

I forced a smile. "Sorry, yes. I was just admiring your scarf."

She touched the Monet flower print and chuckled. "I'll let my boss know. Thanks."

My forced chuckle probably sounded like a hyena, but Kelly went on her way with a happy, clueless smile.

I did my best not to stare, though I probably failed. Stacy had the same scarf.

My mind spun.

Stacy. Scarves. Blood vials.

A job that came with a chauffeur a hell of a lot like those security men.

A job that had made her increasingly nervous, though she wouldn't say why.

Ingo's suspicions about a criminal vampire, Victor Jananovich.

I scanned the "consultants" who'd just enjoyed a good meal. People doing their best to hydrate and top up their iron.

My mind jumped back to vials. Lots and lots of them, a steady order, fifty per week.

Fifty vials with just a few drops each. Shot-glass size, more or less. Enough to remind a person of their loved one...or to savor a sip.

Earlier, my imagination had served up a dozen titillating scenarios about what was going on in this group. Now, it was coming up with a much more frightening one.

I tried doing the math. Fifty vials...fifteen "consultants" with pale, weary complexions, plus wristbands and tight collars.

"Oh, Pippa, I meant to ask," Nancy said when I was back in the kitchen, "are you available to help on Friday? Same client, but this time up at La Puebla."

My eyes bugged out of my head. "La Puebla?"

"Yep. An easy job," Nancy assured me. "All we have to do is bring in the food and drink, set it all up, and leave, then pick everything up the next day. They want to do the serving themselves."

The feeling in my gut got that much more ominous. What did that event entail that the client didn't want us to see?

Nancy must have read my mind, because she gave me a significant look. "If they don't tell, we don't ask. Business is business."

It was, as long as the refreshments were food and drink. But what if the menu went beyond that?

"I'll have to get back to you about that," I stammered.

"Thanks," she chirped, cheery as ever. "Do you want me to wrap up these leftovers for you?"

My voice cracked when I replied. "No, thanks."

I'd long since lost my appetite.

Chapter Fourteen

PIPPA

By the next morning, Stacy still hadn't called, and I was feeling more and more uneasy — about her, that creepy Deirdre who'd picked up the vials, the "consultants," and the dead hiker.

Was Ingo right to be suspicious, or was there a perfectly good explanation for it all?

Tangential to that was my building anticipation about the glass contest, and how that related to my financial problems. I had high hopes, but you never knew how a project would turn out until you opened the annealer door.

So, I decided to start there. One step at a time, as Erin liked to say.

I tapped my fingers on the steering wheel throughout the drive to town and the hot shop. Once there, I hurried straight to the annealer. My heart was in my throat as I lifted out the decanter and held it to the light.

"Wow," I couldn't help murmuring.

Thin black lines crisscrossed the clear glass and curved gracefully over the surface. Small diamonds formed between the lines, each with a tiny air bubble in the center. I turned the decanter around, checking for imperfections but finding none.

"Wow," I repeated.

It was good. Really good. Possibly my best work ever.

The glasses were just as good. Every last one.

Grinning in triumph, I grabbed my phone, intent on sharing the good news with Ingo, who'd helped me get them done in such a tight time frame.

But all I got was his out-of-office message. The usual, in other words.

My spirits sank.

I thought about calling Abby or Erin, just to be able to share my excitement. But they hadn't sweated through this project with me. Ingo had. And while I loved making my sisters proud, nothing beat the feeling of Ingo's pride.

I stared through the glass, not focused on anything in particular. Without Ingo, the world was a little duller, a little emptier. A vessel without anything to fill it, like the decanter I held.

I closed my eyes, replaying our kiss. Was I really ready to deny myself the one person who injected meaning into my life?

On the other hand, that out-of-office message summed things up well. With Ingo, I would always be waiting — or worse, worrying, as I had for my dad.

I thought through all the times I'd waited up for my dad, terrified he or one of his crew might not make it. All the soccer games, all the glass exhibits, all the holidays he'd missed. Was all that worth the trade-off for me and my future kids?

For the first time ever, I was starting to think. . . yes.

I looked at the phone, tempted to call Ingo again. Instead, I checked the contest specifications for the tenth time.

The winning contestant will submit four beautifully crafted glasses and a matching decanter. All must allow for proper aeration and visibility of the liquid inside.

My mind bounced back to the day Stacy had handed me that flyer. *My boss is sponsoring a design contest. I thought you might want to enter.*

That day, she'd been carefree and happy. Now, she was missing in action.

My eyes wandered to the northwest, in the direction of La Puebla.

Best view of Chimney Rock in Sedona, one of the "consultants" had quipped yesterday. The exact same words spoken in the same inside-joke way Stacy had once told it.

Stacy, whom I hadn't heard from in several days now. Stacy, who'd been nervous about something. Stacy, whose boss was sponsoring the glass contest.

I hated unsolved mysteries. I craved clarity. And I was desperate to track down Stacy — for her own sake, and to disprove Ingo's crazy suspicions so I could go back to seeing things positively. But I couldn't.

Or could I?

I looked at the decanter, then the contest flyer. The address listed was a PO box, but what about La Puebla?

The gears in my mind turned in a way Ingo would not approve of. But, heck. The plan hatching there made sense. And I had been so eager to check on my glass project that I'd come to the hot shop two hours early. Plenty of time to pop out for a quick...er, errand, then pop back again. An errand that could give me peace of mind on two counts: Stacy, and my chance of winning that contest.

Ingo, I knew, would shoot down the idea immediately. But Ingo was paranoid and overprotective.

Also, he wasn't around to talk some sense into me.

Before I could talk myself out of a perfectly good idea, I packed the decanter and glasses carefully, locked up the shop, and started driving.

Twenty-five minutes later, I blinked at the cameras at La Puebla's security checkpoint. Two were aimed at my dusty orange Subaru, while a third was slowly pivoting over from a different angle. A big, burly security guy lumbered out of the guardhouse, chest thrust forward.

"Good morning," he growled.

Talk about mixed messages.

"Good morning!" I chirped, going for *dumb blonde* instead of *amateur sleuth.*

He waited for more, then sighed. "Do you have an appointment?"

I nodded cheerily. "Yes. Well, no. Sort of." I lifted the box on the front seat. "I'm here to deliver this rushed order."

"Delivery?" He snorted.

The wind shifted, bringing me a whiff of his scent. It was musky. Woodsy. Bear-y, in other words.

I did my best not to flinch. The guy was a bear shifter, like Ingo's suspects in the death at Gunnery Point.

I nodded. "Stacy said she needed it before Friday."

I watched carefully, but I couldn't catch a flicker of guilt light his expression. No denial when it came to Stacy being associated with the place either.

"Well, you can leave your delivery with me."

I shook my head. "I'd love to, but I have to demonstrate it all. Can you just call Stacy over?"

He shook his head. "No can do, lady."

Damn the man — a master of neither confirming nor denying anything I said.

The camera on my right whirred, and the zoom lens extended.

My skin crawled. Here I was, making myself a subject of interest. On the other hand, my cover story was pretty damn watertight.

A little like the *Titanic*.

I forced myself to give the camera a cheery wave.

"Here's the thing," I said loudly. "Stacy said the boss would like my design, and that he needed it ASAP."

By then, my throat was dry. What if Stacy turned up now to deny that, and I got us both in trouble?

The guards weren't buying it, but I must have succeeded in piquing someone's curiosity, because a phone rang in the guardhouse. A second security guy answered it, frowned at me, and shrugged. After hanging up, he waved to the first guy.

"Let her through, Hal."

The gates creaked ominously open, and I eased my car forward with an enthusiastic wave. "Thank you!"

From a distance, La Puebla was little more than a sand-colored lump in the landscape. Now, I found myself surrounded by a weird blend of squat "earthship" architecture and buildings inspired by Native American cliff dwellings. A row of garages was built into the hill on my right, but none of them lined up with each other or the utility buildings around them. Then came a series of boxy, interconnected buildings that looked a hell of a lot like guest rooms or even dorms.

I turned left, checking the view. *Best view of Chimney Rock in Sedona* was right.

My heart thumped.

Finally, I came to the main house, which was another Jenga puzzle with parts heaped up and sticking out from one another. Was it three stories tall? Four? Five? Every time I started counting, I lost track. A circular driveway with a single, gnarled juniper in the center looped in front of it, and I nearly did a second lap while taking it all in. Then I stopped under an arched breezeway by a huge glass entryway crowded with desert flora. The VIP entrance, no doubt.

I looked around nervously. Catering entrances were more my milieu. What the hell was I doing here?

Still, I'd made it this far, right?

I stepped out of my car, clutching the contest flyer and my box.

A woman appeared at the entrance, and for one terrifying moment, I thought it might be Deirdre, though I was confident in my cover story. But it wasn't, and she stepped aside when a man appeared behind her.

"Not to worry," he assured her. "I'll get this one."

Quiet as a mouse, she scurried away and disappeared back into the woodwork.

I pasted on a smile, though my heart pounded. Then I relaxed a little, because the man was the polar opposite of what I'd been expecting. No dark hair, no fangs, no widow's peak. On the contrary, I was greeted by a slight, amiable man with ginger hair, a matching ginger beard, and green eyes that danced upon seeing me.

More *Sean O'Grady* than *Victor Jananovich*, if you asked me.

I inhaled deeply. I might not have inherited much of my parents' supernatural powers, but I did have a knack for identifying shifters and vampires. The latter's faint ammonia smell was usually a dead giveaway.

I hid an inner chuckle at my own joke. *Dead* giveaway.

Then I thought of Stacy and got real serious, real fast.

But, whew. All I got from this man was a pleasing whiff of cologne. Yves Saint Laurent, I'd bet — the pricey kind.

He approached with a disarming smile. Literally. If I'd been toting a gun — or a wooden stake — I would have stashed it away in embarrassment.

There was no way this was a criminal mastermind. On the contrary, his casual khakis and muted yellow polo suggested tech start-up billionaire. The guy was barely into his forties, and he was way too chipper to be a vampire. He didn't offer his hand, but lots of people didn't these days.

"Hello. I'm Victor. Welcome to La Puebla."

His teeth were white and straight, nary a fang among them.

"Nice to meet you," I said, more truthfully than I'd expected to. "I'm Pippa, from Sedona Glass, here to deliver your design." I held up the contest flyer.

First, his expression was blank. Then recognition flickered in his eyes.

"Yes, of course. The contest."

I bobbed my head like one of those toys people kept in the back of their cars. "Sorry to bother you, but Stacy encouraged me to show you my design."

"Ah, yes. Stacy." A robot couldn't have hit a more neutral tone.

I nodded, keeping up the dumb blonde act. "She was sure you'd love it, so she said to bring it around in person as soon as it was done."

His eyebrows lifted a little, but I'm proud — er, ashamed — to say I'm a good liar, and a moment later, he nodded.

"Well, then. Why don't you come in and let me see? May I take your coat?"

Chapter Fifteen

PIPPA

I shrugged out of one sleeve, then the other, letting Jananovich take it. Shouldering my backpack, I followed him down the dim hall, down two steps, around a corner, up four steps to the right...

The place was definitely the product of a stoned, 1970s, peace-love-granola architect/artist type. The walls were raw cement, which would keep the temperature cool in summer, while the red oriental runner rug helped keep things warm now.

"May I offer you a drink? Tea? Coffee?" he asked, half turning.

"No thank you," I said, tearing my eyes away from a side room we passed. A study, by the looks of it.

No bloodstains. No coffin. No coffee-table books of Transylvanian castles.

Either Ingo had been in his line of work for too long, or Jananovich was as slick as they came. My inner pendulum swung back and forth.

"Oh. Actually, some wine would be good. To show you the decanter, I mean," I added quickly.

"That can be arranged." He smiled and gestured me into an office on the right.

I pointed straight ahead to a glass door leading to the terrace beyond. "Ideally, I'd like to demonstrate outside. I'm afraid I might spill something."

And, shit. Was that a flicker of excitement I'd just glimpsed?

Wine, I wanted to insist. *I mean spilling wine, not blood!* My inner pendulum swung back over to high alert.

"Certainly." He continued to the terrace.

I stepped outside. And stepped, and stepped... The terrace was as big as a tennis court, and that wasn't counting the infinity pool. Something I'd bet was added after La Puebla's days as a commune. There were at least a dozen lounge chairs there, all facing the views, and a barbecue big enough to grill an elephant.

"Wow. Great views," I couldn't help saying, though I did hold back, *Especially of Chimney Rock.*

I turned to see the side of the building. Most of it was taken up by a massive living/dining/entertaining room with three-story windows facing the incredible view. The place had definitely undergone a major facelift since I'd visited on a catering job a few years earlier. I'd never seen so many sofas in a private home, though. Some were more like lounges, and I couldn't help thinking it would be a great place for an orgy.

The question was, sex orgy or blood orgy?

Both made my stomach turn, but I managed another approving squeak.

"Wow."

"It is nice, isn't it?" he conceded.

As far as architecture went, sure. But I did notice extra-thick curtains for the windows, currently pushed away. Vampires weren't allergic to light, as popular myths claimed, but they did avoid blazing sunshine.

Like now? Jananovich, I noted, remained in the shaded part of the terrace.

I pulled myself together and pointed to a table. "May I unpack here?"

"Be my guest."

I'd definitely piqued his curiosity, which could be good or bad. *Good* because it gave me a chance to get a sense of what he was really up to. *Bad* because I had the sneaking feeling he was more interested in me than the glass. And, yikes. If he offered me a consulting job, I would be out of there faster than Road Runner sprinted away from Wile E. Coyote.

While I unpacked the glass and other gear I'd brought, my host pressed an intercom.

"George? Some wine, please," he said when someone answered. Then he glanced at me. "Red or white?"

I gulped. My turn to go for a neutral voice. "Red, please."

The man on the intercom went through a list of fancy labels and years for Victor to ponder over. First-world problems.

"Just an ordinary Barolo, please."

Ha. One of the random things I'd learned from catering was that there was no such thing as an ordinary Barolo.

An older man appeared with the wine, looking every inch the butler. He disappeared just as quickly, leaving no impression whatsoever.

I heaved an inner sigh. Rich men's ideas of perfect butlers were old, gray, nondescript men. Their idea of perfect housemaids were curvy, young, and buxom. The world was so fucked up.

Victor opened the wine, and I handed him a glass. He held it up to the light, studying the design.

"I went for a reticello pattern," I said, watching anxiously for his reaction. "So the glass has its own beauty but still allows you to appreciate the wine."

"Lovely," he murmured, turning it this way and that.

I held out the decanter and watched nervously as he filled it, then poured from the decanter to the glass.

"Lovely, indeed," he said, more to himself than to me.

I showed him the matching stopper for the decanter — and whew. It fit perfectly.

I gave myself an inner high five.

"Just lovely," he repeated, sniffing, then taking a sip.

He nodded in approval, and I couldn't help swelling with pride.

He offered me a glass too, and I nearly accepted. Then I pulled myself together. Much as I wanted — and needed — the prize money, this wasn't only about winning a contest. I was here to help Stacy and learn whether Jananovich was a genuine threat.

And if he was a threat? I had a wooden stake and a pocket full of garlic.

Well, okay. The wooden stake was just a sharpened pencil, the best I could manage on short notice.

"Are glasses your specialty?" he asked.

"Oh no." I whipped out my phone to show him the shop's website, then stopped. "Poor reception here. Do you have Wi-Fi so I can show you?"

The network was LaPuebla2, and the password was *guest*. Apparently, cybersecurity was not an issue up here. Not for his guests, at least.

"Here are a few others..." I said, scrolling through the images for him to see.

"Quite a varied selection," he observed.

When his breath warmed my shoulder, I ended the show and stepped back into my own space.

"I'm so glad you like it." I cleared my throat, working up my nerve to pop the million-dollar question. "I'd love to show Stacy the decanter. Do you know where I could find her?"

"Unfortunately, she's unavailable."

Aha. Well, that proved she *had* been here. Jananovich was her boss, and he was the one who'd ordered the vials. So, Ingo hadn't been overly paranoid.

But, yikes. Now, I was.

"Oh. I hope everything is all right?" I asked.

Again, the neutral voice contest. Jananovich was winning, though.

"I hope so too," he admitted. "She had to leave suddenly. Something about her mother..."

Alarms went off in my mind. Big, whooping ones, like a nuclear weapons silo signaling DEFCON 1. Stacy had lost her mother to cancer years ago. I clearly remembered her mentioning it.

I glanced at Jananovich. Was the man innocently mistaken or a cold-blooded killer? More to the point, was he a man at all or a vampire?

My phone rang, and I pulled it from my pocket. "Hello?"

Metal shop noises came through from the other end of the line as Abby spoke.

"Hi, it's me," my sister said, sounding rushed and annoyed.

Bang! Bang! She hadn't bothered putting her work aside for this call. Which made sense since I'd drastically downplayed the situation.

"Oh, hello," I said loudly, shooting an apologetic look at my host.

"Calling like you asked me to." Abby's sigh was punctuated by another couple of hits of the hammer.

"Yes, that's right," I said, playing out my side of a different conversation. "I'll be sure to pick that up on my way home. I'm at La Puebla right now, but I shouldn't be long."

There. Another layer in my safety net, such as it was. I'd just made clear to Jananovich that someone knew where I was, in case he suddenly decided to off me and claim I'd never been there.

"See you at the shop soon," I finished, then smiled, hung up, and apologized to my host again. "Sorry."

"Not to worry," he murmured, more focused on the glasses and decanter than me.

He liked them. He really liked them!

I could have cheered... until I pictured blood instead of wine.

Maybe it was time to get going.

"I'd be happy to leave the pieces with you to mull over," I said, gathering the packaging.

Just then, the wind shifted, and along with the influx of fresh mountain air, I caught a whiff of ammonia mixed in with the Yves Saint Laurent.

My gut lurched. Shit. He really was a vampire.

"They are appealing," he murmured. "Very appealing."

More like terrifying. All the more so with the abruptness of my realization.

Of course, not all vampires were criminals. But with Ingo's warnings, Stacy's disappearance, and Jananovich's interest in unidentified liquids, I veered way over to the *bad guy* hypothesis.

I made a show of checking my watch.

"Oops. I didn't mean to take so much of your time. I really should be going." I did my best not to rush, but the love vials I'd brought in case I needed another excuse to chat rattled, and one fell to the floor.

Quick as a cat, Jananovich caught it. I reached out a split second too late, and our shoulders brushed. I straightened quickly, but not before my nose wrinkled. Now that I was onto that hint of ammonia, it was all I smelled.

And, shit. Jananovich's nostrils were flaring too, and his eyes gleamed as they roamed over my body.

Crap. Had he sensed my mixed heritage? Vampires had good noses, but I had it on good authority I smelled ninety-nine percent human.

Too bad for that one percent Jananovich had just caught on to. His eyes closed the way a wine enthusiast's might when challenged with a taste test.

Interesting, his glittering eyes purred when they reopened. *Very interesting.*

I thought back to the beautiful consultants. Had they gone through an interview process that included a sniff test and ended with the same predatory purr?

"A pity you have to go. This has been a most fortuitous meeting," he said.

I did my best to sound chipper and walk, not sprint, for the door.

"I'm so glad. I hope you like my contest entry."

"I do. We'll have to wait until the official deadline to declare a winner, but I feel very optimistic."

Funny how quickly $25,000 had fallen off my radar.

"Well, I'll keep my fingers crossed," I said, closing a hand around the lump in my pocket.

And my garlic close by, an inner voice added.

I nearly bolted outside without my jacket, but Jananovich held it out, stopping me.

It took everything I had to turn my back to him and slip into it. The hair on my neck stood, and I swear, a spot on the side of my throat warmed. Was he staring at it?

Time slowed to a crawl. I patted my pants pocket, but the sharpened pencil seemed laughably small now. A dozen doubts filled my mind. Could I whip it out in time to stop him from biting? Was it even big enough to stop a full-grown vampire? Most importantly, did stakes really kill vampires, or was that only urban legend?

Ingo would know all the answers. Why, oh why, hadn't I believed him earlier?

"There you are," Jananovich murmured, releasing my jacket.

Stepping away, I forced a smile. "Thank you so much again. I look forward to hearing from you."

"I'll look forward to that too, Ms...."

"Martin," I stupidly supplied. "Pippa Martin."

He nodded, reaching into his pocket.

My heart went still, and my hand tightened around the pencil.

He pulled out a business card and held it out. "Let me know if you ever happen to be interested in a little work on the side."

I took it slowly. Did I have the nerve to ask what kind of work?

No, I did not.

I stuck it in my pocket, thanked him again, and practically dove headfirst into my car.

Victor Jananovich stood still, watching me go.

Closing the door of my little Subaru made me feel a tiny bit better. Closing the circle of the driveway and heading for the exit even more so. I held my breath for the eternity it took the guards to open the gate.

The bear shifter guards. My knuckles went white on the steering wheel.

I imagined Jananovich's eyes on me the whole time, and the closing scene from *Interview with a Vampire* haunted me all the way back down the mountain. The one where the reporter drives away, believing he's safe, only to have Tom Cruise lean over from the back seat to bite him.

I gulped and checked over my shoulder at least three times.

No Tom Cruise. No Victor Jananovich. Not even Brad Pitt, who frankly wouldn't have been an entirely unappealing option.

A moment later, I chastised myself. Just kidding?

The vacant back seat didn't make me feel better, though. Neither did a last, desperate call I put through to Stacy, hoping against hope that she would answer.

But there was nothing. Not even a voice message.

I raced down the mountain road, and every time I reached a curve, the vials in my bag clinked.

Chapter Sixteen

INGO

It took my contact person until the next day to arrange a meeting, and when he did, it was a good hour's drive to our meeting point in Prescott — a place called the Blue Moon Saloon. The bar itself wasn't out of the way, and it wasn't hard to find. But the minute I walked in, I knew it was different.

Not just thanks to the swinging saloon doors or the sign that read, *Check Your Guns at the Door.* Not even the 1870s Winchester hanging over the beautifully restored, old-fashioned bar or the pianist playing a jaunty tune.

More like the subtler hints that something here was unique, like the scene carved in the oak panel over the bar. A wolf howled at the moon, a bear waded in a stream, and an eagle soared above them.

Then there were the not-so-subtle hints, like the burly bear shifter wiping a glass behind the bar or the perky she-wolf serving customers at the tables.

Clearly, the Blue Moon Saloon was shifter territory.

The moment I walked through the swinging doors, the bear shifter pinned me with a hard stare that said, *You, wolf. Watch how you conduct yourself in my territory.*

The she-wolf gave me a friendlier version of the stare, and a moment later, an even burlier bear shifter emerged from the back, his dark eyes fixed on mine. The guy was a near double of the other. His brother, I supposed.

Like a gunslinger fresh out of bullets, I held out my hands to say, *Not looking for trouble. I just want to ask a few questions.*

Which could be as dangerous, frankly.

It was early evening on a Friday, and the place was filling quickly. The customers were mostly human, predominantly country-western types, and pretty boisterous — but those bear brothers clearly kept the place under tight control. One of the big, street-side window panes was newer than the other, hinting that they wouldn't hesitate to eject an unruly customer the fast way.

I approached the bar, keeping my hands in view.

"Kemper?" one of them grumbled.

I nodded, and he led me down the dim hall to the back.

Well, maybe not so dim, but the guy was so big, he blocked the light streaming in from the rear. He rubbed a thick shoulder against every doorframe as he lumbered along, and my wolf huffed.

Goddamn bears. Always marking their territory.

Not that I could blame him. The pretty she-wolf in the front was his mate — their mingled scents were a dead giveaway — and the whole business, from what I'd gathered, was a tight-knit family operation.

The sun was setting, sending long, colorful rays through the stained-glass windows of the rear room. It was set up for private functions and sported a second bar, not as ornate but just as old and impressive as the one out front.

More impressive yet were the shifters waiting for me there.

I nodded to the only one I'd met before, though just once and briefly. My contact — a wolf shifter with spiky hair — was wearing his police uniform, though he'd made it clear he would only attend in an off-duty capacity.

Like me. Way, way off duty. *Getting my ass suspended* level off duty.

His expression remained guarded as he shook my hand. "Kyle Williams." Then he turned to the others, introducing me. "Ingo Kemper of the ADMSA."

I winced like a Green Bay Packers fan who'd wandered into Chicago Bears territory decked out in all the wrong paraphernalia.

"I'm not here on official business," I said, putting it mildly. "Nothing here ends up on the books."

The tall guy in the middle with thunder in his eyes — another wolf shifter — kept his thick arms crossed, unimpressed.

He was clearly the ranking alpha among a hell of a lot of powerful shifters. There were a couple of other wolf shifters, one wolf/coyote shifter, and even a huge boar — er, javelina — shifter standing in the corner as backup. The women who stood among them could have been textbook depictions of tough Amazonian warriors, apart from their modern clothing.

A straw-haired wolf shifter beside the alpha pointed to himself, then some of the others. "Cody Hawthorne. That's Ty and Tina, and this is Lana. You know Kyle, and our host here is Soren." All were wolves except the bear shifter he finished with.

He didn't introduce the others, so yeah. They were backups in case I hadn't come alone.

I heaved an inner sigh. No squad of agents to back *me* up today. I was well and truly on my own.

"Please have a seat," Lana said.

She was friendly enough, and clearly the alpha's mate, because while motioning me to a chair, she clamped a hand over her mate's shoulder and pushed down in an obvious hint.

The guy scowled but lowered himself into a chair. Slowly.

I'd heard of him, of course. Ty Hawthorne, alpha of Twin Moon pack. The agency listed Twin Moon as an up-and-coming wolf pack, but an update was sorely needed. Not that I would be the one supplying that update.

All my local sources agreed that Twin Moon pack was *the* dominant wolf pack in the Southwest and a positive force that ran their own...well, call it a neighborhood watch program.

A very effective neighborhood watch, and no surprise, judging by their leader's thunderous aura.

Ty Hawthorne's eyes blazed, but Lana cut in before he could growl, *What the hell do you want?*

"How can we help you?" she asked.

Same message, different delivery. Thank goodness for level-headed women.

"That hiker death in Sedona, about a week ago..." I started.

Ty looked at Kyle, their inside man in local law enforcement. Very handy.

"I read the report," Kyle said. "The coroner ruled it accidental."

I shook my head. "They missed the bear shifter scent. It was all over the ledge she fell from."

Soren, the bear shifter and saloon owner, bristled.

"I couldn't ID them," I said before he took it as an accusation.

"Surely the agency has the resources to ID scents," the one named Tina said.

She had a strong family resemblance to Ty, except she was beautiful and she actually smiled. His sister, I figured.

I took a moment to word my reply carefully. "They do, but my request was rejected because it was tied to an unapproved investigation."

Ty Hawthorne's lips quirked, the first glimpse of sunshine in his stormy expression. Any failure of the agency was good news for a pack that liked to run under the radar.

And honestly, I couldn't blame them. As I saw it, my job was to hunt down bad eggs, not law-abiding packs that minded their own business.

"Unapproved investigation?" Soren growled.

Like many bears, his vocal cords didn't seem capable of regular speech. Just growls, snarls, and grumbles.

I nodded. "Unapproved because the evidence so far is circumstantial."

Also because of a certain restraining order, but I glossed over that part.

Ty didn't seem concerned. Clearly, he was more of a trust-your-instincts type of guy than a champion of painstaking forensics. The question was, would he trust *my* instincts?

"On a separate occasion, I identified another suspicious bear shifter, new to Sedona," I continued.

"*Another* suspicious bear shifter?" Soren rumbled.

I shot him a look. No, not all bear shifters were suspicious. Hell, some of the best guys on the fire crew I used to work on were bear shifters. But Stacy's driver gave me nothing but negative vibes.

"He works for a company based out of Park City, which I believe is tied to a place in Sedona called La Puebla."

Lana cocked her head. "The one on Schnebly Hill?"

Kyle scowled deeply. Deep enough to make it seem personal. Why?

"Yes," I said. "It has a new owner, but my requests for information at the agency have all been rejected."

That drew a lot of raised eyebrows, so I went on quickly. "Every time I put in a request related to one particular individual, it's rejected. Even some requests I thought were unrelated — a trace on the license plate of that bear shifter, for example — have been rejected, which makes me believe they are related to the same person of interest."

"And that person is..." Ty stirred his hand impatiently.

"Victor Jananovich. A vampire."

No one reacted, except to look to Kyle, who shook his head curtly. Apparently, Jananovich had managed to keep himself off their radar so far.

"Why would the agency reject requests for information regarding this vampire?" Lana asked.

"I suspect an insider."

It was the only thing that made sense. Jananovich had to have an insider smoothing the way for him at the agency, in the same way that Angelina Saint James had tampered with agency files on behalf of Harlon Greene.

I nearly jolted with a sudden realization. Angelina, a vampire, had used her position at the agency to further Harlon Greene's interests, using my ex-partner, Nash, in the process. Angelina was no longer with the agency — in fact, she was no longer with anyone, having been zapped by a lightning bolt at Pippa's ranch — but maybe Harlon wasn't the only criminal Angelina had sold favors to.

I stared into space, thinking. Had Jananovich gotten Angelina to engineer the restraining order too? The timing fit, because that had been months ago, before Angelina had been outed as a double agent.

Someone cleared their throat, and I forced my focus back to the shifters before me.

"Months ago in LA, I was working on a different case that put me on the trail of Victor Jananovich. Let's just say he's a problem vampire."

Cody's sunny attitude darkened. "We had a vampire problem a few years ago."

Everyone went silent, and it was a while before I worked up the nerve to ask, "What happened?"

Ty shrugged. "Problem solved."

Cody's chest stuck out an inch farther. I took it he'd been the one to do the solving.

A phone rang, and Ty looked around, annoyed, until he realized it was his own. I half expected the device to melt under his wilting look, but when he saw the caller ID, his demeanor did a one-eighty.

His lips cracked into a smile, and his eyes danced when he turned the screen to Lana. Then he cleared his throat, got to his feet, and wandered to the back door, rumbling, "Give me a minute." His voice changed completely as he addressed the person on the other end of the line. "Hiya, pumpkin." He paused. "Sweetie, now is not the best time..."

It was like one of those split-personality psycho movies, but with a really sweet alter ego.

"Okay, but just one..." Ty went on, wandering out of earshot.

The others looked at one another, barely hiding grins.

Cody laughed. "He has to sing his daughter a lullaby."

I stared out the back door. I couldn't picture that guy singing, let alone a lullaby.

Soren bristled at me, as if to say, *Real men sing lullabies. You got a problem with that?*

Hell no. My dad was a badass fire fighter and smoke jumper, and I'd loved his lullabies. I'd always figured I would sing them to my own kids someday.

My chest squeezed. The way things were going with Pippa, I might never have kids.

Then I thought back to our kiss and the way she'd held me. Maybe if I closed this case and put Jananovich away forever, I could be the kind of partner she wanted. I could help around the ranch and spend some more time at her workshop. I could actually use weekends as weekends and not just the chance to clock overtime...

Never had I been as tempted. But it all hinged on one big *if.* The one about putting Jananovich away forever.

My jaw hardened. Back to priorities.

Ty wandered back in a few minutes later, looking as grim and remorseless as ever. But, ha. Now I knew his terrible secret — that under that tough exterior, the guy was a pushover, at least when it came to his kids.

He sat and glared at me, like I'd been the one taking a time-out to sing.

"Before the case was shut down, I was gathering evidence to link Jananovich to a series of murders in LA," I explained. "Mostly young women who worked for him as escorts. Some human, some relics. No pure supernaturals, however."

Tina frowned. "What kind of escorts?"

I shrugged sadly. "The usual. Pretty young women with more looks than sense. But all consensual, from what I could tell."

"Only as consensual as a desperate person can be," Tina pointed out.

True, but I still shook my head. "These were high-end escorts. Not so much desperate as ambitious. Too ambitious for their own good, sometimes. Several turned up dead."

"And you see a link to the dead woman in Sedona?" Kyle asked.

"Just a hunch — and today, a bad feeling about a missing woman. Again, no evidence...just a bad feeling. Bad enough to want to follow up before it's too late."

A tic started up in my cheek, the way it always did when I thought of my one big failure. Jananovich...California...a woman named Bridget, drained of all her blood...

Ty Hawthorne studied me closely, and I swore he could read all that in my expression.

Well, fine. Let him.

A long, quiet pause stretched.

"So, what is it you want from us?" Ty finally asked, not as gruffly as before.

"Information — whatever you have on Jananovich, La Puebla, or those bear shifters," I said immediately.

Ty looked around, but everyone except Soren and Kyle looked blank.

Kyle spoke first. "Stef's company sent her over to La Puebla last fall to put in a bid for a new solar installation."

I didn't know who Stef was, but Kyle's eyes went all dark and protective.

"And?" Lana prompted.

Kyle's expression remained grim. "She said there was a bad vibe to the place, but she couldn't put her finger on why. She was relieved when her company didn't get the bid." He waited a moment, then answered an unspoken question. "I'll ask her more about it when I get home."

Aha. So, Officer Kyle Williams and Solar Power Stef were partners. Another interesting connection — and a reminder that as hard as the agency worked to build networks, nothing beat the real thing. And the wolves of Twin Moon Ranch seemed to have *very* handy connections.

Pippa does too, my wolf pointed out.

True, but those connections could also drag her into trouble. Like now, with Stacy.

Another phone rang — Kyle's this time. He pulled one device from each pocket, then frowned and showed Ty one. His work phone?

Ty nodded, and Kyle stepped toward the door to answer. "Williams here."

Lana seemed poised to continue our conversation until she saw Kyle freeze.

"Where? When?" he asked.

Everyone looked over, listening.

"Roger..." he murmured.

Definitely a work call.

Kyle turned, looking grim. He ran a hand through his hair, making it even spikier. "Has the body been ID'ed?"

My gut twisted, and everyone went very, very quiet.

For the next minute or so, Kyle nodded into his phone. Then he signed off with a curt, "Yes, sir. I'm on my way."

My lips moved, but I couldn't spit out my question.

As it turned out, I didn't have to. The second Kyle's eyes met mine, I knew.

Chapter Seventeen

INGO

It was dark by the time I drove home from the Blue Moon Saloon. A universe of stars lit the sky, but I kept my eyes on the road rolling under my tires. On and on in an endless cycle. Lifeless. Bleak.

Passing Paige Springs, I continued to Sedona. My pulse rose at the turn to Painted Rock Ranch, but I forced myself to drive past it. Half a mile later, I cursed, pulled a U-turn, and headed back.

It was a bad night, and I was in a bad place, but I had to see Pippa. I had to know she was safe.

The dirt road to her place was full of ruts, twists, and turn-offs. I counted carefully, then looked for the big stone on the right a few miles down the road.

There. I stopped and peered into the darkness opposite it. Pure darkness, solid brush. Not a sign of a road or a ranch. Still, I eased the Jeep into gear and turned left with my heart in my throat.

Entering Painted Rock Ranch with Pippa, Erin, or even Nash was easy. The road just appeared, clear as day. Entering alone was harder, because an ancient spell cloaked the place. It was a lot like driving up to that cliff Pippa had taken me to on our Jeep tour. I was sure I would plunge into an abyss.

But my tires crunched over smooth gravel instead of crashing through prickly pears, and a few anxious minutes later, I could not only sense but also see the road. I exhaled, following it through the next couple of bends, where the cloaking spell fell away completely.

My knuckles went white over the steering wheel. What would I say to Pippa? How to break the terrible news? The police had agreed to keep the news of the victim under wraps for forty-eight hours, so Pippa couldn't have heard.

Yet.

The Jeep creaked past the main house, where a single light still burned. Dogs barked, and a curtain moved. I pictured Abby inside, rushing to the window while Claire slept. I hoped she would recognize my car and take my slow speed as an indication that all was well.

I jutted my jaw. If only that were the case.

Continuing slowly, I pulled up to the converted barn Pippa lived in, then stopped and slid to the ground. Pippa emerged a moment later. The light inside cast a halo around her fair hair, giving her an angelic glow as she stood in the doorway.

She frowned, spotting me. "Ingo?"

I nodded and stepped closer, though my legs were full of lead.

"What are you doing here?" she asked.

I forced myself to meet her eyes. My gut lurched, because for a moment, those were Stacy's eyes, and Bridget's and all the other victims I'd been too late too help.

My hands curled into fists. Sometimes, I hated my job. And sometimes — like this — I hated myself.

Pippa's face went slack, and she paled.

"No..." she whispered, reading my mind.

Silent as the grave, I took another step.

"No..." She sank into a chair beside the doorway.

I stopped in front of her as she dropped her face into her hands, then glanced up with a look that gutted me.

"Stacy...?"

I nodded. Once.

"Is she...?"

"Her body was found out near Clarkdale."

Pippa whimpered, burying her face in her hands. A moment later, she was rocking, crying, and murmuring that awful word in an endless loop. "No. No. No..."

I was a pebble. A blade of grass. An inanimate, unfeeling object at Pippa's feet.

When my knees finally unlocked, I sank down beside Pippa and wrapped my arms around her.

"No... Please..." She rocked, and I moved with her, unable to speak, act, or think.

Around us, the darkness was a blanket, providing more comfort than I could.

"What happened?" she whispered through her tears.

My voice cracked as I relayed what Kyle had said, using the same clinical terms. No sense in putting a flowery frame around a picture no one wanted to see.

The body had been found about thirty minutes west. Her throat had been slit, her blood completely drained. The police were calling it a secondary scene, which was probably right. But if they were counting on tracking a trail of blood... good luck. Not with vampires involved.

Pippa hunched over her knees, still rocking. "Why?"

I didn't know, but I swore I would find out.

"Was it whatshisname? Jananovich?"

"Same old, same old," I said grimly. "No evidence. But it makes sense."

And, ugh. Bad word choice. Nothing about a young person's death made sense.

"I mean, my gut says—"

Pippa stood suddenly, wiping her tears. "*My* gut says we hunt him down and kill him, right now. As slowly and as painfully as he deserves."

The glimmer in her eyes said she meant it, but I had the feeling she wasn't thinking through the practicalities. Jananovich was a vampire, and they were notoriously hard to kill. Plus, there was no clemency for killing murderers. And judging by the shitty way the universe worked, Pippa would be the one who got caught.

I looked at her silently until her shoulders slumped.

"Well, we can't sit around and do nothing," she said.

"We won't. But we have to think. We need the why, the how, the when."

Easier said than done. I huffed in frustration, making my breath swirl in the cold night air.

I looked at my car, then the sky. Experience told me I needed a clear mind to think, and that wouldn't happen tonight. Maybe it was time to go. Not that either of us would get a wink of sleep.

Pippa must have read my mind, because she laced her fingers through mine.

"Don't go. Not yet."

I didn't have it in me to say no. She needed the company, and I did too.

We held each other for a long, long time. Long enough for the stars to turn a couple of degrees, until Orion keeled over like a drunk and Scorpio scuttled halfway beyond the horizon.

"Better get you inside," I finally murmured. "It's freezing out here."

She managed a little smile. "I run warm, remember?"

My lips quirked. Pippa had the internal furnace of a pyromancer — or a dragon, like her mother. Way back when, we'd driven her dad's car up a mountainside for a stolen hour of sloppy teenage sex, and it had been me shivering in the cold afterward, not her.

In another time or place, I might have chuckled at what had once passed for good sex. We'd come a long way since then.

Then it hit me. Maybe we hadn't, because we'd broken up.

I swallowed hard and followed Pippa through the open barn door.

Inside, I glanced around the cavernous space. I'd heard the sisters call it a converted barn, but the only part that looked even halfway converted — unless fairy lights counted, because Pippa had those strung all over the place — was the bathroom I spied through an open door. Otherwise, the building was still packed with farm equipment, stalls, and cobwebs. At some point, someone had driven the tractor out and replaced it with a worn red couch. But that was pretty much it.

On the other hand, the place had potential. Even I could see that.

Pippa took my coat and hung it on a whimsical rack in the shape of a moose head, made completely from horseshoes. A housewarming gift from Abby, no doubt. Then she pointed me to the "living room" — the red sofa with a crate for a table in front of it. A second — or third or fourth — hand wood-burning stove had been installed, with a chimney rigged to a hole in the wall, the cracks roughly plugged with fireproof insulation. The firefighter in me couldn't help checking it for flaws. Aesthetically, there were plenty. In terms of safety, though, it worked.

I sat while Pippa headed to the "kitchen," a corner with a microwave, electric kettle, and a tiny fridge. There, she turned her sad, red eyes to me and offered me a drink. She stared at the kettle until it boiled, and my eyes drifted to the wall beyond her. The exposed beams doubled as shelves, and they were all lined with glass. Glass baubles. Glass flowers. Even a rabbit made of fused shards of glass. Each piece exploded with color and life.

So, there it was again — that reminder. For all the bad things in the world, there was beauty too.

My breath caught when I spotted the glass sculpture on a higher shelf. A dark wolf pointed his nose to howl at the moon as a second, gold-hued she-wolf wound around his body.

I swallowed hard. Was he howling in joy or sorrow? Were the two forever bonded or damned to an eternity of *near but so far?*

"Here," Pippa murmured, handing me a mug.

We settled on the couch — me with a coffee, her with a tea — and I watched as she fumbled with a match and candle.

Pippa. Fumbling with fire. If that didn't indicate how upset she was, what did?

On the third try, the match lit in a burst of sulfur. With shaking hands, Pippa brought it to the candle. For a moment, two tiny fires twisted, burning together. Then the match died, and the candle flared a little brighter.

"For Stacy," she whispered.

For a long, quiet minute, we contemplated the dancing flame. I expected Pippa to murmur something like *rest in peace* when she blew it out, but instead...

"I promise I'll get him for you." Her whisper was fierce. "I swear, I will."

Her words scared me, because I didn't want Pippa tangling with Jananovich. But I was glad too, because maybe she finally understood what drove me.

Together, we stared at that empty spot where a bright light had burned just a moment before. My chest went tight, and again, I wished I could turn the clock back.

I would bet anything Pippa did too.

She slammed a hand on the couch, sending up a puff of dust. "You were right. And I didn't listen."

I knew how she felt, because I'd tried that trick a hundred times — replacing grief with anger.

I touched her shoulder. "What could you have done?"

Yeah, kind of hypocritical, me counseling someone about regret.

She puffed out her cheeks, and another long minute went by.

Yeah, I knew that feeling too.

"Okay. Tell me," she demanded. "Tell me everything — what you know and what you suspect."

That second category was packed. The first...not so much. But I did my best to summarize, touching on the same points I'd explained to the leaders of Twin Moon pack.

Victor Jananovich, vampire and criminal warlord with a tendency to drink his staff dry — and not in a good way. Drugs...murders...pricey escorts...

"Escorts?" Pippa whipped around at that.

A minute later, it all clicked in my mind. "The vials..."

Jananovich hadn't been using them for couples. He'd figured out a way to combine his business interests with escorts who provided blood. Fresh from the vein, I gathered, plus a "to-go" version. Hence the vials.

I cursed the agency for the hundredth time. If it weren't for the restraining order, I might have had enough evidence, if not to convict Jananovich, then for a search warrant, at least.

"I gave Kyle the billing address you showed me. The one for the vials," I said. "TTC Limited is True Tastes Consortia, Limited."

"Owned by Jananovich?"

"I think so, but if so, it's hidden under a dozen shell corporations."

Pippa went over to her desk — a board laid across two sawhorses — and returned with a flyer.

"Stacy gave me this."

It was for the glass contest, giving a PO Box in Sedona as the address. I left that as a message on Kyle Williams's phone.

As I hung up, Pippa cursed.

I leaned in to read the contest guidelines.

"I thought that was a strange way of phrasing things," she murmured, then read aloud. "'The winning contestant will submit four beautifully crafted glasses and a decanter. All must allow for proper aeration and visibility of the liquid inside.'" She tapped the last part. "Liquid, not wine." She shook her head bitterly. "God, they make me sick."

I could relate.

Then she looked at me expectantly.

I raised an eyebrow. "What?"

"Tell me what I have to do to bring down that slimeball," she grunted, all angel of revenge.

"I'm working on it, believe me. But it's not that simple."

"Sure it is. We sneak into La Puebla and kill his sorry ass."

She started stalking around, thinking. Candles stood all over the place, and any one she passed flared to life of its own volition. Some fizzled and died again, while others remained flickering.

I watched her move. Was she even aware of what she was doing?

No, I decided. The woman was a walking fire hazard.

Then again, I'd bet she also had the power to snuff out any ensuing blaze.

Hopefully.

"Sneaking into La Puebla won't be easy," I warned. "Jananovich will have security. Plus, he's a vampire. They're hard to kill. And even if we could, what's to stop the agency from prosecuting us as murderers of an 'innocent' businessman?"

She thought it over for exactly five seconds before launching into a new plan. "Okay, so we sneak into La Puebla, grab incriminating evidence, and *then* kill his sorry ass."

I let her contemplate that for a minute or two.

Suddenly, Pippa sat straighter, and every candle in the place burned higher. "Oh! I know how to get in without sneaking at all."

"How?"

"Catering."

I shook my head. "There's no way I'm letting you get close to Jananovich. If anyone goes in, it will be me."

She snorted. "Ha. I can just see you serving canapés."

I frowned. "Serving what?"

"I rest my case." She sighed.

"Well, you're sure as hell not going," I declared.

Bossy? Yes. But that was nonnegotiable.

"Erin and Abby can be my backup," she said.

When I shook my head, Pippa stuck a finger at my chest. "Admit it. You want him dead just as much as I do. We both know he deserves it. Why bother going by the books?"

"Tell that to the judge prosecuting you for murder," I said.

In truth, my wolf was all for her plan, and my human side was definitely tempted. But the agent in me knew better.

I took a deep breath, willing her to do the same, then announced, "Okay, we're there."

She looked around, confused. "Where?"

The nearest candle flickered and swayed.

"At the point where we need to stop, get some rest, and reevaluate."

"Reevaluate what? Stacy is dead. I can't just accept that and move on."

"I'm not saying you should. But if we don't think this through, things could get even worse, and Jananovich could get away with more than murder." I did my best to hit a note of finality. "So, we'll reevaluate our options — tomorrow."

I looked at the door, trying to work up the resolve to go. Not really succeeding, though.

She must have read my intent, because she took my hand, and her voice softened. "You're not going, are you?"

I held her gaze. Was there another option?

Her throat bobbed. "Stay," she whispered. "Please."

Stay the night, her eyes begged.

Good idea? Bad idea? I was too worn out to decide.

"To think things through, I mean," she added. "Once we're ready."

I looked toward the bedroom, then at the couch. Which was she offering?

Every candle in the place burned a little brighter, giving me a hint at her reply.

Chapter Eighteen

PIPPA

Every nerve in my body tensed as I waited for Ingo's answer. Would he stay the night?

I wanted him to. Desperately. And no, I didn't have it in me to fight the ever-present temptation he posed. In fact, I wouldn't even call it temptation. More like pure need, because I'd never felt more alone, and I'd never felt safer than with Ingo. Especially when we were all cozied up.

His eyes glowed, though his furrowed brow said he was trying to be rational.

"Ingo..." I whispered, reaching for his hand.

He didn't mirror the gesture, which hurt. But it wasn't lost on me that I'd subjected him to the same *I want you, but I know I shouldn't do this* torture.

I closed my eyes, vowing that we would be finished forever if he turned me down. This *so close, yet so far* state wasn't doing either of us any good.

My hopes dimmed as my hand hung in the air, all lonely and cold. But then Ingo wrapped his warm fingers around mine, and I had my answer.

A switch flipped in me, and I dove in for a kiss, finding his lips even before my eyes opened.

Then I closed them again, because his answer was loud and clear.

He pressed his lips hard against mine, he slid his arms around me, and held me tight. For a while, all our pent-up passion was laser-concentrated on our lips, as if the rest of our bodies didn't exist.

But then I remembered, and my hands immediately set off on a new mission.

As a kid, I'd spent most of the year with my father in Colorado. But I'd spent most of each summer with my aunt on the ranch, and every time I arrived, I would whoop and run around, assuring myself my favorite places were still there.

Which was exactly what I did with Ingo now. I skimmed my hands over his back, then chest, revisiting all those familiar contours. As a kid, I would climb the paddock fence to whistle to the horses, and now, it felt just as urgent to wind a leg around his and press my core closer. The heat between us flared, and my heart hammered.

I broke off our kiss just long enough to chuckle. "Remember that time out at Sunset Point?"

Ingo nibbled his way down my neck, pausing here and there to reply. "I'll...never...forget...it."

That had been our first time, back as teenagers, and it had been desperate and sloppy. But, hell. We'd both glowed with satisfaction for days after, and we'd gradually refined our technique in the weeks, months, and years that followed.

This felt much the same. A door opening. A new world, full of hope and promise.

I pushed my fears and worries to the edge of that world the way I'd pushed all the farm equipment to the periphery of the barn. Someday, I would have to face sorting through it all. But right now, I had a working solution.

And boy, did that solution work for me. Especially with Ingo sliding his hands over my rear, pressing me closer. He guided me back until I was anchored against one of the roof posts. That gave us a nice, firm surface without any give, the way I worked molten glass against a metal surface in the hot shop.

I chuckled again. *Molten. Hot shop.* All so fitting.

"You're laughing with me, not at me, right?" Ingo murmured between kisses.

His lips were at my collarbone, his hand sliding from my belly to my chest.

"Just thinking of the hot shop," I said. "Suddenly, everything is full of innuendo."

"Like at a firehouse?" He laughed.

I nodded, reaching for his... er, apparatus. "Yeah. Like hose control."

"Doing my best," he rumbled. "But you're not making it any easier."

We both laughed, and the sound echoed through the barn.

"Head pressure..." I murmured.

"We'll test that soon," he promised. "But first..."

He closed a hand around my breast, and I moaned, tipping my head back.

A frontal assault, in firefighter talk. I was all for it.

My nipple peaked like one of those timers that popped up when the Thanksgiving turkey was ready. The fact that I didn't mind the crude comparison said a lot about my state of mind. Because, yes, oh yes. I was ready to be all gobbled up.

Soon, I was, and most thoroughly. First, through the cotton of my knee-length sleep shirt, then skin-to-skin. The fabric bunched as Ingo tugged it, blocking my view of the best show in town, so I pulled off the shirt and tossed it aside.

"Not cold?" Ingo asked.

On the contrary. I needed an air conditioner.

And, wait. Who'd started that blaze in the fireplace? I caught a glimpse of it crackling, then frowned. The mystery occupied my mind for all of two seconds before more important things took over. Like how to strip Ingo naked without interrupting our momentum, for starters.

Another part of me relished every second. After years of terribly misguided celibacy, or so it seemed now, we were finally getting close.

Ingo switched from one side to the other, cupping my soft flesh with his hand. I wasn't built big, but Ingo was a master at making maximum use of the resources at his disposal. And now that I was naked — convenient! — even more raw materials were available. Like my core, which he thoroughly explored with his free hand.

"Firefighters are supposed to extinguish fires, not start them," I scolded between throaty sighs.

"Laying the blame on me, huh?" he mumbled without a hint of complaint.

I laughed. "What was that terrible line about firefighters?"

"Find 'em hot, leave 'em wet."

His voice was all growly, and between that and the actual message... let's just say he was making swift progress on the second part of that promise.

"Speaking of which..." I mumbled, guiding his head lower. And lower...

In no time, he was knocking at heaven's door — or rather, circling, probing, licking. At that point, I had one leg slung over his shoulder, and it was only by dint of that support pole that I remained upright. Ingo gradually guided my leg outward, opening the pearly gates, so to speak.

I knew I wasn't in heaven. But it sure felt like it.

I ground against him, making enough noise for the soundtrack of a dirty movie — the director's cut. Then I shook, shuddered, and came with a howl.

Everything went hazy for a while. Eventually, I found myself comfortably propped between Ingo and the support pole. Or the support pole and Ingo. It was hard to tell one from the other until I reached around, identifying Ingo's contours, right down to his... er, personal support pole.

I gripped it, congratulating the instincts that had guided me there.

"What are you smiling about now?" Ingo chided.

I shook my head. "Inside joke, sorry. Another dirty one."

He laughed, then went serious and kissed me.

"Mm," I mumbled, swirling my tongue.

His body stiffened, and his kiss went harder and deeper, stoking my inner fire all over again.

Chapter Nineteen

INGO

Over the years, I'd entertained many hot dreams, all starring Pippa. A survival method, you might say, since I couldn't have the real thing, and other women aroused nothing in me.

It still felt like a dream, even though I knew it was real.

All too real, I realized, thinking of the tragic events that had brought us here.

But I hadn't been kidding about the need to stop, rest, and reevaluate. And step three — reevaluate — wouldn't swing around until morning. Until then, I intended to do a hell of a lot of resting. Resting my mind, at least.

"That way," Pippa murmured, breaking out of our kiss.

She pointed toward the bedroom section of the barn, then cupped my jeans, making it hard to move, even if I wanted to.

Yes, Pippa had always been a woman of contradictions.

My eyes slid half shut. And, whew. Now I knew why Pippa found that roof post so handy. I gripped it, barely keeping my balance as Pippa worked me over. The post helped when she pushed my jeans down too, trapping me in the denim while she had her wicked way with me.

My wolf howled in glee, and my teeth ached as my wild side climbed closer to the surface. Then I caught her hand, stopping her before my hips started pumping. I'd had to settle for DIY hand jobs over the years, but I could do better now. Much, much better.

"Bed," I grunted, kicking my jeans away.

"Shirt," Pippa insisted, continuing our one-syllable conversation. "Now."

She helped me get it off, not even teasing this time. Well, barely. She did stop long enough to circle, then tweak my nipple. Tiny bolts of lightning zipped down to my toes and, um. . . other important places.

"Bed. Room," I growled in caveman talk.

Pippa led the way past the couch, past the bathroom, and down the two-story central "hall" of the barn. Bits of hay poked out from the rafters overhead, where more fairy lights twinkled. Then Pippa turned right, into the stall she'd converted into a bedroom.

Again, "converted" was putting it loosely. She'd scrubbed the place and rolled out an old rug, but we were still surrounded by rungs where previous occupants had rubbed noses with their equine neighbors.

Now, it was just the two of us, and one. . . two. . . three flickering candles.

The number increased with every step Pippa took. If I hadn't been otherwise occupied, I might have glanced around in awe. That had never happened before. On the other hand, pyromancers were known to be late bloomers. And a good thing, too. I didn't want to imagine an angsty, frustrated teenager who could ignite fires — with or without consciously intending to. Half the schools in the country would be burned down, along with a lot of orthodontic clinics.

In any case, I wasn't up to imagining much at that moment. I didn't have to, especially once I laid my true love out on the big mattress and admired her for a while.

She held out a hand impatiently, but I shook my head. Way back when, Pippa used to deride people who didn't admire a sunset or beautiful vista with anything but a quick glance or a single snapshot. I intended to soak in this stunning view for a while.

Her lips quirked, and she slid her hands to her breasts. "What about this view?"

Again, the mind reading. Not that I objected.

"I like, but. . ."

I tested her, picturing a different place.

Her eyes sparkled, and she slid a hand lower. Lower. . .

My throat bobbed, and I forgot to breathe for the next minute or so. I definitely sucked in a huge lungful of air, however, when Pippa spread her legs and slid a finger inside, then circled around.

Her eyes glazed, though she kept them fixed firmly on me. Reading me like a book, no doubt — or a dirty magazine. Whatever I imagined, she did, from probing deeper to adding a second finger to—

I pounced, and we collided in a deep, possessive kiss.

You are mine, my wolf howled over and over.

Always have been, I heard her mental reply. *Always will be.*

I moved over her, driven by the instinct to mark and claim my territory. I scrubbed my stubble over the soft flesh of her breast, then touched, kissed, and stroked every inch of her.

"Oh..."

Her groan took on an achy note, telling me I was pushing her limits.

Don't you dare stop, she warned in a mental growl.

Good to know I wasn't the only one desperate for more.

Her mouth consumed mine. The nails of her left hand scraped my back. Her legs wound around mine, which put us in the perfect position to—

"Yes," she moaned as I slid home.

Inside, my wolf howled. Outside, my mouth hung open, echoing the sentiment. Then I sucked in a deep breath and began to move.

Earlier, I'd caught Pippa's thought about how amateurish our lovemaking had been way back when. Now, I was determined to remind her how far we'd come since then. Every one of my thrusts was smooth, hard, and absolutely, positively on target.

Pippa moaned, squeezing my ass harder.

We moved in perfect rhythm for another few strokes, then switched to a new position like dancers showing off dueling moves before the big finale. That meant me on my knees with Pippa lying sideways, one leg under mine, the other over.

I growled out loud.

"So good..." Pippa moaned as I continued moving.

Yes, it was. Deep and achy, but in a good way. And when she squeezed her inner muscles in a rippling motion—

I threw my head back with an animal howl.

Around us, candles swayed, casting shadows. Beneath me, Pippa's skin glowed with their fiery tint, and I caught our silhouettes dancing erotically on the wall.

"Yes..." Pippa cried, crushing me closer.

I managed to power through three more thrusts. Then I exploded.

The candles flared so high, their light swirled around me. I lost all sense of direction, knowing only that I was joined to Pippa. We could have been spinning through space or stuck in a whirlpool, but as long as we were together...

Gradually, the walls of the room — such as they were — reappeared around me. The bed was there too, along with tangled sheets and blankets, but all I cared about was Pippa.

Our eyes locked and held for an eternity, telegraphing a dozen short, silent messages.

Love you so much.

We belong together.

Let's stay this way forever. Please.

Her chest rose and fell with each heavy breath. Mine too. Gradually, our pulses dropped, and we relaxed into the mattress. Eventually, after wiping off with the corner of a sheet, we spooned together. Pippa pulled a blanket over my shoulders, though she kept her side open.

"I run hot, you know," she murmured.

I laughed out loud, then snuggled closer. "You sure do."

Chapter Twenty

PIPPA

I woke up slowly, relishing the warmth of my bed — and Ingo. He was wrapped around me, with one hand over my belly and one thumb stroking my skin. So, he was awake too.

Awake, happy, but preoccupied, just like me.

I rolled to face him, and we each mustered a smile.

"Good morning," I whispered, keeping tight hold of his hand.

He kissed my knuckles. "Morning to you too."

I gazed into his eyes, wondering. Wishing. But neither took me in a good direction, so I shut my eyes and snuggled in, listening to his steady heartbeat. The day ahead, I sensed, would be a doozy, and I intended to tank up on calm while I could.

Which worked surprisingly well. So well, I started to wonder if we might actually make *us* work again someday. Ingo didn't shoot out of bed to rush back to hunting bad guys, and I didn't feel the usual lethargy that made it hard for me to get into gear most mornings.

On the contrary, I had a whole mental list of missions to be accomplished, though they were all tempered by the *why rush off?* feeling that came with the afterglow of stunningly good sex. So, while I wasn't capable of heading out yet, I did prioritize my agenda.

Item one, breakfast, combined with strategizing with Ingo.

Item two, a quick round of chores on the ranch, while working out the details of that strategy.

Item three, heading out to wreak my revenge on Victor Jananovich.

Item four, live happily ever after?

Outside, the sun was just over the horizon, and the horses roamed quietly in their paddock. I listened, trying the mindfulness thing, but I could sense a dark cloud slowly gliding in over the horizon.

"You're frowning," Ingo observed quietly, cupping my cheek.

Maybe. Still, what a treat to have him within whisper-distance so early in the morning.

"Not at you. I'm thinking of Victor Jananovich."

Ingo arched an eyebrow. "I'll try not to take it personally that you're thinking of him while in bed with me."

"You know what I mean."

He chuckled a little, then sighed. "I do. And sorry. I think I finally get how you feel now."

My brow furrowed. "How?"

"Waking up with someone whose mind is on the bad guys definitely puts a damper on the fun."

My throat went all dry, and I blinked back tears.

"I didn't mean to—"

Ingo pressed a finger to my lips. "Not an accusation. More like a look in the mirror."

I gulped. Hard.

"I'm sorry. I really am," I said. "Now I understand how hard it is for you to turn off work. Especially knowing the bad guy is still out there, ready to hurt someone."

Ingo nodded. "It is hard. I definitely need more practice in switching off."

I thought for a moment, then pointed outside. "How about we give ourselves until the sun is over the fence line?"

"Is that your alarm clock?" He grinned, stroking my side until his eyes sparkled. "Whatever will we do to distract ourselves until then?"

I chuckled. "Oh, I have a few ideas. . ."

More than a few, as it turned out. I stroked his side, then his steely rear. Then. . . other places. Ingo guided me around, and soon, I found myself straddling him, my body rippling over his, my pulse quickening.

Ingo tilted his head back and lowered his eyes to half-mast, succumbing to sheer pleasure.

As good as it felt, I found myself straining for something just out of reach. Then, in a brilliant lightbulb moment, I stopped and leaned to one side.

Ingo's eyes popped open in a question.

"Remember this one?" I rose and swung a leg around, swiveling over him.

He groaned when we lost contact, then growled when we reconnected, now in reverse cowgirl. The view wasn't as good for me, but Ingo seemed to enjoy his, and the angle was just what I needed.

"Oh yeah," he murmured, all throaty. "I remember."

As teens, we'd gotten hold of a magazine illustrating different sex positions, and we'd tried out every one. Some left us laughing too hard to muster any passion, while others had us moaning. Most turned out to be too complicated for anyone but a contortionist. We'd usually resorted to three tried and true positions: missionary, cowgirl, and wolf-style, as Ingo liked to call it.

Back then, as diligent students, we'd checked reverse cowgirl off the list and moved on. But now...

My body heated, and rapture filled my mind the way bright fog lit up the creek on beautiful spring mornings.

"Gorgeous..." Ingo hummed.

Yeah, the view definitely worked for him. I made a mental note to keep up the tight tummy/flat fanny exercises I'd found in that online video.

I braced my arms on his muscled legs and pressed down, mumbling incoherently. The inner thigh exercises were coming in handy too.

I leaned forward, grinding my hips. And when Ingo reached around and touched me—

My breath cut off, and my whole body jolted.

I moaned, moving faster.

Ingo's breaths came louder and rougher, telling me he was close too. I closed my eyes, grinding more deeply. Then I threw my head back, swept away by an intense wave.

Ingo hissed, coming at the same time, and ecstasy locked us in that position for a while.

Seconds — minutes? — later, I wiggled slowly around to face Ingo. Once cleaned off and snuggled in, I chuckled.

"If we knew then what we knew now..."

Ingo laughed. "A good thing we didn't. We would have turned into addicts." Then his eyes sparkled. "Maybe we should try out some of those other positions we gave up on. There might be another gem among them."

I laughed, then went serious, gazing into his eyes. Maybe position wasn't the deciding factor. Maybe it was maturity and lessons learned the hard way.

Of course, I would be happy to test his theory. Most thoroughly.

I wrapped my arms around him and held him tightly. Maybe if we gave ourselves another chance...

Outside, the horses nickered, and I sighed. The sun was over the fence line — already.

In the distance, footsteps crunched over gravel, and car doors squeaked open.

"Oh! Isn't that Ingo's car?" I heard Claire chirp.

"Looks like." Even from this distance, Abby's disapproval came through loud and clear.

"Did they have a sleepover?"

Ingo grinned. I buried my face in the pillow.

"Maybe," Abby grumbled.

"Definitely," Ingo murmured, kissing me.

Outside, Abby changed the subject. "Come on, sweetie. Time to go to school."

Whatever Claire said next was lost in the sound of the car starting, thank goodness.

Still, I kept my face hidden until the sound of the engine disappeared down the driveway.

Ingo tapped my back. "The coast is clear."

I shook my head without turning. The coast was never clear when you shared a property with your sisters. Even when the property was a ranch with hundreds of acres.

At least Erin was out. Ballooning was an early-morning business.

"Come on, sleeping beauty." Ingo tugged on my shoulder.

I sat up slowly, then met his gaze.

At first, we smiled, but then my thoughts turned to Stacy, and my heart went all heavy.

Ingo kissed me again, then swung his legs resolutely over the side of the bed. "All right, then. Time to bring down the bad guys. Or make a plan anyway."

∞∞∞∞∞

We brainstormed while going about my morning chores. Ingo was a star, helping me feed the horses and check the cattle without so much as a grumble. He helped with breakfast and cleaned up afterward too.

The kind of morning I could get used to, if it hadn't been for the dark cloud hanging over it. A cloud that got darker the longer we threw out ideas. And the longer we did that, the more I was convinced I had a solution.

Yet Ingo shot it down every time, with the same reason.

"Too risky."

"It's the *least* risky."

"It's not like Jananovich will leave evidence lying around for the catering crew to find," Ingo pointed out. "At least, nothing compelling enough for the agency to use as an excuse to charge in."

"If the timing is right, there will be evidence. Believe me."

My mind played out gratifying images of law enforcement agents busting in at the height of a blood orgy, just in time to save innocent people and put away the bad guys, without risking their own lives. That's what happened in the movies, right?

I made a mental note to pitch the idea to a Hollywood agent someday. It was brilliant.

On the downside, I had the sneaking suspicion real life and Hollywood mirrored each other about as well as horses and pigs.

"If the timing is wrong, I lose my job and Jananovich goes free," Ingo growled. "Or worse, another person ends up dead." He pinned me with a significant look that said, *Someone like you.*

For some reason, that didn't worry me. But my heart bled when I thought of Stacy, Janet Sullivan, and their families.

My hands formed fists. It was time to put Jananovich away for good. Hell, I would *plant* evidence if I had to and call the agency with an anonymous tip.

The latter was actually an echo of our first backup plan — to ask Kyle Williams, Arizona law enforcement officer, to call the ADMSA with an urgent request for immediate agency intervention. But the wolves of Twin Moon pack were loath to get involved — with the agency *or* with vampires — for fear of opening a Pandora's box that would plague their peaceful little corner of paradise.

I would really have to visit one day, if they let me. I made that my second mental note of the morning. Plus, it was positive thinking. Visiting Twin Moon Ranch one day meant I would survive my plunge into a pool of sharks. (Ingo's inspiring analogy, not my own.)

"I've already been to La Puebla once," I pointed out. "I survived that."

Ingo scowled. Well, that was better than him flipping out the way he had earlier, when I'd admitted to dropping in on Victor Jananovich.

"Once is already too many times," he grumbled.

"I doubt I taste good anyway," I joked, but it went flat.

"It's not just the taste the vampires are after," Ingo said. "It's the power infusing the blood. Especially magical power. The stronger the victim, the bigger the boost their blood gives the vampire."

I felt strangely comforted, because I hardly had any magic powers.

Then I remembered the bonfire.

I gulped. I'd never wittingly conjured any real power, but sometimes it happened unintentionally. Not a very useful kind of power — not to me anyway. But to a vampire...

I stuck my hands on my hips. "Do you have a better idea?"

I knew he didn't, because his best idea had been *him* sneaking in. Jananovich's security would be all over him in a New York minute, whereas I'd already been let in once. Plus, Ingo had *law enforcement* written all over him. I was just innocent ol' me.

I fluttered my eyelashes at Ingo to reinforce the point.

Five minutes later, I was on the phone while Ingo listened in, not at all pleased.

"Hi, Nancy. It's Pippa. Sorry for the late notice, but I'd love to help with that catering job today." I waited, then nodded smugly to Ingo. "Yes, exactly. The easy in-and-out job." I waited again, then smiled into the phone. "Perfect. See you soon."

Chapter Twenty-One

PIPPA

Hours later, I watched the gate at La Puebla slide open, admitting the catering crew — and me. Somehow, the motion pulled the plug on my confidence, which drained the moment we were through.

Make that, whirlpooled away with a dramatic slurp. Suddenly, Ingo's worries didn't seem like such exaggerations any more.

Security personnel. Vampires. Cold-blooded killers.

Shit, shit, shit.

Thank goodness for Nancy, who directed her helpers — Wendy, me, and two guys from the staff at La Puebla — in unloading supplies with her usual efficiency.

"Start with the drinks, please. Those four crates need to go straight to the fridge, and those four can stay on the floor in the kitchen."

Every time I shuttled between the van and the kitchen, I eyed the landscape beyond the fence. Somewhere out there, Ingo was stalking around — in wolf form? Human? I wasn't sure. He'd packed enough equipment for an entire commando force before setting off, though I had a hunch he relied more on raw animal instincts than technology. I sniffed the air, not that I had a chance of locating him. He would be downwind, for one thing, and blended in with the scenery.

Back and forth I went, van to kitchen, then kitchen to living room, where Nancy had me stack plates, silverware, and napkins on a table. I did so, then held a knife up to the light, checking for any blemishes. Then a fork, and so on. In between, I slid a hand into my pocket, pulled out the nanny cam Ingo had given me, and set it quickly on a shelf. It was already programmed with the Wi-Fi password, so it ought to be transmitting to Ingo.

I raised another knife, checking the camera angle out of the corner of my eye, then decided to declare my mission accomplished.

Wow. I was practically a secret agent now.

I even went in search of a bathroom and "accidentally" detoured toward Victor's office next. But when footsteps sounded down the hallway, I lost my nerve and scurried back to the kitchen.

Okay, maybe not that great a secret agent.

I was so frazzled, I genuinely lost my way back to the kitchen, opening the door to a utility closet instead. I closed it just as quickly, then froze, thinking.

I looked left. Right. The coast was clear, but my heart was hammering.

The utility closet door squeaked when I opened it for the second time. I stared at the conveniently labeled circuit breakers there, including one marked *sprinkler system.*

Click.

I flipped it. Because, well. . . you never knew.

And, yikes. I could now add *saboteur* to my résumé too.

Then I shot out of there, wincing in anticipation of alarms going off.

They didn't, but my pulse still hadn't dropped when I entered the kitchen. Especially not when I spotted the butler talking to Nancy.

I skidded into a sharp turn and stepped into the walk-in cooler before he spotted me. I could explain myself readily enough if anyone recognized me from my previous visit — after all, I really did moonlight for Nancy's catering company — but ideally, I would prefer to stay off the radar.

I snorted. Ideally, Ingo would have La Puebla surrounded by dozens of secret agents, and I would be miles away. Ideally, Stacy would have lived to see this day and many, many more.

I took a deep breath and worked my determination back into place like a bad hairdo. It didn't sit well, but I would have to live with it. Because right now, I needed evidence. Fast.

But, shoot. How likely was I to find that in a walk-in cooler?

My skin prickled the moment I entered the cold, dim space. Wendy was already there, rubbing her arms against the temperature.

"God, it's freezing in here," she complained. "And the sticky notes aren't sticking."

One fluttered off a tray of hors d'oeuvres as I walked by, and I chased it around like a butterfly.

"Dammit. . ." I kneeled down and peered into the back corner it landed in.

Reaching it meant moving one big box, then another.

"I'll be right back with some tape," Wendy said, stepping away.

The note was still out of reach, so I shifted another box, then froze at a familiar *clink*.

I sat back on my haunches and stared. Except for the dull whirr of the refrigerator's cooler, silence reigned.

I glanced at the open door, then back at the box. Ten loud thumps of my heart later, I pulled the box closer.

Ten more thumps. Two more glances at the door. A couple more screwdriver twists to my determination. Finally, I eased the box open and tipped it toward the light. My shadow fell over the contents, but I already knew what was in there.

Vials. Dozens and dozens of vials.

I plucked one out, pinching it with the tips of my fingers, more like a dead mouse than a piece of glass I'd shaped with my own hands.

With one important difference. I'd delivered them empty. Now, the vial was full of sluggish red liquid.

My stomach lurched as I held the vial up to the light.

Neat, rounded script graced the label, recording a name, a date, and a symbol.

Saanvi, it read, with last week's date and the sketch of a tiger.

I gulped and plucked out another.

Rob, that one said. Same date, different sketch. A lion.

A good thing I'd been too keyed up to eat earlier. I might have spewed my lunch over the vials.

Becca, the next one said. I didn't understand what the fishtail sketch indicated until I thought of the plus-sized beauty who'd been lounging in the hot tub that day I'd catered to the "escorts."

Then it clicked. Becca, the mermaid relic.

My blood went cold, and not from the refrigerator.

Evidence. Sort of. Maybe.

I pulled out my phone and snapped several pictures, zooming in on some labels as well as getting an overhead shot of the entire box. I'd delivered the vials in recycled "peanut" packaging, but now, they were stacked in neat racks like so many test tubes in a mad scientist's lab.

Or neat racks like the ones Nancy used for hors d'oeuvres, just as clearly labeled as these.

My stomach twisted the other way, forming a pretzel. Partly from the blood, partly from the fear that pictures of vials might not cut it as evidence. But I sure as hell wasn't sticking one of those vials down my bra to smuggle out of there.

I settled for grabbing two and working them gingerly into my pocket.

And, boy, was that gross. The vials were just cool glass, but my skin crawled as I pictured blood dripping down my pant leg. Double gross — and how the hell would I explain a stain like *that*?

"Okay, next try." Wendy stomped back into the cooler.

I shoved the box back into place, wincing at the clinks that ensued.

"You want a wine label for that?" Wendy asked.

My throat was too dry to gulp. "No. The box is labeled."

It wasn't, but I was desperate to get out of there. So desperate, I rushed into the kitchen — directly into a hulking, familiar body.

"Sorry," he said.

I blinked into a handsome, all-American face. It was Rob, the escort I'd pegged as a football player.

He tilted his head. "You okay?"

Other than having a vial of his blood in my pocket? Sure. Perfect.

"Yes. Thanks. Sorry." I flattened my hand over the side of my pants.

He grinned in the manner of a confident, airheaded football player — a lot like Ryder, my occasional dance buddy — and tapped his chest proudly.

"I'm on grill duty tonight."

I pinched my lips together before I blurted something like, *I hope not.*

"Can you show me where to find the steaks?" he continued.

I could picture it now — vampires trading small talk with "escorts" out on that beautiful terrace while bloody steaks simmered on the grill.

"Um, Wendy would know." I motioned toward her.

The good news was, he hadn't recognized me. The bad news was, I had a goddamn vial of his blood in my pocket, and I feared he'd be "donating" more soon.

I watched him go. How much desperation, greed, or twisted desire did it take to sign on as a vampire escort? How could the money possibly be worth it?

Grabbing a dish towel, I hurried over to one of Nancy's portable coolers, wrapped the vials in the cloth, and dropped them into the ice at the bottom. Those coolers had been brought in full and would soon be shuttled away empty. I snapped a picture of the cooler number, then hunched over my phone in the walk-in pantry, working my thumbs at warp speed.

Evidence? was all I had time to write before attaching the pictures and hitting *send.*

The symbol on my phone turned in agonizingly slow circles.

Then, whew — a check mark. They were on their way.

My thumbs flew over the screen again, erasing every picture, then emptying the trash.

I exhaled, stuffing the phone back into my pocket. There. I'd done it. Evidence... hopefully. Even if it wasn't, I'd had enough of La Puebla. It was time to pack up and clear out with Nancy.

I turned back to the kitchen, so eager to depart that I bumped into Rob again.

"Sorry," I said, drawing back.

Then I froze. It wasn't Rob or Deirdre or the butler. It was my worst nightmare.

Victor Jananovich.

Thin, pale lips curled into a tight smile as he took me in.

"Ah, Ms. Martin, the glass artist."

Shit. The average guy took five tries to get my name right. This vampire had it memorized.

Worse, the way he looked at me said he had *me* memorized.

His nostrils flared, and his eyes flickered. If I could have ordered my blood to stop swishing through my veins, I would have.

"To what do I owe the pleasure?" he asked.

I forced a smile. "Pleasure's all mine." I waved toward Nancy. "I moonlight for the catering company."

"A woman of many talents," he said amiably.

His eyes, however, dropped to my neck. Right about to where my pulse was hammering.

The laugh I forced came out as more of a cackle. "I guess you could say that."

I looked at Nancy, desperate for her to snap her notebook shut and announce, *Well, we really must be going.*

But she went right on talking garnishes and sauces with George, the butler.

My heart thumped harder while sinking to about the level of my liver. As tempted as I was to get the hell out of Dodge, was my mission here really over? Would pictures of vials constitute hard evidence?

Doubtful, my heart — or my liver — concluded.

Certainly not enough to usher the agency in for a raid tonight, just in time to catch Jananovich at his game and rescue the likes of Becca, Saanvi, and stunning, stupid Rob.

I yanked the sentiment back an instant later. Maybe Rob wasn't stupid. Maybe Saanvi wasn't reckless and Becca perfectly sane. Maybe they were here for noble causes, like saving money for a relative's cancer treatment or to pay off crippling loans. Maybe, just maybe, one of them had a ranch that meant everything to their family, and they couldn't find any other way to meet a sudden hike in back taxes.

That one sure sounded familiar.

So, was my mission here accomplished?

No. Not by a long shot.

My mind spun as a whole new idea hatched. A foolproof way to collect evidence... or one that would prove me a fool.

"And, my. What a coincidence." Jananovich raised his eyebrows at my *moonlighting* remark.

He looked at me, then around the kitchen, working out the odds of such a coincidence.

Not very high, and we both knew it.

It was time to take the offensive.

I pulled his business card out of my back pocket. I'd brought it as a *get-out-of-jail-free* card in case one of the security guards questioned my presence on the premises. That way, I could always claim to have been invited by the big boss.

I never imagined selling a different version of that story to the big boss himself, but here I was. And Stacy was waiting for me to avenge her.

"Actually, I jumped at the chance to come here again," I lied, showing him the card. "I was hoping to talk to you about that opportunity you mentioned."

His eyes lasered through me in a mixture of temptation and suspicion.

"Did you, now?"

I did my best to ooze honesty. "I did. But I see it's not a good time."

"Not the best... but perhaps opportune in a different way."

My pulse quickened.

"Oh yes?"

His eyes flickered ominously, but Nancy called out before he spoke.

"Thank you, everyone. We'll be going now. Pippa. Wendy..." She nodded us toward the door.

The left side of my body burned to join her. The right side hung back, ready to play avenging angel. Both impulses canceled each other out, and in the end, my body simply jolted, getting nowhere.

"Pippa?" Nancy cocked her head.

Leave while you're still ahead, my mind screamed.

Not done here yet, my heart insisted.

I opened my mouth, but no sound came out.

"Give us a minute, please," Jananovich murmured.

Like that, the kitchen emptied. Even Nancy went after a last, questioning look.

"I'll get a ride home later," I assured her.

Another promise I really, really hoped to make good on.

Silence fell like a curtain. Jananovich leaned in slowly, ominously, putting the onus on me to begin.

A very big, very creepy onus.

I took a deep breath, then started.

"As I said, I was hoping to see you."

Somehow, my voice didn't waver. Bonus points for me.

"Indeed." His voice was as smooth as ever, but his eyes took on a hunter's sheen.

I took a deep breath, then let it all out. Go big or go home, right? I just hoped it wouldn't be in a body bag.

"I know you're a vampire," I started as matter-of-factly as I could.

Jananovich's eyes sparkled in a way that said, *Now, this sounds interesting.*

"I know what the vials are for. I know what the escorts are for. I know your guests are interested in exotic *flavors,*" I said, using air quotes.

He looked neither surprised nor offended, which really pissed me off.

"Aha. Let me guess. You're here to blackmail me."

"Ha. Like I'm stupid enough to blackmail a vampire. I'd be looking over my shoulder for the rest of my life."

"As long as your life lasted," he agreed, oh-so casually.

I snorted. "Like I said, not stupid."

On the other hand, I was in his lair and laying out every-thing I knew. Well, almost everything. So, stupid? Maybe.

Vampires were a pale bunch, but Jananovich's cheeks were practically ruddy with curiosity.

"Then what exactly are you offering?"

I lifted my chin and stuck my chest out. In for a penny, in for a pound, right?

"What do I have to offer? Simple." I looked him straight in the eye. "Me."

Chapter Twenty-Two

PIPPA

Wow. Using the direct approach was pretty damn effective. Pretty damn terrifying, too.

Jananovich listened intently as I explained how much money I needed and how desperately. In fact, he nodded like he'd heard that story a hundred times, and he probably had. With Stacy. With Janet Sullivan. With Rob, Saanvi, and the others, no doubt.

And, shit. Was I truly going to add myself to that list?

As I spoke, he raked his gaze over my neck, and his nostrils flared again. Ick.

"Well, we are a staff member short with Stacy away," he finally mused, stroking his chin.

Away, my ass. She was six feet under, or soon to be.

And I swear, I will make this murderer pay, I vowed quietly.

"What's your asking price?" he asked.

"What's your going rate?"

He mulled that over. "For an entry-level position?"

My imagination only came up with two positions. Number one was eyes squeezed tight with my head tipped back while a vampire got off on sucking my blood. Number two was eyes squeezed tight with my legs spread wide while a vampire got off on other aspects of my body. Both had zero appeal.

But, hey. I had a few moves of my own planned. Number one, a kick to the balls. Number two, a stake to the heart.

Number three, a little voice whispered. *Burn the place down.*

"Five thousand a night," he said. "Assuming you don't need room and board."

He assumed right.

But, damn. What would he offer next? Medical plans? Retirement benefits? Dental coverage?

I frowned at the image. Dental...vampires...

Ick.

The crazy thing was, I actually found myself doing the mental math. Six nights with Jananovich, and our tax hike would be paid off. Just three weekends...

Then my sanity won out. There was no way I would prostitute my body or my blood.

I shook my head. "No room and board. My safety, on the other hand, is nonnegotiable."

He waved a hand, dismissing the thought. "I can assure you, we see our consultants as investments. It's not in our interest to hurt anyone."

Oh yeah? He'd probably assured Stacy too.

His eyes twinkled. "In fact, I'm told the experience is quite pleasurable for the escort. A real rush, apparently."

On a scale of one to ten, with one being slightly crude and ten being absolutely, positively disgusting, I gave that a nine — and only because I was reserving ten for the real thing rather than just imagining it.

"So I gather," I said dryly.

His brow furrowed. "From Stacy?"

"No, she didn't say a word," I said in her defense, though that wouldn't help her now. "I figured it out on my own, though it took a while."

Things went on in that vein — ew, *definitely* no pun intended — for a while. Eventually, I found myself signing a nondisclosure agreement, then bustled off to join the escorts. Jananovich called me back before I got both feet out the door, though.

"One last thing, Ms. Martin. We usually vet our escorts carefully, but time is short."

A helicopter buzzed overhead, and Jananovich rose to his feet.

"Therefore, Deirdre will remain with you at all times. To orient you to our customer-friendly approach, of course."

Deirdre? The bitchy brunette with the three-inch nails who'd picked up the vials?

Yep, that Deirdre. She stepped out of the shadows, and it took everything I had not to blanch. Especially when I caught the scent she must have masked earlier. Vampire.

Still, I forced myself to nod. "Of course."

She stepped closer in a stilted walk dictated by that tight cocktail dress. The sequins flashed, just like her eyes did.

Orient me? More like kill me if I stepped out of line.

"Follow me," she grumbled.

And just like that, I was in. Well, out the door, but in with the escorts, who were primping for the night in a big, ground-floor room in another building that was part of the La Puebla rabbit warren. The place was set up like a fashion show dressing room, with racks of clothing and a row of light-studded mirrors.

Deirdre introduced me curtly, and everyone looked over with the air of sorority girls, already judging if I was cool enough to join their exclusive club.

I wished I could assure them I really, really didn't want that. Not at all.

Luckily, the din of hair dryers drowned out any attempt at conversation, and no one seemed to recognize me. Either I was completely forgettable, or they had all been so dazed that no one remembered me from before.

I recognized them, though. Kelly, Rob, Becca, Saanvi, and the others. Poor, meek Delaney was there too, looking like a deer in headlights as she followed the others through the motions.

Ingo and I had guessed at what was going on, but seeing it made the details sink in.

The vials. The escorts. The big event with VIP guests.

Jananovich wasn't just selling sex or blood. He was running a twisted business catering to vampires — connoisseurs, one might say, not of fine wines, but rare blood types. Why settle for an ordinary human "vintage" when you could sample a fine blend of the best bouquets? A human-mermaid blend, for example. A hint of dragon. Maybe even a splash of pegasus.

My eyes misted as I thought of Stacy. Had she even been aware of her heritage? Had she dreamed of galloping and flying over open plains the way I dreamed of controlling fire?

I looked around the room. Did any of the escorts know about their own heritage?

Somehow, I doubted it.

But Jananovich knew. I could picture him hiring a couple of bear shifters with good noses — like the one who'd kept an eye on Stacy — to scour bars and gyms for promising new "talent."

Worse, I could picture the rest. Blood samples drawn and poured into vials. Vials used to lure high-end paying clients to events like tonight's highly anticipated "dinner."

A hundred thousand per person, I'd heard one of the escorts say proudly.

Nancy's catering was good, but not *that* good. The main draw — the secret sauce, one might say — was Jananovich's escorts.

I thought back to all the vials Stacy had picked up over the past weeks. Many more than necessary to draw in customers for one dinner. Unless...

My stomach turned. I would bet good money — say, $30,000 — that Jananovich was running an entire business based entirely on small amounts of blood. Targeting a different segment of the vampire market, in other words, who paid a premium for handpicked samplers sent monthly, the way some folks paid for a coffee subscription.

My pulse rose, and I yearned to explain it all to Ingo.

I couldn't — not now — but I did use a trip to the toilet to text him a choppy, telegraph-style message. Then I checked the nanny cam — and nearly cursed out loud. Someone had put a wide-screen TV in front of it, and all it showed now were blurry cables.

Shit, shit, shit. I would have to get back in and reposition that camera.

I sent another text, explaining the problem in staccato bursts of misspelled text. That was the best I could do before Deirdre cleared her throat outside my stall. If I didn't exit, pronto, she would drag me out and frisk me.

I hit send, then deleted the conversation and cut the link to the camera before emerging with a ditzy smile. In no time, I was squeezed into a pleated chiffon dress and matching emerald pumps, with my hair done in long, loose curls.

And, oh. A glance in a full-length mirror told me I looked pretty damn amazing. Not a good thing, though. Not tonight. I ruffled my hair and plucked at the dress, doing my best to spoil the effect.

The escorts started lining up at the door, where a security guard patted everyone down before letting them walk over to the main house.

I hung back, wide-eyed.

"Is that really necessary?" I whispered to Kelly.

Her look said *Duh,* though her words were kinder. "All part of the rules. No phones, no devices, nothing. Makes sense, though."

I stared at her. Sure, it did — if you were running a criminal organization and didn't want any evidence leaked.

"Don't worry." She shrugged. "It's just like airport security."

No, it wasn't, because that was designed to protect the good guys.

My pulse raced as I eyed the rear door. It was high time to get the hell out of here. . . somehow. The nanny cam might catch something useful, and the vials I'd stashed might also serve as evidence. The escorts would probably survive the night, and eventually, the law would catch up with Jananovich. I'd risked enough tonight.

If our roles were reversed and Ingo were the inside man instead of me, I would be screaming at him to get the hell out. That it wasn't worth his life. That he didn't have to be a hero.

But since it was me. . .

Slowly, understanding dawned on me. This wasn't about being a hero. This was about responsibility. Not responsibility to an employer or agency, but to my own conscience. I couldn't stand by and do nothing.

But, shit. I'd never, ever done anything as dangerous as this. Posing as an escort was bad enough. If Jananovich caught on to what I was really doing, he would kill me. Slowly.

Correction. He would drain my tasty pyromancer/dragon blood, then kill me. Slowly.

My gut wrenched. My sisters would be gutted. My father would be destroyed. My mother...

I sighed. Mom might be saddened, but she would get over it.

Ingo, on the other hand, would never forgive himself, and I shuddered to think what he might do to himself or others if I didn't make it out.

It hurt just to imagine causing so much grief to so many people. But I understood why Ingo would go through with it if he were in my shoes. It was the right thing to do, and he couldn't live with the guilt if he backed away.

Just like I couldn't live with myself if I didn't.

I patted the clothes and personal effects I was leaving behind gently, wondering if I would ever see them again. Then I pulled up my big-girl pants — figuratively, because pants would look really weird with that dress — and joined the line to get patted down.

Outside, the last rays of the setting sun warmed my skin. I threw a look at the surrounding wilderness, praying Ingo would understand why I had to go through with this.

Another wave of realization washed over me. Ingo probably murmured the same prayer every time he undertook a mission, and I had never, ever shown him the slightest understanding. I'd never made impossible choices easier on him, only harder.

God, I'd been so selfish.

I bent my head with a final vow. If I got out of this alive, I would love Ingo long and hard. I would make him part of my life — if he would have me — and celebrate every moment we had together. I would do my best to keep him out of trouble, but I would let go when necessary. And I would make damn sure he headed out knowing I was proud of him.

Be proud of me, Ingo, I thought loud and clear, hoping he might hear me. *And I swear, I will do everything in my power to get back to you.*

I gulped, then allowed myself to be swallowed up by the darkness of the hallway.

Chapter Twenty-Three

PIPPA

"Places, everyone. Places," Deirdre snipped.

The escorts scattered throughout the living/dining area of the main house. Delaney and I were assigned the drinks table — to begin with, at least. Once things got into swing, we escorts were supposed to mingle with the guests.

Mingle. Such an innocent word. Such horrifying connotations.

Well, I, for one, had no such plans. I was going to fix that nanny cam, then mingle my ass right out the door.

I eyed the giant screen that blocked the camera. It showed a stage, where curtains slowly drew open. A red dot and tiny text in one corner said *Live from the Met*, and a stout woman in a red dress and a very hardworking push-up bra started to sing in warbly, ear-piercing notes.

An opera. I knew that much, even if I couldn't tell *Tosca* from *Aida.* I was pretty sure they both died at the end, though.

The volume was low enough to stay in the background, as were the muted optics.

I slid my eyes over to Deirdre. The woman had the eyes of a hawk, and they were right on me.

Shit, shit, shit. How was I ever going to pull this off?

My throat was dry, and my fingers tingled as I fantasized about turning the whole place into an inferno. But that wouldn't put Jananovich away, and it would risk innocent lives, like Delaney's.

Her hands shook as we poured juice and water into glasses.

"You don't have to do this, you know," I murmured, keeping my eyes down.

Her head whipped around in surprise. Then she looked down and continued pouring. "I do. I have to."

Her voice was thin and shaky but packed with determination, and I wondered what misfortune had led her here.

Another helicopter thundered overhead, and we all followed it with our eyes.

I swallowed hard. The VIPs were arriving. Whatever was about to go down was officially in motion.

I closed my eyes briefly. Whatever happened tonight, I would get at least two people out alive. Myself and Delaney.

"They're coming!" Kelly chirped from the doorway in excitement.

Excitement, like she couldn't wait to lose a little — or a lot — of blood.

I'm told it's quite a pleasurable experience. Jananovich's words echoed through my mind. *A real rush.*

Ha. As much of a rush as Russian roulette, I figured.

The door opened, and the escorts lit up expectantly.

The first two guests were middle-aged men who would have fit in at any ordinary business shindig. Well, a high-end shindig, given those tailored suits and silk ties. They looked around with appraising eyes, then winked at each other. My sisters and I probably mirrored them when we stumbled across a great deal on brownie mix or ice cream at the supermarket, but yeesh. These were vampires.

Victor Jananovich strode in next, chuckling to the man at his side — a tall, thin man with gray hair and round glasses — the spitting image of John Lennon, if only he'd lived to old age. My stomach turned at the deceptive similarity. John Lennon had been an artist, not a vampire, and he'd written beautiful songs about peace, love, and some really out-there psychedelic trips. This look-alike sucked innocent victims' blood.

The flames in the fireplace beside me leaped and crackled. Deirdre frowned and fiddled with the damper.

My mind spun with ways to play that to my advantage.

The next guests were a man and a woman — er, vampire and vampiress — who wouldn't have looked out of place in Marie Antoinette's ballroom, minus powdered wigs and shoes with buckles. Otherwise, their clothes were just old-fashioned and flouncy enough to give off that rich, excessive vibe, and their teeth extended at the sight of the scrumptious menu spread out before them.

The *human* menu.

The couple looked to be about forty, but my gut told me they were much, much older. How many victims had they sucked dry over the centuries?

The blood drained from my cheeks when the vampiress made a beeline for Rob, while the man headed straight for Kelly. Astoundingly, the two escorts looked delighted. Maybe they were big tippers? That, or the vampires were so powerful, they could enthrall from a distance.

More guests entered until over a dozen were scattered throughout the huge living room. I glued a smile on my face as a distinguished Latino man approached with a dangerous gleam in his eye.

My heart rate tripled, then slowed down as he took a glass of wine and turned his back, more interested in surveying options other than me or Delaney. Whew.

But I wasn't accomplishing anything from behind the drinks table. Not when the nanny cam was blocked. Working up my courage, I grabbed two glasses of wine and headed across the room.

I could sense Deirdre's eyes on me as I moved in the direction of the wide-screen TV. I made it over to the shelves, but John Lennon was already there — and he turned to me expectantly.

"Wine?" I offered, handing him one.

And, dammit. The escort he'd hooked up with — wouldn't you know it, a cute Asian girl — grabbed the second glass. That meant I had to make a second trip.

And a third and a fourth, as it turned out, with Deirdre tracking me the whole way. Then, halfway across the room on my fifth try, I jerked my elbow at the fireplace.

Whoosh! The flames doubled in size, leaping and crackling.

Deirdre turned to look. I ducked behind the TV screen and snatched the nanny cam down from the shelf. Sliding back into the open, I made a stretching motion and stuck it on a different shelf, then grabbed the wineglass just as Deirdre's seeking eyes found me.

So, whew. Camera repositioning, check. Now I could work on getting my ass out of there.

A guest came over to me. A tuxedoed John Jacob Astor type, with the manners and elegance of a bygone age, if the *Titanic* movie was anything to go by.

"A beautiful evening, isn't it?" He gave me a slow look-over.

I inched away, forcing a smile. "Beautiful. Victor sure knows how to throw a party."

"He certainly does."

Minutes ticked by in agonizing small talk. I didn't have much choice, with Deirdre pinning me with a stern look the whole time.

I gulped and did my best to play along, though I made myself as unappealing as possible.

"New to Arizona? No," I said in answer to his question. "I've spent most of my life here. Small-town girl," I chuckled loudly to underscore the *not your type* message.

Unfortunately, that didn't deter him.

"College? Yes, I studied as a veterinary assistant specializing in bovines," I lied. "I love cattle."

His interest waned, so I pressed on.

"Just this week, I got to run rectal checks." I mimicked working on a shoulder-length plastic glove. "I got to reach all the way in and everything!"

His nose wrinkled. "All the way?"

"All the way." Nodding happily, I sniffed my arm, then chuckled. "Whew. It takes days to shake the smell sometimes."

He set aside his glass and scurried off. "If you'll excuse me, I meant to get back to Victor on some important business. . ."

My flash of triumph died an instant later, because Marie Antoinette and Rob were making out by then. Kissing, touching… Her long hair hid the details, but I could swear she was homing in on his neck. His eyes were closed, his head tipped back with an expression of sublime expectation.

I was pretty sure I'd looked like that last night with Ingo. But, ugh. The *suck my blood* variation was so not appealing.

Saanvi was in a similar position with a guy best described as John Travolta gone wrong, and she raked her fingers over his back in *Feast, baby, feast* mode.

I made for the relative safety of the drinks table but froze a moment later. Another vampire — a rakish guy who brought the Prohibition era to mind — was across the room, talking to Delaney. Make that, crowding Delaney. Running his finger over her shoulder, then along her collarbone.

He tipped her chin up, exposing her throat. She clenched her fists as he leaned in to sniff, then kiss her cheek. A moment later, he took her hand, whispered seductively, and led her away.

Alarms shrieked in my mind, and I took a step to follow — but Deirdre stepped in first.

"She's doing her job. You do yours," she barked, pointing to the drinks table. "Serve and mingle."

I'd never wondered how it felt to be a slave at a Roman orgy, but now I knew. And it turned my stomach.

I took one slow step, then another, thinking frantically. How to stop Al Capone before he bit Delaney? How to get the hell out of there?

I slid behind the drinks table and fiddled with bottles, trapped by Deirdre's icy stare. The only comfort to be found in that cold, heartless space was the fireplace, though the flames had gone low, as if they, too, were ashamed to play any part in this.

On the TV screen, the opera singer belted out a song of pride and defiance.

Come on, Pippa. I tried pumping myself up. I had to do something, and fast.

When Deirdre glanced away, I flicked a hand at the fireplace.

Whoosh! The teepee of logs collapsed, and a flaming log rolled onto the rug.

"Put it out! Put it out!" John Lennon yelled frantically, but everyone jumped back.

Apparently, vampires didn't like fire any more than humans did.

When Deirdre turned her back to deal with the chaos, I grabbed a bottle of champagne — the kind with the thickest, heaviest glass — and hurried out of the room. The minute I turned a corner, I ran.

My heart hammered as I rushed down the hall. Which room had the vampire taken Delaney to? I paused at one, then another, listening. Nothing. I jogged on. Still nothing. I held my breath and prayed for some clue.

A muffled cry came through a door across the hall, and I kicked it open.

"What the—" Al Capone protested.

"Run, Delaney!" I yelled, brandishing the champagne bottle.

I had no plan for what to do next. But even before I finished speaking, the vampire coughed and fell forward.

I jumped back, staring at the object protruding between his shoulder blades. A stake?

His outstretched hand went from pale to dull, and his skin shriveled in a time-lapse of a grape under a heat lamp. His clothes collapsed inward, and the smell of ash hit my nose.

"You staked him?" I sputtered, more at the body than Delaney.

"Bet your ass, I did," she said.

My eyes shot to her — or maybe it was her stunt double, because shy, meek Delaney was gone, replaced by Uma Thurman in "Kill Bill." She stood taller, stronger, and wow — she even spat on the rapidly disappearing body. "That was for Janet, asshole."

I did a double take. "You mean Janet Sullivan?" The woman found dead at Gunnery Point?

She nodded. "My sister. I begged her to get out of this place. But she was hell-bent on finding something concrete to bring down Jananovich."

I gulped. A little like me.

"He must have figured her out, because he killed her. Or had her killed," Delaney finished bitterly.

My mouth hung open. Delaney wasn't Bambi. She was pretty damned badass. She'd managed to work her way in with Jananovich's escorts and onto the premises to avenge her sister.

Wow.

"We have to get out of here."

I jerked my hand toward the door, but she shook her head. "Not going anywhere until I finish this."

Finish Jananovich, she meant.

I was all for that... in principle. In practice, though...

I glanced at Al Capone's body — or all that was left of it. Gingerly, I reached down and touched the stake. It crumbled instantly.

Delaney made a tsk sound and reached into her high, lacing boot. "There's more where that came from."

Holy shit. She was either a superhero or a lunatic. But, hell. She was certainly well-armed, and she seemed to have a plan, which was more than I could say.

So, great. I could turn things over to her and hustle my ass to safety, right?

But then I thought about Stacy, and my rubber nerves toughened up a little.

"What about you?" Delaney asked. "Did you lose someone too?"

I thought it over. "Not a sister." *Thank God,* I could have added. "But Stacy..."

Delaney nodded sadly. "Every once in a while, one of the others mentioned her, but someone would shut them up." She scoffed. "They had to have suspected, but somehow, they decided to kid themselves."

Disgusted, I pointed to the door.

"We have to go. Now. I planted a camera. That should find enough evidence."

Delaney scoffed. "The police won't do anything. They thought I was crazy for believing in vampires."

"Not the police. A supernatural law enforcement team."

She still looked skeptical. "Somehow, the law doesn't apply to Jananovich. He always gets away. The only way to end this is to end him. Permanently."

I wanted to protest, but I knew she was right. Besides, the other escorts were still in danger.

My darker side yelled to forget about them and save myself. If they were stupid enough to get involved with — and stick with — the likes of Jananovich, they deserved whatever fate threw at them. No one was begging for me to be their hero.

But my good side reminded me that each was someone's son, daughter, brother, or sister.

That last part resonated with me most. Sister. Where would I be without mine? Where would I be if fortune hadn't given me a loving father, a decent job, opportunities — and, best of all, Ingo?

My heart swelled, and I squared my shoulders. He was somewhere close, but still too far. In any case, he wouldn't stop until this was finished. Well and truly finished.

And I wouldn't either.

"You go," Delaney urged me, pulling a second stake from her boot. "I've got this."

I shook my head, correcting her. "*We've* got this."

I held out my hand, and she grinned, handing me the stake. "All right, then. Let's get those suckers."

Chapter Twenty-Four

INGO

I paced by the fence of La Puebla for the hundredth time, then swore. The nanny cam had been blocked for ages, and when it did come on again, it showed Pippa heading down a hallway — and not coming back.

I threw down my night vision goggles and started ditching the other equipment I'd brought.

"Fuck this. I'm going in."

I couldn't mind-speak to Pippa from this distance, but I could sense her general state of mind, and her anxiety had just spiked.

Kyle Williams, police officer and member of Twin Moon pack, grabbed my arm. "Not yet. Backup isn't fully in position."

"To hell with backup," I grunted, heading for the fence.

Pippa had disappeared minutes ago, and every second had been an eternity. Was she all right? Had Jananovich caught on to her? Was she being attacked by a vampire right now?

She'd sent a series of pictures and brief comments an hour ago, but since then, there'd been nothing. Nothing but the sounds of a party in the main house. A vampire party.

My blood boiled.

The chain link fence surrounding La Puebla rose and fell with every contour of the mountain, but my concern for Pippa carried me over easily.

Kyle grabbed the fence from the outside. "Wait!"

I shook my head. Waiting meant death. I was sure of it.

"Stand by," I grunted. "If we're not out in fifteen minutes, I need you to come in. All of you." I shot a meaningful look at the shadows in the slope above us.

A contingent of wolves from Twin Moon pack had concealed themselves all around La Puebla, but concern over drawing the attention of the agency or making a powerful vampire enemy meant they would only rush in as a last resort.

As far as I was concerned, this *was* our last resort.

Apparently, they had different ideas.

Let me out! my wolf howled as I ran in a crouch.

I was dying to release my inner beast and let him rage, but human form was best for now. A fact proven two minutes later when I took out the man standing guard at the delivery entrance to the main house. I could muffle his shout with one hand and wring his neck with the other.

Brutal? Yes. But I wasn't taking any prisoners tonight.

Human form also came in handy for silently turning door-knobs and stealing through the halls. The house was a god-damn maze, but instinct guided me around every turn without so much as a pause.

That way, my wolf pointed, urging me on.

I threw open one door, then stared at the pile of ash on the floor.

My wolf cheered. *Pippa one, vampires zero.*

I hurried onward, checking the adjoining rooms. Earlier, I'd seen a dozen vampires enter the premises. Even eliminating one left many, many more to go.

And what the hell was Pippa doing, killing vampires? She was supposed to set up the camera, then get the hell out.

The party was in full swing down the hall, but to the right... The scent trails were confusing as hell, with lots of movement back and forth. Pippa had been by several times.

Right, my wolf barked.

I took off at a jog, then slowed to check a corner. Four steps later, my nose caught an acrid smell, and I peered into a room on the right.

"Shit." I cursed, halting my right foot an inch above another pile of ash. I crouched and poked at the remains of a sequined cocktail dress. A female vampire? I narrowed my eyes on the shape protruding from the back. The remains of a stake, though it was mere charcoal now.

As far as I knew, Pippa hadn't gone in armed with stakes. She hadn't gone in armed with *anything* but a tiny camera and her own wits. What the hell was going on?

A bump sounded in the next room. I froze, then rushed into the hall and burst through the adjoining room just as a body thumped to the floor. Two women leaped back when I entered, and—

"Pippa?" I stared.

"Ingo!"

My wolf howled in glee. She was alive!

Her eyes filled with joy, then panic.

"Wait!" she cried to the second woman.

I turned in time to grab the woman's arm before she staked me too.

"Watch it," I ordered, gripping her arm tightly.

The woman was a terrier — small but ferocious.

"It's okay." Pippa hustled closer. "He's with us."

I stared. Who exactly was us?

"Ingo, meet Delaney. Delaney, meet Ingo."

I nodded but didn't let down my guard. Honestly, the woman looked borderline deranged.

Not deranged. She's on a mission, Pippa murmured in my mind. *There's a fine line.*

Well, maybe. But Delaney was definitely teetering toward the dark side.

Pippa touched me, and every nerve in my body calmed. Slowly, I released the woman's arm, and we both stepped back.

"Delaney is Janet's sister," Pippa explained softly.

My brow folded. Police research hadn't come up with any such relation.

My skepticism must have shown, because Delaney chimed in next.

"Technically, her stepsister, through her mom marrying my dad. Eventually, they divorced, but Janet and I were always close." Her eyes shone with grief and anger. "Sisters, through thick and thin."

So that was why police hadn't found the link — and why Jananovich hadn't caught on to Delaney either.

I eyed the stake. "Have you two been..." I trailed off, incredulous.

"Luring in vampires one by one and offing them?" Pippa supplied.

Delaney gave a proud nod, and they exchanged high fives.

"You bet your ass, we have," Pippa finished.

I didn't know whether to cheer or yell.

"What happened to setting up the camera and getting out?" I asked.

Pippa shrugged. "I guess we had a better idea."

Delaney moved to the door. "Now, if you'll excuse me..."

I stared. How long was her hit list?

Long, I decided. With Jananovich at the top.

Still, I tugged her back.

"Offing them one by one will only work for so long. Sooner or later, Jananovich's security guards will catch on, and what will you do then?"

And, uh-oh. Delaney had an eerie sense of calm about her. Kamikaze-style calm.

"That's why I'm going for Jananovich next."

Her tone was as flat and emotionless as a person giving driving directions. *Go left, then right, then stake a vampire in the heart...*

I eyed the stake in her hand. "How many of those do you have?"

"Last one. And it has Jananovich's name on it."

Literally. I could see the letters etched into the wood. Wow. She really had it in for the guy.

Pippa hurried to the desk, then motioned to me.

"This is the office. *Jananovich's* office." She tapped the desk with both hands.

I met her eyes, then looked at the desk, wishing for X-ray vision.

"So?" Delaney asked, annoyed.

"Evidence," Pippa whispered.

"Evidence?" someone echoed from the door, and we all whirled.

My hackles rose, and I spat his name. "Jananovich."

The son of a bitch ignored me, keeping his eyes on Pippa. Two more vampires crowded the doorway behind him.

"Evidence of breaking and entering," Jananovich said, smooth as can be. Only then did he acknowledge my presence. "Evidence that will put you away, Agent Kemper, for a long, long time. Not just for harassment, but for corrupting and enlisting these innocent young women to do the dirty work in your misguided cause."

"Corrupting?" Pippa screeched. "You're the criminal here."

I curled my hands into fists. As absurd as Jananovich's accusations were, he'd found ways to make false allegations stick before. He could find a way again, especially if he still had an insider at the agency.

Pippa bristled from head to toe, while Delaney seethed.

But this wasn't another ambush where all it took was timing to plunge a stake into an unsuspecting foe. That required a hell of a lot of moxie, but still. Taking on a vampire head-on was a whole different kind of fight. A quick one, and the vampire wasn't usually the one to spill blood.

"Criminal?" Jananovich shook his head sadly. "I can see Agent Kemper has presented you with his twisted facts." He sighed and turned to his guests. "Gentlemen, I regret the disturbance."

The big, olive-skinned guy on his left grinned, showing the points of his fangs. "On the contrary. A dinner party is always nice, but nothing beats a good digestif."

I'll show you a digestif. Pippa's eyes blazed.

I glanced around for a way out. A wolf's odds of beating a vampire were fifty-fifty at best. But a vampire with backup on his home turf... Those odds were closer to nil, even with Pippa and Delaney at my side.

Not good.

Edge toward the window. I shot the message into Pippa's mind. *Get ready to open it.*

I'm not running away from that jerk, she retorted.

I shook my head a tiny bit. *Not to run. To call in Kyle and his pack.*

And, whew. Pippa inched toward the glass expanse.

"The only question is, who gets whom?" One of Jananovich's bloodsucking buddies grinned.

Jananovich smirked. "As a good host, I'll share, of course..."

I growled.

Ignoring the warning, Jananovich pointed to Pippa. "However, I would appreciate getting to sample that one first."

My wolf tore out of me so fast, I only felt the pain of the lightning shift after a delay. By then, I was hurtling through the air, aiming at his throat.

And just like that, the fight was on.

Pippa! I yelled into her mind. *Call for help!*

Then I grunted and rolled, body-checked aside by Jananovich's buddy. The swarthy vampire was obviously itching for a fight. The shorter Latino stepped forward too, stripping out of his jacket like a gentleman getting ready to duel.

Vampires. Such fucking snobs.

I whirled, lashed out with my claws and fangs, then skittered back and snarled.

Jananovich remained behind his buddies, more focused on Delaney than me.

"Now, now," he said in an annoying, singsong tone. "I'm sure we can clear everything up."

Delaney stared at me — but to her credit, didn't run or scream at the sight of a wolf — then turned to Jananovich, clutching her stake. "Clear up killing Janet? Not happening, asshole."

"Janet?" he cocked an eyebrow. "Her death was a tragedy, but it had nothing to do with me."

Delaney snorted, and I growled, then jumped aside as one of the vampires lunged forward. The next minute passed in a blur of fists and fangs. Then we broke apart, panting.

Cool air kissed my cheek, telling me Pippa had the window open.

"Help! Over here!" she yelled into the night.

Jananovich tsked and turned to the burly guard who'd just arrived on the scene.

"Check on that, please." Jananovich sent him off again — but not before I caught a whiff of the man's scent.

Bear shifter. The one who'd driven Stacy.

My hunches had been right. But we needed help, and fast.

Kyle! I yelled at the top of my lungs. It came out as a guttural roar, closer to a lion than your average wolf.

But I was not your average wolf. Not when fighting for my true love's life.

Jananovich's friends stood shoulder to shoulder, preparing their next attack. The swarthy one seemed familiar, though I couldn't place him.

Meanwhile, Jananovich continued speaking to Delaney. "Just put that down, and everything will be all right."

In my peripheral vision, I saw her go stiff. Shit. Jananovich was enthralling her, and it was working. Worse, it seemed to be working on Pippa too. She froze by the window, staring into space.

Shit, shit, shit.

Jananovich chuckled. In the same instant, his buddies lunged for me.

Vampires were lightning-fast, with long, claw-like nails. One sliced across my shoulder in the tussle that ensued. Hissing in pain, I landed my own blow, sending the smaller vampire careening into the first. Then I stepped back, snarling at Jananovich.

The bastard chuckled, focused on Delaney and Pippa.

"That's right. Put down the stake. Step back. Take a deep breath."

And, crap. Delaney did as she was told, moving robotically. Pippa wore an equally vacant expression.

I screamed inside. *No, Pippa! Don't fall for it! Don't listen!*

Fear struck me, because what if this was it? The wolves of Twin Moon pack weren't charging to our rescue — yet.

Neither was the agency, which I hadn't involved — except for sending Nash a last-minute message to notify them. Pippa and Delaney were my only allies on the inside, but Jananovich was neutralizing them both. The moment I fell — and sooner or later, I would — Jananovich and his guests would devour them in a gory feast.

I unleashed another loud growl, praying for help from Kyle or Nash. Without them, we were doomed.

Then my eyes caught a tiny movement. It was Pippa, slowly bending her fingers in a motion I'd seen before. The night of the bonfire, when she'd left even her father spellbound.

Maybe she wasn't enthralled. Maybe she was working on her own trick. I didn't dare look closer for fear of alerting the vampires, but I could sense her mind ticking away.

My hopes soared, or at least peered up from rock bottom. If I could hold off Jananovich and his men a little longer, Pippa might be able to catch him by surprise, and the tables would be turned.

That, or I was imagining things and we really were doomed.

The vampires flexed their claws, preparing for their next attack. I growled and stepped forward, sliding all my chips to one spot in a last, desperate gamble.

Chapter Twenty-Five

PIPPA

I nearly screamed when Ingo threw himself into another lethal round with the vampires, but I couldn't. Not because Jananovich had me enthralled, though I was happy to let the bastard believe that. I had better things to do, like focus, and focus hard.

Not the easiest thing for me to do on a good day, and not at all with a pitched battle raring a few steps away. But I had no choice.

Delaney and I had already succeeded in killing several vampires. I'd harbored some moral reservations about staking the John Lennon look-alike, but Delaney had not. And she was right. He was a vampire and no relation to the Beatle.

But this was different from the two-versus-one odds we'd enjoyed so far. It was time to dig deep and end this for good. And my greatest weapon was fire.

My greatest weakness, however, was... me.

I let out a slow breath, trying to pull myself together.

A whirl of horrifying action unfolded before me, but I forced myself to shut my eyes and call to the fire. Any fire, dammit.

What seemed like an eternity later, my senses located two fires. One was the fireplace in the huge entertainment room, and another was a candle burning in a room several doors down. The room I'd seen a vampire lead Saanvi to. Delaney and I had planned to head there next, but we'd been stopped by Jananovich on the way.

I raised my hands and called to the fire.

It took a while, but I felt the candle, then the hearth sway in response.

Okay. Step one accomplished, just like my dad had explained way back before we'd both given up on me ever controlling fire.

Step two was convincing the fire to listen, and that was the hard part. Fire was a little like a stray dog in a public park. You could whistle to get its attention, but good luck convincing it to heed your beck and call.

Over here. I moved my fingers gently. *Over here...*

I sensed the candle lean my way, and the fire in the living room followed suit.

So, whew. But fire couldn't jump time and space any more than I could. I had to steer it over like a guide for the blind.

The open window created a weak draft, and my mind tapped around the intervening space, identifying different airstreams.

Over here...

Inch by inch, I coaxed the fire closer. Closer...

Ingo yelped, and my eyes flew open, severing my connection to the fire. My heart wept at the blood matted in his dark, thick fur and the fury in his midnight eyes.

I'd seen him in wolf form countless times, but never in such a rage. And never, ever in such danger.

Don't worry about me, he panted into my mind. *Focus! You can do it. I know you can.*

I closed my eyes and reached for the fires again.

"Get him!" one vampire grunted to the other.

"That's right. Just stay there," Jananovich cooed — at Delaney? At me?

I doubled my efforts. Vaguely, I sensed minds growing alarmed. The fire in the living room had to be blazing high by then, and if someone grabbed an extinguisher...

I cursed the inspector who'd ensured every building in La Puebla was up to code.

I strained, caught in an invisible tug-of-war. My weak powers struggled at one end of the line, while natural forces that kept fires stationary resisted on the other.

No matter how hard I tried, the fire wouldn't budge, and I was losing hope.

Help, I wanted to scream. *Dad. Erin. Abby. Anyone...*

Worse, Ingo was running out of steam in his mismatched fight, and Jananovich's voice was starting to wheedle its way into my mind. *Just stay there...*

No, no, no! I screamed inside. I couldn't fail. Not this time.

But, hell. It sure seemed like I would.

Finally, the fire budged. I could sense it creeping down the hallway, one tiny ember at a time. I strained to maintain the connection and coax it this way.

Shouts broke out, and Jananovich muttered something, though I barely heard over the sickening sounds of Ingo's struggle against the vampires. I hung on to the thread in my mind, slowly reeling in the fire.

More shouts. Footsteps pounded down the hallway.

"Fire! Fire!" someone yelled.

An acrid smell reached my nose, and smoke filtered in under the office door.

Keep going! You can do it!

I must have really been pushing my limits, because now I was imagining my sisters cheering me on.

"Dammit..." Jananovich growled at the encroaching fire.

I cracked an eye open, though my mind was still with the fire. Ingo roared, leaping at the smaller vampire's throat. A sickening squelch followed.

Jananovich cursed, then yelled at the second vampire — the bigger, swarthier one.

"Get him, Gregor!"

I strained harder, pulling the fire closer. Thick smoke poured in from under the door.

Yes! I cheered. *Yes! Over here...*

Smoke billowed, and the temperature rose. Crackling sounded just outside the door.

Yes, yes, yes! I cheered feverishly.

It was a heady experience, controlling fire. I could do anything, beat anyone. I could burn this place to ash and dust. I could smite any foe and make my enemies tremble in fear.

Then I caught myself, remembering what my father had always said. To control fire, you have to control yourself, because its power has a way of corrupting.

I blinked hard, renewing my focus.

Jananovich was standing just outside the radius of the fight raging between us, staring at me. His eyes were dark and menacing, not at all like the charmer I'd met earlier.

He raised one arm, holding it toward me in a silent command.

A wave of pressure closed in around my mind, like the mother of all migraines creeping in after a bad day. The bastard was trying to enthrall me.

I focused on my powers instead of his. Or better put, *our* powers, because I realized I wasn't alone in my struggle. It was just like that night on the ranch when my sisters and I had tapped into a vortex and directed its power.

But I wasn't on the ranch now, and there was no vortex.

On the other hand, my sisters were on the ranch. And if they'd sensed my emergency...

They had, I realized. And they were helping — somehow.

You can do it, I sensed Abby telling me.

I pictured her leaning against one of the secret vortexes back on the ranch, straining to funnel its power toward me.

I didn't have the brain space to work out how that was possible. I just kept on fighting, because even with that boost, Jananovich was a hell of an opponent. His powers worked on my mind, casting a fog over everything.

I wiggled my fingers, coaxing the smoke toward his feet. It wound around his shoes, then climbed around his ankles.

Yes, I murmured. *More...*

The smoke wound around his legs like a vine. Or even better, twin pythons.

The smoke thickened, and Jananovich looked down, alarmed.

"Hey!" he protested, like I'd broken the rules or something.

Ha. If he didn't play nice, neither would I.

Still, that was just smoke. I needed fire.

The scary thing was I *really* needed it. Fire was my drug, and I craved it.

Wow. Dad hadn't been kidding about the power complex.

Meanwhile, Ingo was fighting hard but flagging. His opponent seemed just as strong as ever. So strong, I feared he was toying with Ingo. But my faithful wolf refused to back down, and that only made me angrier.

I raised my arms, redoubling my efforts.

In the distance, sirens wailed. People shouted. Smoke poured into the room from every edge of the door. Ingo and Gregor whirled, kick, and bit. And somewhere in the increasingly dim chaos of the room, something else moved.

It was Delaney, creeping along the wall. Trying to escape? I sure hoped so.

Then I spotted the stake in her hand and the fury in her eyes.

She wasn't trying to escape. She was seeing this through, as I should.

And just like that, I released my inner brakes and unleashed my full fury.

Jananovich was a manipulator and a killer. He was worse than a bloodthirsty vampire — he was a bloodthirsty businessman with no boundaries or morals. Whatever suited him, he did. Whatever — or whoever — didn't, he cast brutally aside.

Like Stacy. Like Janet. Like so many others.

A loud crack sounded, and fire joined the smoke pouring in around the edges of the door. The smoke around Jananovich's legs thickened, miring him in his own movements.

"Stop that!" Jananovich batted at it.

No. No, I wouldn't.

I shaped the smoke with my hands, building a ghostly figure as tall as the vampire. Vague at first, then more and more lifelike.

"Stacy?" His eyes went wide.

It was just smoke, not a ghost, but hey. Let him tremble. I shaped the air, making Stacy bigger, meaner, and angrier than she'd been in real life. More vengeful. I let her stare at Jananovich long and hard while I plucked fire from the edge of the door and added that to the smoky image. It flickered around the edges of her body, illuminating her like an angel.

"Leave me alone!" Jananovich shouted.

His words only stoked my fury. I moved my hands faster, reworking the image. It blurred momentarily before details began to emerge. A longer face. A bigger, more elegant body.

Jananovich's jaw went slack as the smoke gave way to a fire in the shape of a horse. And, *snap!* The mighty horse opened huge wings and reared up before him.

Pegasus! I remembered Claire cheering at the bonfire.

But that had been a friendly one. The huge, fiery creature facing Jananovich now was very bitter and very, very angry.

It reared higher, lashing at Jananovich with its front legs.

Whoosh! A wave of heat followed the motion, and sparks streamed through the air.

"What the..." Gregor, the second vampire, stumbled away, breaking off his fight with Ingo. They both stared.

Jananovich raised both arms, trying to drive the pegasus back. But the fire had taken on a life of its own. Now that it had locked on its target, I couldn't redirect it if I wanted to.

By then, the wall behind Jananovich was obscured by smoke, but I did catch another movement.

Delaney. With the stake. Sneaking closer and closer.

The pegasus flared its nostrils, and its eyes reflected the gold and red flames of its body. Every beat of its powerful wings sent waves of heat pulsing. It shook its mane and flicked its hoofs at Jananovich, driving him toward Delaney.

The vampire stumbled back, shouting in anger. But the sound turned into a cry, and he arched awkwardly. His chest thrust forward, and his eyes went wide.

"Victor?" the second vampire called out.

Frozen in an awful grimace, Jananovich toppled forward as if he'd been kicked by Delaney, who stood behind him. Then he face-planted on the floor. The stake in his back smoldered, then burst into flames, and after a few anguished contortions,

Jananovich went limp. In seconds, his body desiccated, then turned to ash.

The fiery pegasus pranced and shook its mane, leaving flames in each hoof print.

Delaney gulped, then nodded at the Pegasus.

"For you," she whispered. "And for my sister, and all the others."

The pegasus tossed its head, and I imagined a whinny that echoed the cadence of Stacy's laughter. Rearing again, it beat its wings in triumph, and the message was clear.

Jananovich's victims had been avenged. No amount of magic could bring them back, but they could rest in peace, knowing he would never hurt another person.

Tears blurred my vision, and the pegasus blurred too, until it was no longer a winged horse, but an ordinary inferno.

And, uh-oh. That inferno was filling the room rapidly.

I blinked, then reached for Delaney. Clasping hands, we whirled — only to face the towering figure of the second vampire.

"Interesting. Very interesting," Gregor murmured, taking me in slowly.

Not a *Yikes, I'd better not mess with you* kind of slowly. More like a *Yum, I can't wait to taste your blood* kind of slowly.

Behind him, Ingo crouched, and my heart thudded.

"Interesting?" I goaded Gregor. "I'll show you interesting."

He laughed at my raised fists, and I forced myself to focus on his face rather than over his shoulder, where Ingo coiled, then leaped, his jaws wide.

When he bashed into the vampire, they both stumbled. Delaney and I jumped back as snarls and shouts broke out. Muffled snarls, because Ingo had buried his teeth in the back of the vampire's neck. Not enough for an instant death blow, but if he held on long enough...

Gregor fought back, kicking and reaching around to gouge Ingo with his long, sharp nails.

"No more stakes?" I coughed at Delaney. The smoke was growing thicker, the flames higher.

She shook her head, then ran to the office fireplace and started rooting through the woodpile with her collar pulled up over her nose and mouth.

Amid the din of the fire and the fight, a sickening crack sounded. Ingo had just snapped a bone in the vampire's neck. Even then, Gregor fought on.

"Here!" Delaney made a tossing motion, then threw me a thick piece of kindling.

I stared at it, feeling sick. It was more *stick* than *stake*. Was it up to the job? Was I?

"Do it!" Delaney yelled.

I raised the stake high and thrust down with both hands. Gregor jolted, and his nails scraped my side. But the worst part was the soft give of his body, the gush of blood.

Still, the vampire fought back.

Using my body weight, I drilled deeper. My hands went cold as frigid vampire blood flowed over them. Then another crack sounded, and his eyes bulged. A moment later, he went limp.

I scuttled away as the body collapsed, then turned to ash. I stared, then hurried to Ingo.

He backed away from the vampire, spitting blood and ash.

I kneeled and threw an arm over his furry, bloodstained back. "Are you all right?"

He snarled and spat in disgust. *Could be worse,* he said, speaking into my mind.

I sagged in relief, then glanced around, because it was one of those *Out of the frying pan, into the fire* moments. Literally.

"Can you stop it?" Delaney motioned to the flames consuming the door.

Coughing, I shook my head, terrified of what I'd unleashed.

But *no* wasn't good enough. A peek out the window earlier showed me we were high above a stone ledge. Too high. It was the door or nothing.

I pulled my shirt over my nose and mouth, then faced the door with my hands in prayer position. Tilting them forward, I shouted at the fire.

Move! I commanded, sweeping my hands apart.

The fire barely crackled.

"Pippa..." Delaney urged.

I tried again.

I said, move! Now! Even in my mind, my voice was hoarse.

Still nothing. I gulped, then closed my eyes, reaching out for the power I'd sensed before. Reaching...reaching...

Ingo pressed gently into the backs of my legs. *You've got this, Pippa. I know you do.*

My skin pinched, and sweat dripped down my brow. The heat was that intense.

You've got this, Pippa, I sensed Abby echo.

Move! Now! I ordered the fire.

The heat wavered, and the flames intensified at the edges of the door.

"Do it again!" Delaney cried.

I repeated the chopping motion. Flames flared out the sides of the door, while the middle dimmed.

I did it again and again, shoving the flames away from the center of the door. Then I stepped aside as Delaney ran at the door with Jananovich's rolling chair. It battered through in a cascade of sparks, and Delaney stumbled forward. I leaped through next, and Ingo followed.

The hallway was ablaze, but successive sweeps of my hands cleared a narrow escape path. Standard procedure in a fire was to drop and crawl, but wielding magic was a little like wielding a bat, so I stayed on my feet and plowed forward, barely able to see through the smoke. Every time we advanced one step, fire and smoke flooded in behind us, pushing us ever forward. Our first few steps were tentative, then faster as the fire thinned, until we burst through a door at a run. All three of us crashed to the ground, coughing and sputtering.

"Wow," Delaney managed between hacking coughs.

Sputtering, I pulled her and Ingo away, then turned to stare at the inferno. An inferno I'd kindled.

Considering the circumstances, Dad would be proud.

Ingo flashed a weak canine grin and licked the side of my face. He was proud too.

Me three, I decided a moment later. *Me three.*

Chapter Twenty-Six

PIPPA

Ingo, Delaney, and I sat in the sweeping driveway, watching the building burn. And burn and burn.

Jananovich was dead. Several other vampires too. Ingo, Delaney, and I had survived. So, mission accomplished.

But damn, had it been close.

Ingo leaned into me, his furry shoulder soft against my leg. I wrapped my arms around him and held him close.

Years ago, we'd sat together like this on mountaintops, wondering about the future. Now, we were in that future, and for all the chaos around us, hope blossomed in my heart. Especially when Ingo sighed wearily and turned, coming nose-to-nose with me.

My chest warmed. We used to do that too, back when we were head over heels in love.

I spoke into Ingo's mind, quickly correcting myself.

Still madly in love.

He flashed a tired canine smile, then nudged my side. *Are you all right?*

I sighed and plucked at my sleeve. "Not bad. Just a little ashy. What about you?"

He dipped his muzzle in a nod. *Good enough.*

He was playing it down, because I'd seen the blood. Thank goodness for accelerated shifter healing. I only had a few bruises myself, though I was dead tired from directing the fire.

Sirens blared in the distance, and people ran to and fro. From the looks of things, Kyle had enacted Plan B — calling

217

in local police, claiming he'd received an urgent, anonymous tip about human trafficking at La Puebla.

So, whew. The police had acted quickly enough that the wolves of Twin Moon Ranch didn't have to reveal themselves. I could sense them nearby, though, keeping a close eye on things.

Then, *whoosh!* A pair of dark shadows fell over us, and we all flinched.

Delaney looked up, and her eyes went wide. "Dragons?"

I nodded as Erin and Nash swooped by in dragon form.

I leave my kid sister alone for a short time, and this is what happens? Erin joked into my mind.

I grinned. *You were the one who dragged me into a lightning fight.*

She chuckled, then glided in a long, smooth arc while glancing around. *Do we care that people are fleeing?*

We do if they're vampires, I replied.

Ingo must have communicated the same sentiment to Nash, who roared into the night and took off, belching fire. Erin joined him, and I couldn't help being a little awed.

My sister, the dragon shifter.

And she wasn't the only one who'd rushed to help me. I could sense Abby back home on the ranch, panting from the exertion of tapping into a vortex. Somehow, she'd channeled some of that power to me despite the intervening distance. When I got home, I would hug her.

Ingo leaned against my legs, telling me I was just as amazing. And thinking back on the past few hours... Well, maybe I was, at least a little.

"Wow." Delaney stared as staccato bursts of dragon fire lit up the mountainside.

I decided she won my vote for *most amazing* tonight. She was just human — well, mostly — but she'd kept herself together enough to kill vampires, to handle the sight of Ingo shifting into wolf form, and now, to process the existence of dragons.

I was sure she was a relic, but I doubted she was aware of that part.

"No one can know," I warned her.

She snorted, her eyes still glued to the dragons. "No one would believe me anyway."

We watched Erin and Nash. Their eyes glowed in the dark, their wings beat, and their massive tails lashed. Every now and then, when they spat fire, an anguished cry would slice through the night.

Delaney nodded in approval. "Another one bites the dust."

I made a mental note to ask Ingo if the agency was recruiting for vampire hunters.

But first things first. Police were pouring into the area, and fire trucks were grinding up the mountain behind them. *Human* police and *human* firefighters. It was time for Ingo to shift back to human form. But Delaney had already gotten up close and personal with enough supernatural activity for one night — plus, shifting would leave Ingo in the buff. A very *buff* buff, so to speak, but still.

"Over here."

I led him to the dressing room I'd used earlier. It was eerily quiet now, except for the flash of red and blue police lights against the windows.

I retrieved my belongings while Ingo gave himself a massive nose-to-tail shake, making ash and dust fly. A short time after I rejoined Delaney, Ingo emerged in human form, wearing a pair of slacks and boots and fiddling with a shirt.

My girl parts fluttered. Did I mention my true love was buff?

He pulled on the shirt, then wrinkled his nose. "I still reek."

We all did, though I was more concerned with the gashes on his arms and shoulders.

"Are you really okay?"

"I'll be fine," he assured me, though he winced a little, then sighed. "As far as injuries go, at least."

I squinted into the flashing lights of law enforcement vehicles. "Is the agency already here?"

"No. But they will be."

And when they appeared, they would question why Ingo had been on the property of a vampire he'd been ordered to avoid.

I tapped my lips, thinking. "Well, who's to say you were here at all?"

He tilted his head. "What do you mean?"

Slowly, I worked it out, then whispered my plan to him and Delaney. Shortly after, Ingo disappeared into the darkness while Delaney and I walked directly toward the police.

"Remember, no mention of vampires, dragons, and definitely nothing about a wolf," I whispered as we drew close.

"Wolf? What wolf?" she murmured. "And I didn't see Ingo either. Never even met him."

We raised our arms and walked into the melee at the security entrance, where a handful of police were doing their best to corral witnesses and potential suspects — including Delaney and me. Within minutes, though, Ingo appeared among the law enforcement officers.

"Who are you?" the nearest policewoman demanded when he asked to be let through.

"Special Agent Kemper," he said.

"He's with us," another officer — a really hot one with spiky hair and soulful eyes — assured the first.

And just like that, Ingo was through. A few minutes later, he and Spike led us to a squad car parked close to a thick patch of woods.

"Thanks, Kyle." Ingo patted the officer's shoulder.

Ah, so this was Kyle Williams, the wolf shifter from Twin Moon Ranch.

"Thanks for keeping us out of this." Kyle nodded at the woods.

The bushes rustled, and I glimpsed canine eyes glowing in the dark. When low snarls sounded, three men hurried back into the lit area, turning themselves in to the police with their hands raised.

Delaney looked at me, but I signaled that I would explain later. The Twin Moon wolves were keeping a low profile but still contributing by keeping Jananovich's cronies — human or otherwise — from fleeing. With Erin and Nash incinerating any escaping vampires, I decided I could sleep soundly that night.

Ingo squeezed my hand, and I grinned. I would definitely sleep well tonight.

I'd done a quick head count, and all the escorts had made it out alive. They were now in police custody, but that sure beat vampires. Whatever happened next, I hoped they would steer clear of pointy-toothed supernaturals in the future.

"How will they explain themselves to the police?" I murmured, watching Kelly and Rob being led to a squad car.

"The truth, more or less," Delaney said. "That was part of escort training. If we ever got picked up by police, we were supposed to say we were part of an escort service, and we didn't know the details of anything higher up. Which is the truth — except for omitting the *vampire* part."

A big omission, but it made sense.

Another blast of fire appeared higher up the mountain. How would Kyle explain *that* to his human colleagues?

He must have caught my expression, because he answered with a totally straight face. "Drones."

I chuckled. "Drones that do what?"

He shrugged. "That will be for the ADMSA to figure out."

Ingo sighed. "If I'm still on the job by then."

I meant to console him, but I did a little fist pump instead.

"Hey!" poor Ingo grumbled, thinking I meant his job.

"No — I meant that. Him." I pointed to Stacy's bear shifter driver being handcuffed by the police.

A female officer waved for Kyle's attention, and he excused himself. Delaney leaned against the front of the squad car, while Ingo and I moved a few steps away, watching the blaze light up the night.

"What a mess," I murmured.

He shook his head. "A mess is when things end with a high body count. And luckily, vampires don't leave bodies."

"That's the only good thing you can say about them."

He slid an arm over my shoulders. "I just feel bad about your glass."

I pictured my beautiful decanter and glasses. The heat of the fire would melt them to lumps, much like the raw materials I'd started with.

"Yeah, all that work... Totally worth it, though," I decided.

Ingo shook his head sadly, and his voice cracked. "Not sure any of this was worth it. My obsession with Jananovich could have gotten you killed."

I turned, clasping his hands. "You're not obsessed. You're highly principled."

He looked rueful. "Probably a bit of both, to be honest."

I gave his hands a little shake. "I chose to go in there, and I chose to stay after I got the camera set up. So, I get it now — why you do what you do. And I'm sorry — so sorry — for giving you such a hard time about that."

He shook his head. "Well, I get it now, too — what you always said. Knowing you were in danger killed me."

I wrapped him in a hug, then whispered in his ear. "Maybe we can find some kind of compromise."

"We will." He held me tighter, rocking from side to side. "I promise."

∞∞∞

I did sleep well that night. At least, what was left of the night after we stumbled home — my home — in the wee hours of the night. Ingo and I even slept in, though sleeping wasn't all we did when the sun came up. But, hey. I'd survived an evening with a hoard of hungry vampires. I deserved it.

After dozing off, I woke up feeling dreamy, satisfied, and so proud of myself, it was practically criminal.

Leave it to reality to bring me down a few notches.

"Wakey, wakey, sleeping beauties." Erin knocked on the frame of the stall that served as my bedroom.

The clock showed nine — which really wasn't *that* late, considering.

"We have company," she finished, keeping her eyes averted.

I cringed. "Is it Mom?"

"Even worse," she said, dead serious.

Ingo groaned. "Captain Edwards?"

"Bingo," Erin said. "He's over at the main house, demanding to see Ingo, pronto."

Ingo flipped the covers over our heads. "Leave it to Edwards to know where to find me."

The question was, what else did Ingo's boss know?

We washed and dressed quickly, then headed over to the main house, where a tank of a man sat on the porch, surrounded by Claire and her horses.

Abby winked as Ingo and I approached. *I told him he'd have to wait, and he got all huffy. Then Claire worked her magic.*

I grinned. Ah, to be a cute eight-year-old again. The things I'd gotten away with back then...

Ingo cleared his throat. "You wanted to see me, Captain?"

Edwards spun, his gaze going from soft to blistering. "You bet your ass, I did." Then he froze and looked at Claire. "Er, I meant ass, as in donkey."

Claire giggled, while Abby sent him a withering look that said *How dare you use such language around my daughter?*

Never mind that Claire had heard worse from Abby and the rest of us.

"Let's go, sweetheart," Abby snipped, gathering Claire and her toy horses.

"Bye, Mr. Eddie," Claire called sweetly. "Say bye, Seabiscuit."

She made a nickering sound, and Captain Edwards waggled his fingers. The minute she left, he transformed back into a hard-nosed law enforcement officer.

A very hot, silver fox of a law enforcement officer. Not my type, but still.

Except, ugh. He was my mother's type — or had been when they'd had a fling many years ago. I'd met Edwards once under equally regrettable circumstances, when his ire had been aimed at Nash. Now, it was aimed at Ingo, who had defied direct orders to keep away from Jananovich.

"Bye," Abby muttered on her way to the car with Claire.

I raised a hand, then dropped it. Thanking Abby for her help would have to wait. She and Claire were already late for school and work.

We moved inside, and Edwards took a seat at the dining room table. Ingo and I stood, and for a long minute, the only sound was the tap of Edwards's fingers over the table.

I crossed my arms firmly. This was my house — sort of — and my property. Well, one-third my property. But still. He'd better not expect me to obey any commands.

Tap, tap, tap, went his fingers as he glared at Ingo.

I wondered what that spelled in Morse code. And, huh. Was Edwards old enough to know Morse code?

Tap, tap, tap.

What kind of supernatural was he? Dragon? Wolf? Warlock? All I got from his scent was Calvin Klein Eternity.

Tap, tap, tap.

I rolled my eyes. "How can we help you, Captain?"

His eyes strayed toward the kitchen. Had the tapping been Morse code for *Aren't you going to offer me a coffee?*

I kept my gaze level. No. I wasn't.

He made a face, then spoke, studying us for our reactions. "I'm here about the fire." When neither of us replied, he scowled and went on. "The fire at Victor Jananovich's property."

I lifted one shoulder. "Oh. *That* fire."

Edwards snorted. "What were you doing there?"

The question was aimed at Ingo, who answered evenly. "I heard the call on local police frequency and followed it."

"Despite the restraining order?"

"Yes, sir. I felt it important an agency member was present to pick up on what human law enforcement might overlook."

Edwards didn't look impressed. "What a coincidence." Then he turned to me. "What about you?"

I flashed an innocent smile. "I was in the catering crew."

"Catering," Edwards echoed in the same disbelieving tone. "And what about the fire? Any idea what set it off?"

I opened my mouth, nearly blurting something like, *Yes, I did, and it was awesome. I had to coax the fire over from all the way across the house.*

Ingo coughed into his hand, and I reworked my answer. "I don't know, but Jananovich did have a fire going in the fireplace and lots of candles. Maybe that started it."

And, oh, the irony. I had finally controlled fire, but I couldn't even take credit for it.

Edwards made a show of checking a notebook that probably didn't hold anything more incriminating than pizza delivery numbers. "I understand your father is a pyromancer."

I arched an eyebrow. "And my mother is a dragon. But you know that, don't you?"

Ha. A hint of a blush showed on his cheeks. I just hoped that was chagrin and not a flush of longing.

"Ah. Your mother. I don't suppose she's in town?" His firm voice went wobbly for the first time.

God, I hoped n—

The door swung open, and my mother sauntered in. Just like that, as if this were her home and not ours.

"What is this I hear about vampires?"

No hello. No hug. No *Oh my goodness. Are you all right, sweetheart?*

Edwards lit up like a golden retriever greeting its long-lost owner, but she took no notice until he whispered dreamily.

"Virginia..."

She glanced over, dismissing him in a nanosecond. "Oh. Hello, Todd."

"Tom," he murmured.

Textbook proof that hope springs eternal.

Edwards dragged his eyes away from Mom's svelte figure just long enough to check his hair in the mirror.

"I didn't know about the vampires when I took the catering job," I fibbed.

Edwards scratched his chin. "Well, you and your sisters certainly have a way of finding trouble. That was quite a blaze that consumed the property."

Mom beamed with pride. "So I hear."

I heaved an inner sigh. All those soccer games I'd played my heart out in as a child... Had she ever shown any interest?

No. Never.

My most beautiful glassworks... Did any of them elicit the slightest hint of approval?

Not a glimmer.

But burning down a multimillion-dollar property — that tickled Mom's pickle. Maybe that came with descending from generations of fire-breathing dragons — the love of reducing things to ashes.

"It was terrible," I told Edwards, and it had been. Just not the way he imagined. "All I could do was call for help and do my best to get people out of the building."

And stake a few vampires along the way, I wished I could add.

"There. You see?" My mother sniffed. "All quite innocent. And there wouldn't have been any trouble to get caught up in if you had been doing your job at that agency of yours." She looked at Edwards, all miffed and haughty, like she was the one who'd dedicated her life to public service.

"That was *his* job," he grumbled, pointing at Ingo.

"Not when it came to Jananovich," Ingo said. "As per your orders, I couldn't go near him or investigate his activities."

The sour look on Edwards's face was priceless.

My mother scoffed. "Vampires."

As if dragons had such a spotless track record.

Edwards continued his monotone interrogation. "Jananovich is presumed dead, as are several other vampires, including Gregor Hadik. I don't suppose you saw him there?"

I shook my head. "I didn't recognize any of them, sorry. Well, one looked like John Lennon..."

Edwards didn't seem interested. Not in that one anyway.

I shrugged. "It was my first time catering for vampires."

"First and last," my mother grumbled.

She didn't mean the vampires part. More like catering, a job beneath the dignity of a dragon.

Edwards pulled out one of those sketches the police made when they didn't have a photo of the suspect. And, oh. Was it just that they'd never snapped one, or because vampires didn't show up in photos? Or had modern technology changed that since digital cameras didn't use mirrors?

I made a mental note to ask Ingo later.

Edwards tapped the sketch. "Gregor Hadik. Ring a bell?"

"Not the name, but I saw him there," I said.

I also saw Ingo kill him, but why bore Edwards with such details?

"Gregor?" My mother snorted at the sketch. "No loss there. Such a prick." Then she chuckled. "Ha. Get it? Prick? Vampire?"

I frowned. "I could have died, Mom."

"Don't be so dramatic. I didn't raise my daughters to die foolishly."

More accurately, she hadn't raised us, period. But there was no winning with my mother.

Captain Edwards returned to the original subject. "I can't say I'll mourn Hadik. Been wanting to put that bastard away for years."

My hopes rose. If Edwards was pleased about that, he might not push hard about Ingo's involvement in the whole episode.

"Well, then. All's well that ends well," my mother concluded.

It would be if law enforcement operated that way. But, heck. My mother had worked her magic on Edwards when Nash had been in the hot seat. Maybe she could do the same now.

When she yawned and asked for coffee, I seized my opportunity.

"We're all out. But there's a great place in town for brunch. Great views, great service..."

Mom didn't look interested, but she did perk up when I threw *Cute waiters* into her mind.

"You really must buy a decent coffee machine," she grumbled.

Yeah, just for her and her infrequent, unannounced visits. I would make a note to add that to our list of priority expenses, right up there with the thousands we owed in property taxes.

I drooped at the thought. We'd solved our vampire problem but not our financial issues. My hopes of winning the $25,000 prize had died with Jananovich.

Ingo touched my back, reminding me to look on the bright side.

I threw him a grateful smile. Yeah, it had definitely been worth it.

"Brunch is a great idea," Ingo told Edwards. "I could write a full report of the incident while you're there. I mean, the little I witnessed," he added quickly.

"It's an all-you-can-eat brunch, and they have the best espresso in town." I threw a pointed look at my mother. *Ask for Conrad.*

Her eyes glittered. "Maybe I will try it..."

I nodded eagerly. "You really should. Plus, it would give you a chance to catch up with Todd — er, Tom."

I was operating on Pavlov's principle, because it could come in handy for Edwards to associate our ranch with the positive reward of my mother.

Which struck me as ironic, but I supposed one man's reward was another's worst nightmare.

Edwards scowled at Ingo, but his longing eyes betrayed hope when it came to my mother. Finally, he grumbled and stood.

"I expect a full report in two hours."

"Or three," my mother murmured, licking her lips. Was she thinking of coffee, Conrad the cute waiter, or Captain Edwards? Maybe all three?

I cut off the thought. I really, really didn't need to go there.

Ingo nodded curtly. "Yes, sir."

Edwards stepped to the door, nodding absently.

I ushered them outside. "The brunch place — the Chinchilla — is right in the middle of town. You can't miss it."

They stopped on the porch, sizing each other up. Then Edwards stuck out an elbow in a shy, hopeful gesture. My mother sighed — so much suffering, all before ten in the morning — but finally wound her arm through his and sashayed away. And — double shocker — I even saw her flash Edwards a coy smile when he opened his car door for her.

Dashing little bastard, wasn't he?

"Wow. That went well," I murmured as they drove off.

Ingo grinned, sliding an arm over my shoulders. "It did. Though, the last thing I want to do now is write a report."

I looped my arms around him, coming face-to-face. "Ah, but when you're done, you can take a few days off..."

He smiled ruefully. "True. I have accumulated a lot of vacation time..."

A lot? He probably had *months*. But I vowed to help him work that down in the near future.

I grinned, studying his lips. "You think you can survive a whole day off?"

He slid his hands up my sides. "Oh, I think we can find some way to fill the time."

"Like helping me at the shop?"

He laughed. "If you need it, yes."

"Or lending a hand around the ranch?"

He looked around, smiling at what he saw. "Just what I need for a little work-life balance." Then he went all serious. "I swear, I'll work on that."

I smiled. "I swear, I'll help you."

We hugged, rocking back and forth slightly. Then we drew apart, and I walked him to his car, sending him off with a pat on his perfect ass.

"Go get that report written, mister."

"And the request for vacation time filed," he added, sliding into the Jeep. "See you later?"

I nodded firmly. "The sooner, the better."

Chapter Twenty-Seven

INGO

In the end, Captain Edwards let me off lightly. He was more focused on the demise of Gregor Hadik than my involvement, for one thing — and even more focused on Pippa's mother. When I'd headed over to the Chinchilla to deliver my report, I found them deep in... well, not exactly conversation. More like a cross-fire of lusty, heated looks.

The Chinchilla also offered a couple of hotel rooms, and I couldn't help but wonder if they offered day rates.

I also submitted a request for time off, but after two days of radio silence from Edwards — who might have claimed his own days off — I called in to the head office and made my request a statement of intent. Not, *Can I take time off?* but *I am now taking time off.*

And for the first time ever, I did. And I truly turned work off.

Pippa turned everything else on, and we spent the next couple of blissful days in bed or in slow, lazy meanderings around the ranch.

"What a day," Pippa said, taking in the sky, the space, the peace. Peace we felt inside and out.

We'd hiked to the top of the mesa on the west side of the ranch and sat with our legs dangling over the side of a boulder with views that went on for miles.

"I could spend forever unwinding like this." I sighed, stroking her arm.

A full minute passed before she quietly asked, "Could you, though? I mean, once you start back at work?"

My heart ached for all I'd put her through. And, yes, I had to go back to work in a few days. But I could already feel the difference that closing the Jananovich case had made. My old enemy was gone, and a raw, personal wound had healed.

I nodded firmly. "Yes. I can't swear to never working another hour of overtime in my life—"

"I wouldn't want you to," Pippa interjected. "Not when it comes to putting away dangerous criminals. I get that now. But less risk and more downtime would be nice."

"All on board with that plan, believe me. Especially with more projects to do in my downtime."

"Projects?" Her eyes sparkled with hope.

Mine, too. I could feel them heat.

"You know, maybe finding a fixer-upper to turn into a home..."

Pippa chuckled. "Maybe even converting a barn?"

"For starters. Then there are those art projects I wanted to assist with..."

"Art? You? Since when?"

I poked her. "Since the day I got to help at a local glass shop. It was fun, actually. Plus, the woman who works there is pretty cute."

Pippa laughed. "Oh yeah? You think you have a shot with her?"

I nodded firmly. "I think I might." Then I took a deep breath. "I plan on proving it to her too. Every day for the rest of my life."

She leaned into my shoulder and nuzzled my chin. Her cheeks were pink, her eyes bright. "Sounds good, but you never know. She could have a really messed-up family."

I chuckled. "Nah, they're all right. Her sisters are pretty awesome, and one happens to live with my best friend." I glanced at the cabin Erin and Nash shared.

"Handy," Pippa murmured.

"I actually have a lot in common with her father..." I went on.

"That's good, but you could be getting a nightmare as a mother-in-law."

"Well, that could be entertaining."

Pippa snorted. "How little you know."

"I know she has an in with my boss. That could be useful."

Pippa sighed. "She has an in with lots of men."

I turned, cupping her face. "Doesn't matter. What matters is how much I love her — the glass artist, not her mother."

"Better be what you meant," Pippa growled.

I chuckled, then stroked her cheek. "It was. I love you." I kissed her gently, then rested my head against hers. "And I know we can figure the rest out. Jobs, mothers-in-law..."

"Ranch debt?"

I wrapped her in my arms. "That too. Somehow. Even if it won't happen overnight."

"Well, it had better happen soon," she muttered, more to herself than to me. Then her eyes narrowed on a plume of dust rising from the road. "Looks like we've got company."

Alarmed, we headed back down at a sharp pace, aiming for the dusty pickup parked by the main house.

Claire was on the porch, showing her horses to a girl of about the same age, and inside...

I pulled up short, staring at the guests.

"Hi, Pippa. Hi, Ingo." Abby nodded. "Meet Lana and Tina from Twin Moon Ranch."

I extended a hand slowly. "We've met."

They seemed friendly enough, but I couldn't help wondering if I had pissed off the most powerful wolf pack in the Southwest.

Abby motioned us to join them at the dining room table, which was covered in paperwork.

"Tina does the taxes for Twin Moon and Seymour Ranch, and Lana knows a hell of a lot about... well, a lot," Abby said.

Lana grinned. "Jack-of-all-trades when it comes to land and resource management, I guess you can say. A little law, a little real estate, a little mediating between interest groups..."

"Nice to meet you," Pippa said, though her eyes held a question mark.

"Kyle put us in touch," Tina explained.

"Lana was just saying..." Abby nodded for Lana to pick up where she'd left off.

"This property assessment is full of holes." Lana waved the document that had caused Pippa and her sisters so much heartache. "I'm confident you can contest it and get a more favorable assessment."

Pippa's eyes went wide, and Abby nodded to her gleefully.

Tina picked up from there. "In fact, you have grounds to file for a refund on what you've overpaid over the past few years." She tapped the tax forms lying before her. "You could be declaring a lot more deductions than you currently have. The storm damage, for example..."

Abby and Pippa exchanged loaded looks. The *storm* was their encounter with Harlon Greene. I'd arrived late on the scene with a squad from the agency, and while the details were hazy, it was clear an epic fight had taken place. The sisters had won with a little help from Nash and a big boost from the vortex they remained tight-lipped about.

I'd never asked, and I intended to keep it that way. The less I knew, the more I avoided a conflict of interest with my job. And, heck. Edwards had said it himself. *It's not possible to investigate all supernatural activity in an area. Just the ones causing concern or harm.*

"Then there are the animals you rescue," Lana chimed in.

That was mostly Abby, but all three sisters shared the costs.

Lana went into details on favorable tax scenarios, but I slowly tuned out when it became clear Pippa and her sisters could stop worrying about the ranch.

"I can't wait to tell Erin!" Abby grinned from ear to ear.

"Speak of the devil..." Pippa turned as another car came down the drive. Erin and Nash were just returning from their super-early morning shift. Pippa waved them over to the main house, made introductions, and shared the good news.

"I can't believe it. That's great!" Erin said, hugging Nash, her sisters, Nash, me, and — you guessed it — Nash. Again.

Lana and Tina kindly offered to help with the paperwork, and Erin set a date to sit down and do just that. Apparently, the ranch accounts were her department. A good thing too, because Pippa... Well, each of the sisters had her own particular talents, and paperwork was not Pippa's.

The guests departed, and I had the distinct impression of a great friendship being born — not just between Claire and Lana's daughter, but between the women too.

"Oh, I nearly forgot. I picked up the mail." Erin pulled several letters from her bag. "Business, business, junk mail..." She tossed each in a separate pile. "One for me, more junk, one for you..."

She handed a letter to Pippa, who studied it, then hissed. "Jananovich?"

Everyone froze.

Pippa locked eyes with me, then studied the envelope. "Postmarked Friday morning — before everything went down."

No one spoke as Pippa tore the flap of the envelope and removed the letter. A second slip of paper fluttered to the rug. Erin bent to retrieve it while Pippa read aloud.

"*Dear Ms. Martin. It was a pleasure to have met you and have the chance to admire your glasswork. It meets our needs perfectly...*" She snorted and murmured, "Bet your ass, it did." Then she went on reading. "*Although the committee has not yet met to judge all submissions, I wish to reserve the rights to your work with this small token of my appreciation...*" Pippa flipped the paper over to check the back. "What token?"

Erin straightened slowly, staring at the paper she'd retrieved. A check.

"This." She turned it around.

Abby stared. "Five thousand dollars?"

"Five thousand?" Pippa shrieked.

"Poetic justice." Erin grinned.

"If she can cash it," Abby pointed out.

Pippa rushed through the rest of the letter.

"*This sum is separate from the contest prize purse. Should the committee deem your work the winner, you will receive the entire purse in addition to this payment. I hold your work in high esteem and look forward to seeing more soon. Sincerely, Victor Jananovich.*"

She turned the check over twice, dumb struck. "Wow. But even if I can cash it, wouldn't it be taking blood money?"

"No, it would be compensation for the glass you lost in the fire," Abby growled.

I wasn't too hopeful, but when Pippa went to the bank the next day, the check cashed.

I agreed with Erin and Abby in accepting the money as compensation for everything Pippa had been through. However, she'd decided to give it to Delaney — but Delaney declined, telling Pippa to put it to good use.

And she did, using it to install a decent kitchen and bathroom in the barn. I'd never had such fun shopping, and we found a great deal on secondhand cabinets and appliances. We threw everything we had into the project during my week off work and in the weeks that followed — the perfect antidote, I discovered, to falling into the overtime trap. When my work hours ended, I was happy to hurry back to the ranch and squeeze in another few hours on a home that felt more and more... well, *homey*... each day.

Every night, Pippa and I fell into bed tired but satisfied. Every morning, we woke up snuggled close. Breakfasts turned into together time rather than just shoveling down food on the run. We drove to town for work together, too, and met up again for the drive back.

A perfect rhythm. A perfect life. Which only left one stone unturned.

The mating bite. A time-old rite of passage that turned a wolf and his mate into partners for life.

I kept reminding my wolf to be patient while Pippa came to grips with everything that had transpired. But one evening when we were putting the final touches on the kitchen cabinets and counter...

"Looking good," Pippa declared.

"It does," I agreed, admiring the space.

She patted my rear with a grin. "I wasn't talking about the cabinets."

I laughed, then dusted off the counter, checking our work.

Pippa tapped the counter. "We need to test this sucker."

I nodded, too stuck in construction mode to pick up what she really meant.

I caught on fast, though. Especially when Pippa perched on the edge of the counter and drew me into the space between her legs.

"I think we need to check the joints," she murmured, working her lips against mine.

I pulled her to the very edge of the counter until all of her was pressed against all of me. Especially the good parts.

My wolf howled at the sensation of all my *hard* against all her *soft.*

"Definitely need to check the joints." My voice went all hoarse.

Good thing I wasn't a singer. Besides, it was Pippa's voice I wanted to hear, preferably loud and throaty as she called my name. That way, we could check the acoustics too.

To hell with acoustics, my wolf growled. *Let's get this show on the road.*

My hands were already roaming, working out a plan. Her shirt off first or mine?

"Yours," she breathed, reading my mind. "Definitely yours."

The second it fluttered to the floor, she zeroed in on a nipple and circled it with her tongue, then nipped.

I hissed, all the while making mental notes. Pippa was giving me a blueprint for what she wanted when our roles were reversed.

She was wearing an old flannel work shirt of mine over a tank top and bra, and it was a lot more fun to take the flannel off her than myself. Her top and the bra followed soon after.

Pippa threw her head back with a moan when I swirled my tongue around the tight beads of her nipples, then hissed in need when I nipped.

"More..." she whispered. "More..."

I slid a hand lower, and she spread her legs wider, breathing hard.

When I paused and looked over my shoulder, she growled. "You are *not* stopping now."

"Just checking for open flames."

We'd learned the hard way that her fire-wielding powers peaked when she was worked up. But power didn't always come with control, so I had a good look around for safety's sake. No candles, no fire in the hearth. Not even a pilot light in the stove. It would be a shame to burn the barn down now.

The pause put us at a good juncture to strip her out of her jeans and me out of mine. The moment I kicked them aside, we hurried back to checking the structural integrity of the counter.

"Yes..." She pushed forward as my fingers parted her folds, then slid in.

She danced against my hand, making my wolf howl.

"Ingo..." she moaned, clutching my hips.

Seconds later, I filled her, inch by hot, straining inch.

Pippa made a sound that was half sigh, half growl.

The counter wasn't wide enough for her to lie back, so she slung her arms around my shoulders and pushed her hips forward, meeting every thrust.

Red-hot embers sparked in her glazed-over eyes. My vision blurred as a primal beat drummed in my veins.

There, my wolf rumbled greedily, eyeing her neck. *Right there...*

I licked my lips, watching her pulse tap against her skin.

"Here," she murmured, brushing a hand over that exact place.

Apparently, she'd had the same thought at the same time. *A mating bite.*

For a wolf shifter, the urge was instinctive. Pippa knew all about it, having grown up around wolf shifters and other supernaturals. We'd even talked about it — fantasized, really — years back, but we'd known the time wasn't right.

But now, the inner mechanism that had once slammed on the brakes was revving the other way. Our time had finally come.

You're sure? I asked — quietly and only in her mind, afraid to utter the question aloud.

"Never been more sure," she panted.

My heart soared, but I had to check. *Really sure? That you want me — forever?*

Never wanted anyone else. And I can't wait for our forever *to finally begin,* she added.

Like I needed any extra impetus.

Extending your teeth and plunging them into your true love's throat might not sound all that appealing, especially after a vampire encounter. But a mating bite was totally different. No sucking, for one thing. No taking, no stealing, no endangering. Just connecting — a permanent connection forged at the height of sex that pushed the experience beyond the physical realm.

My mind exploded with raw, intense sensations. Lust. Pleasure. Unfettered desire.

Pippa clamped a hand over the back of my neck, urging me on. I pushed — with my jaws and my hips — and soon, we were rocking to a primal rhythm.

"Ingo..." She chanted my name, almost like a synonym for *forever.* In my mind, I did the same, echoing her name.

When I plunged deeper, Pippa dug her heels into my ass and held my head close.

Yes... she breathed into my mind. *Oh yes.*

My blood surged, and my ears filled with the crackle of a blazing fire. It burned higher and higher, shooting off fiery, swirling tornadoes. Entire nerve chains detonated, and lightning zipped through my veins. I clung to Pippa as we catapulted off the face of the earth and careened through space.

I braced myself, ready to shield her from a hard landing. But we fluttered down, featherlight, instead. Gradually, my sense of orientation returned. My knee bumped the door of a wood cabinet, and the new kitchen counter was in front of me, along with Pippa.

My canines retracted, and I pressed my tongue over Pippa's skin before easing away. The wound healed as I did, and I exhaled, slumping over her shoulder. Only my arms retained the slightest tension as I held her tightly.

Never letting go, my wolf rumbled.

"Never ever," Pippa echoed, stroking my back gently.

Chapter Twenty-Eight

INGO

One month later...

My lungs burned as I scrambled over hard-packed dirt, fighting the urge to glance back at the wolf chasing me. I had to make it to the top of the mesa first. I just had to. I rushed through the dim light of the full moon, avoiding a prickly pear, only to brush by a yucca. Its sharp tips scraped my side, raking parallel furrows through my thick wolf pelt.

I surged forward, then leaped, straining for the top of a big, flat-topped boulder bathed in moonlight. Then I spun to face my adversary.

Gotcha! Pippa sailed onto the rock beside mine with a cry of triumph. The word sounded in my mind and into the night in yippy wolf-speak.

My tongue lolled as I panted.

Got what? I was here first. I pranced in place.

She snickered, prancing on her own boulder. *The race was to the highest rock. And it's all mine, baby.* Her paws tapped a silent jig over the boulder.

I'm on the highest rock.

Then it hit me that I was staring into her beautiful blue eyes straight on, not slightly downward as usual due to my height advantage.

I checked at my rock, then hers, and stopped wagging my tail. Damn. I'd ended the race a step too early.

Ha! Pippa danced around on her boulder. *Who's the best wolf, huh? Who's finally learned to coordinate four feet and a tail? Who beat the big bad wolf to the top of the mesa? I'll tell you who. Me! I am the greatest!*

Below us, the scattered lights of the ranch formed the background of her little solo. I grinned, letting her enjoy her Mohammed Ali moment without commenting that her wagging tail and floppy ears diminished the comparison ever so slightly.

Oh, Great One, I barked. *May I join you on your throne?*

I'll think about it. She turned her nose up in a pose hauntingly similar to her mother's.

Then she grimaced, catching my impression. *Oh God, no. I swear, I was just kidding!*

I grinned. Ha. Now I knew the ultimate weapon to use against Pippa: any comparison to her mother.

Her teeth showed in a snarl. *Don't you dare.*

I echoed back her own words. *Just kidding.*

A shadow blotted out the moonlight momentarily. We looked up, spotting a pair of dragons soaring through the inky sky. Apparently, we weren't the only two lovebirds out enjoying the night. Erin and Nash were too. They glided soundlessly over the landscape, banked into graceful turns, and disappeared into the darkness.

I couldn't help glancing at Pippa out of the corner of my eye.

You wouldn't rather be a dragon like Erin? I ventured. After all, Pippa was half dragon — and she loved fire.

Nah. The sky would be lonely without you. She circled me, rubbing her body along mine the entire way. *Got all I need down here.*

She butted my head gently, demanding space to nuzzle my neck and shoulders.

I grinned. As if she hadn't thoroughly marked me from day one.

Gotta keep the competition away, she murmured, still nuzzling. *Let all those women in town know you're mine.*

I nuzzled her just as fiercely. *Ditto for all the men when it comes to you.*

My wolf snarled, picturing it. We'd gone to Buffalo Bill's the previous Wednesday and danced to every tune in their oldies lineup — and I swear, every man had his eyes glued to Pippa's perfect ass the whole time. Well, they did until my glare had them studying the labels of their beers like there would be a quiz on breweries of the Southwest soon. One or two of the boldest might have peeked again by the time the last notes of "Islands in the Stream" faded, but they'd gotten the message. Pippa was mine — forever.

My neck tingled at the spot where she'd marked me with her own mating bite.

Finally, I feel complete, she'd murmured afterward, and I could only echo the sentiment.

Mine, my wolf hummed happily.

I'd never heard of any "convert" — as wolves jokingly called humans turned shifter — mastering the fine art of wolfery as quickly as Pippa had. Maybe being half dragon helped?

No. That's just Pippa being Pippa, my wolf hummed proudly.

True. Whatever Pippa did, she did with the joyous enthusiasm — and élan — of a golden retriever chasing a tennis ball. She'd been all in from day one.

I'm so happy, I could howl, she said, then grinned. *Wait. I'm a wolf now. I* can *howl.*

She lifted her muzzle and let her soft, smooth soprano drift over the landscape.

Arrrooooo. . .

I tilted my head back, harmonizing with her. Our voices mingled and carried over the vast, undulating landscape.

I can't believe humans say this sounds sad, Pippa muttered in the breath between two long, soulful howls.

Well, humans just didn't have an ear for wolf tunes. And some howls really were mournful, like mine, back when Pippa and I had lived apart.

Never again, my wolf declared, releasing a joyous howl to prove it.

I can't wait to show Dad everything I can do now, Pippa said after we wound down our duet.

I flashed a toothy wolf grin. *You can show him when he visits tomorrow,* I reminded her.

She pranced happily. *I'll show him how fast I can run and how far I can jump. Oh! And my favorite part — digging!* She leaned down, sending dirt flying between her back legs.

You can show him almost *everything,* I joked, thinking of home and the big, sturdy bed.

Pippa flashed me a naughty grin. *Race you to the bottom, hotshot.*

She leaped into a sprint. With a yip, I took off after her.

Watch me win again, she taunted, flicking her tail.

As it turned out, we were both the winners. Pippa got home first, but when we shifted into human form and fell into bed, I claimed the top, and we both enjoyed two sizzling rounds of sex before fading off to sleep.

We picked up where we'd left off the next morning, then grudgingly showered, ate, and headed to work. I snuck over to the glass shop during Pippa's lunch break and helped her find a whole new use for the workbench in the storage room. That round of sex had been on the slow, careful side, what with all the glass around us. But satisfying, nevertheless, despite the *wolf in a china shop* jokes Pippa cracked.

"Will I ever stop lusting after you?" She sighed when we finally dragged ourselves back to work.

I waggled my eyebrows. "I hope not."

We were just doing what any freshly mated shifters would do — though, I swear, we were setting new records when it came to heat levels. As high as the blazing bonfire Pippa's father treated us to that evening.

Everyone gathered around, as before — Erin and Nash, Abby and Claire, Pippa and me, and Greg and Mike.

"You two really are like a couple," Erin quipped to her father, referencing the story Mike had told at our last bonfire.

"I do love him." Mike smacked his lips in the air. "Just not that way."

Greg pretended to look hurt. "And here I was, thinking we had the makings of something beautiful."

Mike laughed. "Sorry, bud. My Harley and I already have something beautiful."

Pippa stood to clear the plates from our barbecue. "Marshmallows, anyone?"

I smiled at the echoes of our previous bonfire, and so many before it back in Colorado. Having said that, the bonfires here on Painted Rock Ranch were developing their own traditions and inside jokes, a lot like a family Thanksgiving celebration.

And a celebration it was. A terrible threat had been eliminated, Pippa and I had finally surmounted our differences, and the ranch was at peace again. I hadn't suffered any consequences as a result of my involvement in the Jananovich case. On the contrary, I'd been commended for finding a promising new recruit for the agency. Delaney had aced the grueling basic training that weeded out all but the best candidates and had started training for undercover missions. Apparently, she'd even started dating a nice bear shifter in the agency.

I just hoped he would help her find a little work-life balance.

Jananovich's escorts had all been questioned and released on probation. One had made the Phoenix Suns Dance squad, while another was forging a new career as a social media influencer specializing in hydration and nutrition. Two others had started dating each other, and yet another had started a vampire-themed podcast that the ADMSA was keeping an eye — er, ear — on. Hopefully, that would be the closest any of them ventured to vampires again.

Meanwhile, I'd also rooted out the double agent who'd acted as Jananovich's inside man at the agency — or rather, inside woman. It had been Angelina Saint James, as I'd suspected — the very vampire who'd caused Nash so many problems.

Fucking Angelina, he'd growled when we'd worked it out together.

She hadn't just been working with Harlon Greene, but with Jananovich and a number of other supernaturals. The agency had already created a task force to identify which other cases she'd tampered with.

However, I was off duty now, and I'd learned to draw a firm line between working hard and enjoying private time.

Like right now, at the bonfire.

I took in the happy faces, from Claire snuggled in Mike's lap to Erin and Nash nestled together. Pippa blew me a kiss before stepping away to find the marshmallows. Even Abby gazed up at the stars with a dreamy expression.

"For you, Grandpa." Claire held her stick toward Greg a short time later.

He plucked the marshmallow off the end and made a show of relishing it. "Yum! Perfectly toasted on the outside yet gooey on the inside. A born pyromancer!"

"God, I hope not," Abby muttered, half joking, half serious.

Everyone laughed, though I couldn't help wondering about Abby's father. Was he "just" a human or something else?

Not human, I decided, judging by her mother's penchant for powerful supernaturals. But what kind? A warlock? Dragon shifter? And what about Claire's father?

I blinked into the fire, reminding myself it was none of my business. Not until the day a teenage Claire startled us all by turning into a dragon or burning down a barn by accident.

But, heck. As long as it wasn't the barn Pippa and I were converting…

"Is it story time yet?" Claire asked after a few more marshmallows.

Mike had been the lucky recipient of her second one, then Abby, then Erin and Pippa, and finally Nash and me.

We're way, way down the pecking order here, I joked, shooting the thought into his mind.

Nash grinned, keeping his arm looped around Erin's shoulders. *Just happy to be part of the club, man.*

I raised my beer bottle in a silent toast, seconding the sentiment.

"I thought we'd try something different tonight," Greg said. "Like make-a-wish night."

Pippa rubbed her hands. "Oh, I love this."

"Just tell me what you wish you could be or have or do, and I'll do my best to show it to you," Greg explained. He pointed to Mike. "Get us started, big guy."

Mike closed his eyes, thinking. It was easy to imagine his wish, and I fully expected an even bigger, louder motorcycle to appear in the flames of the bonfire.

Mike opened his eyes and looked at Greg in silent communication. Greg nodded, then raised his hands toward the fire.

"Aw..." Erin clasped her hands to her heart as a scene slowly formed in the blaze.

It was a bonfire within the bonfire, with each of us sketched in flames around it. Even Nash was there.

"That's my wish," Mike murmured, rumbly as thunder — a weathermonger's version of emotional. "This. Exactly this. My family safe, sound, and happy."

Erin beamed. Abby wiped a tear from her eye. Claire patted his thick arms.

And Nash... I caught his throat rippling in an emotional gulp. Nice to see he was gradually being accepted.

Erin was next. Seconds after she'd whispered her wish to Greg, a hot air balloon formed in the flames and wafted skyward, circled by a dragon.

"Mine is kind of like Dad's," she explained shyly. "Going flying with everyone I love. See? You're all in the balloon, and that's Nash beside it."

The figures in the basket started out a little hazy, then developed more detail when Pippa raised her hands and moved her fingers like a conductor.

"Thanks, sweetie." Greg beamed.

Pippa too.

Mike chipped in next, stirring up a breeze to mimic the sensation of flying. It toyed with Pippa's long hair and the hood of my jacket.

Slowly, the image faded, and Greg turned to Nash.

"Your turn. Anything you wish you could be or have or do."

Nash cleared his throat and waved a hand. "I think the first two have me covered."

Erin tipped her head against his shoulder and rubbed his arm. Then she straightened abruptly.

"Oh! Can I take his turn?"

Pippa and Abby booed. "Not fair!"

It was easy to picture the three of them huddled around a board game as kids, saying the same thing.

Greg intervened, as their aunt probably had once upon a time. "I think we can accommodate one extra."

"I'd just love to see myself landing smoothly for a change," Erin said. "I still bobble."

"Just a little," Nash reassured her.

A fiery dragon zoomed around the fire, then zipped past Claire, heading out into the desert. Everyone swiveled their heads, watching it glide to a perfect landing. A trail of embers tumbled in its wake, then slowly disappeared, along with the dragon.

"Bravo!" Mike patted Erin's shoulder. "That's my baby. Perfect!"

"Not yet." She sighed. "But I am getting there."

Pippa was next, fixing her father with a hazy look that indicated they were mentally communicating. Moments later, they both raised their hands.

One wolf, then another, gradually emerged from the heart of the fire. They cavorted around the edges, then reunited in the middle, brushing against each other. When they raised their muzzles to the sky, their howls were silent, but the snaps and crackles of the fire filled in nicely.

"So sweet," Erin sighed.

Greg slowly let the image fade, then heaved a theatrical sigh. "Just three words: it's about time you two got together."

"That's not three words, Dad," Pippa pointed out, but her look was forgiving.

Claire started counting on her fingers.

Like Nash, I passed on my turn. There was nothing I could wish for that hadn't already been covered.

Continuing clockwise around the bonfire would have put Abby next, but she mumbled something about finding the fixings for s'mores and excused herself quickly.

Pippa watched her go, then glanced at Erin. Their dads appeared equally concerned, and Greg looked like he might go after her. But Mike shook his head curtly.

"Let her be," he murmured. "Nobody has to share if they don't want to."

A cloud drifted overhead, and a few seconds ticked by in awkward silence. Well, awkward for everyone except Claire, who was still counting.

"Your turn, Dad," Pippa said.

Greg shook his head curtly. "Yours covered my wish perfectly. Although I would have added a few grandpups."

Pippa rolled her eyes. "Dad..."

Personally, I was all for it. But it was probably better to save that conversation for a less public occasion.

"Which means it's..." Mike drummed his fingers on Claire's shoulders.

"My turn! My turn!" she cheered.

Greg leaned over, and she cupped her hands around his ear, whispering.

"Oh, good one," he said, rubbing his hands. "Ready?"

"No, we have to wait for Mommy," she said, hollering to Abby.

"Coming, coming," Abby murmured, settling back down in her spot.

"Now we're ready," Claire announced, staring eagerly into the fire. Hell, we all did.

The sharp edges of the fire grew softer — almost liquid — and a sleek body leaped out of the blue heart of the flames.

"Dolphin!" Claire clapped in delight.

Everyone grinned. Over the past few weeks, Claire had moved on from pegasi to marine wildlife.

With a flick of his hands, Greg sent the dolphin leaping high into the night sky. Mike helped by whipping up swirling clouds that mimicked the ocean, and the edges sparkled like seafoam, lit by starlight.

Everyone oohed and aahed, and Nash and I exchanged wide-eyed glances. We had definitely found our way into one crazy, lovable family.

It was like Erin liked to say. A very functional dysfunctional family. Right down to the shifters and warlocks.

When the dolphin faded, Greg lowered his hands and coaxed a new one out of the fire.

"Help me, sweetheart," he murmured, keeping his eyes on the image he'd created.

Pippa raised her hands and stared into the fire, waiting. Catching the beat, almost, the way kids did before hopping into a rotating jump rope.

And, *whoosh!* Another dolphin rose out of the fire to join Greg's, and the pair spun around each other, spiraling up into the universe.

"Wow," Abby breathed.

Everyone was rapt, including me. I did drag my eyes away from the fire long enough to glance at Pippa, though. Her cheeks glowed, reflecting the firelight, and the smile on her face was a thing of beauty.

My chest rose with a happy sigh. She'd always dreamed of harnessing powers like her father's.

Finally, I feel complete, she'd said earlier.

Me too, I nearly whispered. *Me too.*

The dolphins put on a show better than that in any Orlando theme park, leaping, flipping, and spinning. How Greg and Pippa pulled off the watery illusion within a blazing fire was beyond me, but it was amazing.

Watching them at work was equally entertaining. I loved how Pippa's lips tightened in concentration and how she lifted or dropped her eyebrows while guiding the dolphins' movements.

For the grand finale, Greg took over both dolphins while Pippa juggled her hands, tossing fire from one to the other. Then she waved her arms, releasing a ring of fire for the dolphins to spiral through.

"Wow," Abby murmured.

"Incredible." Erin shook her head in amazement.

"I want to be a Fire Dancer when I grow up," Claire announced.

"So do I," Nash murmured, only half joking.

Magic. Like being with you, Pippa whispered into my mind. Then she blurted *Whoops!* and saved her careening dolphin.

"Nothing's going to top that," Nash murmured as they wrapped up the show.

I agreed, but then again, I'd entertained that sentiment many times over the past few weeks, and I would bet Pippa would go on surprising me for... Well, forever.

She chuckled into my mind. *I'm game if you're game.*

I grinned. This was my life now, and it couldn't be more perfect.

Sneak Peek: Dream Weaver

In a town where magic stirs the air, a fiery blacksmith must forge her destiny, fight for her family, and gamble on love as boundless as the Sedona scenery.

Single mom and badass blacksmith, Abby Carson, has spent years hammering out a life on her own terms, raising her daughter, and avoiding trouble — especially the masculine kind that comes wrapped in a flannel shirt and a spellbinding smile. But in Sedona, where vortexes hum with mystical energy, trouble is as persistent as the visions that color her dreams.

When the town's famed vortexes start misbehaving, the town buzzes with talk of energy shifts and cosmic nonsense. Abby suspects something darker is afoot — especially when her deadbeat ex shows up out of the blue, suddenly interested in playing dad.

As Sedona's magic begins to unravel, Abby uncovers an evil scheme to drain the vortexes of their power. Turns out, she's more tied to that magic than she ever dreamed of, and tapping into it might be the only way to save her home and her family. To do so, she finds herself reluctantly teaming up with a rugged bear shifter who's as infuriating as he is intriguing. Cooper is big, broody, and full of secrets... But then again, so is she.

Books by Anna Lowe

Spellbound in Sedona

Wind Whisperer (Book 1)

Fire Dancer (Book 2)

Dream Weaver (Book 3)

Sherwood Forest Shifters

Tempting the Sheriff (Book 1)

Tempting the Outlaw (Book 2)

Tempting the Maiden (Book 3)

Aloha Shifters - Jewels of the Heart

Lure of the Dragon (Book 1)

Lure of the Wolf (Book 2)

Lure of the Bear (Book 3)

Lure of the Tiger (Book 4)

Love of the Dragon (Book 5)

Lure of the Fox (Book 6)

Aloha Shifters - Pearls of Desire

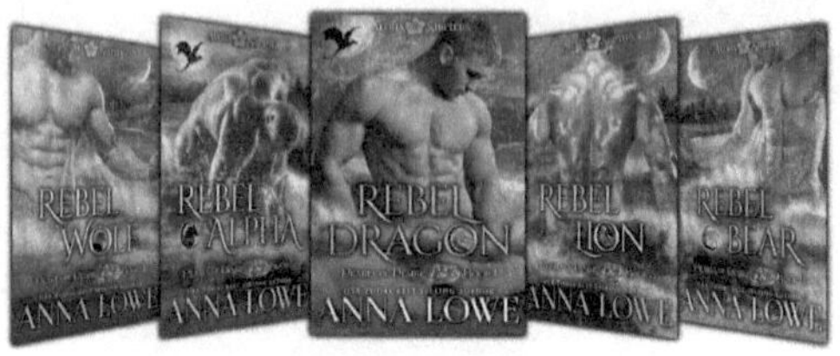

Rebel Dragon (Book 1)

Rebel Bear (Book 2)

Rebel Lion (Book 3)

Rebel Wolf (Book 4)

Rebel Heart (A prequel to Book 5)

Rebel Alpha (Book 5)

Fire Maidens - Billionaires & Bodyguards

Fire Maidens: Paris (Book 1)

Fire Maidens: London (Book 2)

Fire Maidens: Rome (Book 3)

Fire Maidens: Portugal (Book 4)

Fire Maidens: Ireland (Book 5)

Fire Maidens: Scotland (Book 6)

Fire Maidens: Venice (Book 7)

Fire Maidens: Greece (Book 8)

Fire Maidens: Switzerland (Book 9)

The Wolves of Twin Moon Ranch

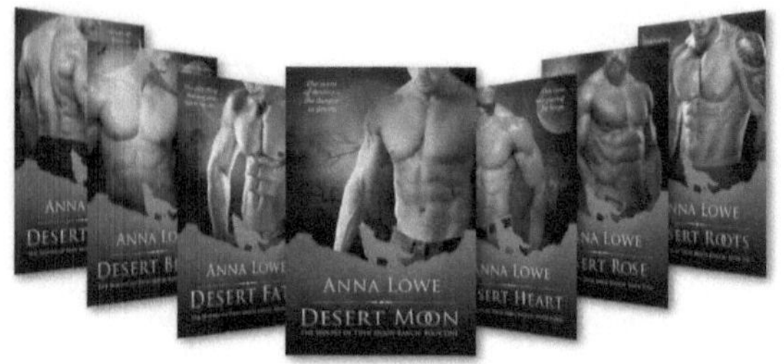

Desert Hunt (the Prequel)

Desert Moon (Book 1)

Desert Blood (Book 2)

Desert Fate (Book 3)

Desert Heart (Book 4)

Desert Rose (Book 5)

Desert Roots (Book 6)

Desert Destiny (Book 7)

Sasquatch Surprise (Book 8)

Desert Yule (a short story)

Desert Wolf: Complete Collection (Four short stories)

Blue Moon Saloon

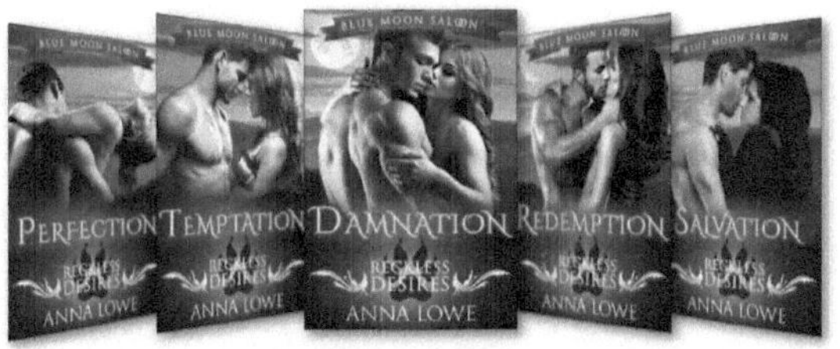

Perfection (a short story prequel)

Damnation (Book 1)

Temptation (Book 2)

Redemption (Book 3)

Salvation (Book 4)

Deception (Book 5)

Celebration (a holiday treat)

Shifters in Vegas

Paranormal romance with a zany twist

Gambling on Trouble

Gambling on Her Dragon

Gambling on Her Bear

Gambling on Her Panther

Serendipity Adventure Romance

Off the Charts

Uncharted

Entangled

Windswept

Adrift

Travel Romance

Veiled Fantasies

Island Fantasies

www.annalowebooks.com

About the Author

USA Today and Amazon bestselling author Anna Lowe loves putting the "hero" back into heroine and letting location ignite a passionate romance. She likes a heroine who is independent, intelligent, and imperfect – a woman who is doing just fine on her own. But give the heroine a good man – not to mention a chance to overcome her own inhibitions – and she'll never turn down the chance for adventure, nor shy away from danger.

Anna loves dogs, sports, and travel – and letting those inspire her fiction. On any given weekend, you might find her hiking in the mountains or hunched over her laptop, working on her latest story. Either way, the day will end with a chunk of dark chocolate and a good read.

Visit AnnaLoweBooks.com